Going To See The End Of The Sky

When the Scouring Robot tore the lid off his pod, Beyar knew his only chance to survive was the Long Run. But fear seemed to hold his feet glued to the pod bottom until the whirling arms of the robot closed in behind him, stirring up clouds of dust, blinding and confusing Beyar. Driven by desperation he ran, losing all sense of direction in the storm of dust. He didn't feel the clump of debris when his foot hit it, and, caught in sudden nightmare, he scarcely realized he had fallen even when he hit.

All he knew was overwhelming terror as, prisoner of the dust, he waited helplessly for the robot's deadly arms to begin tearing into his suit...

Also by
William John Watkins

The Centrifugal Rickshaw Dancer

Published by
POPULAR LIBRARY

Going To See The End Of The Sky

WILLIAM JOHN WATKINS

POPULAR LIBRARY

An Imprint of Warner Books, Inc.

A Warner Communications Company

POPULAR LIBRARY EDITION

Popular Library® and Questar® are registered trademarks of
Warner Books, Inc.

Cover art by Richard Corben

Popular Library books are published by
Warner Books, Inc.
666 Fifth Avenue
New York, N.Y. 10103

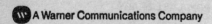

A Warner Communications Company

Printed in the United States of America

First Printing: July, 1986

10 9 8 7 6 5 4 3 2 1

For Shana, Desirea, and Jay,
The children of the future
And
For Sharon & Jim,
The guardians of their present

CHAPTER
ONE

Beyar stood looking out on the bigness of the moon. It was the whole of the sky from the Nearside Window. Beyond the Farside was only darkness and the other five stationary habitats of the LeGrange League, but Beyar did not think of them; they were separate and distinct, the children of Catchcage, which had made the metal to build them.

The great magnetic gates flashed as they slowed the momentum of the mineral payloads from the Lunar Accelerator. Beyar watched them come, down the Slope, into the Dip, and finally up into Catchround, which guided them around Catchcage to the Dumper where they would be opened and their contents of moondust poured into the Separator on its way to the smelter. The empty ones gave a disappointing pop as they came through the magnetic fields that turned their momentum into energy, but the others flashed and flared with the bursts of power that had lured the chemists and physicists of Catchcage into space.

Off to his left the empty kidneycars hurtled back toward the moon and LUNAC, forty thousand miles in the airless dark, three days there with only a Time Lump for food and water and, after the ordeal, three days back. Three days in the Little Death, and then the awakening into the terror of the Scouring Robot, a scramble, a run, the squeeze of acceleration, and then the Little Death again. But it was the price of going to see the end of the sky.

He had paid that price only four years before. Push and Chancey, young as they were, had the right to pay it as well, and as their specialbrother, he had the obligation to fasten them into the kidneycar they would make their pilgrimage in. Other brothers had done it before him, year after year, one Catchcage generation after another. And yet it worried him, and justifiably so, just as it had worried brothers and sisters, Bios and co-parents, ever since children began playing the game of Going to See the End of the Sky.

The game was played in the kidney-shaped metal pods the gravitational accelerator lobbed moonrock up to Catch-cage in. No one over fourteen ever played it. No one under twelve was allowed. Those who did, when no one was looking, almost invariably died. Survivors always grew up to be either very powerful people in the LeGrange League of Stationary Habitats, or Skyshockers, itinerant lunatic-saints, fanatic followers of URdon Wee. They were loved or pitied by practically everybody for the marks skyshock had left on their minds.

Still, there were those who said the Skyshockers were only pretending to be crazy and that they were the eyes and ears of the Fist, the LeGrange Police. But most of the people in Catchcage didn't care if they were; the Fist had only lip-service jurisdiction in Catchcage, anyway, and when Skyshocker craziness took an artistic form, as it almost always did, they were the best entertainment in the League. Small bands of them traveled everywhere in the six habitats, providing entertainment the way people wanted it, uncensored. They were a kind of living news service, acting out the events of Catchcage, Hardcore, the Big and Little Wheels, Henson's Tube, the Grand Sphere, and even Earthside. Or making it up. Nobody really cared about that, either; a Skyshocker lie still bore more resemblance to the truth than anything the LeGrange News and Entertainment Network put out.

The Skyshockers were crazy, of course. There wasn't one of them that didn't bear the mark of having scrambled screaming around the inside of those kidney-shaped ore shells pursued by the huge shearing arms of the Scouring Robot. No one who lived through that horror could ever forget it, and yet almost everyone in Catchcage risked it. Going to See the End of the Sky was a rite of passage from childhood to adulthood, and how you went through it determined everything you became. It gave Catchers an aura of power that never left them, no matter what they did afterward. It was why Catchcage tolerated the cost of it in life and sanity year after year. They had been tolerating it for a long, long time.

Catchcage was the first true habitat. Some of the cargo containers and dormitories that made up Hardcore predated it, but it had been catching the kidney-shaped ore pods from LUNAC long before the other habitats had been built. The solar furnaces on its middle levels had been converting the moon dirt into aluminum, and fiberglass and other metals even before half of the OBees, the Original Builders from Hardcore, had come up. In the close but stormy family of the League, Catchcage was generally accorded the status of elder brother, even in Hardcore.

The habitat itself was shaped like a truncated cone. A large, clear tunnel curved around the upper third, where the ore pods were emptied and rerouted to the moon again. A series of huge frames funneled them into the tunnel from ten miles out and recaptured their momentum for conversion into the energy the gates beamed to Catchcage to feed the smelter and the Torch. The original idea of hurling up forty-pound loads of dirt wrapped in plexiglass was scrapped in the experimental stage when it was found that almost every load had to have some course correction after it left the moon, and the loads mysteriously came apart on their way to the prototype ore-carrier that was supposed to catch them. In their place the final lunar accelerator launched one-ton kidney-shaped pods that opened lengthwise like a peanut.

Everything about the construction of the LeGrange League was a matter of shady deals and huge profits, and the kidneycars were no exception. The Corporation claimed the cars were kidney-shaped because it "offered the best storage to wind-resistance ratio." But the truth was that the cars were shaped that way because Spencer LeGrange wanted to build a bigger and more expensive lunar accelerator than most of the sponsoring governments wanted to pay for. He had his engineers support the design, and after a bit of money changed hands, nobody mentioned the embarrassing fact that there *is* no wind between the moon and the habitats.

Since the LeGrange Corporation was the only one geared up to produce such a ridiculous-looking thing to begin with, it got the contract, and Spencer LeGrange got an excuse to build his jumbo accelerator at a more than jumbo profit. It was generally believed in the League that the original accelerator payloads were blown up by Corporation agents on the moon so that the ore pods and the larger accelerator would be needed.

The kidneycars were full coming up, and they were supposed to be empty going down. But every year, on the twenty-seventh day of the Second Lunar, they were filled with children testing themselves for adulthood, all hoping to become an Exceptional Person.

Beyar was already an Exceptional Person because of his birth. He was the largest baby born in the Cage in the history of the yearly Lottery to determine whose genes would be used to fabricate the newest generation of Catchers. The Lottery, like most things in the League, was a matter of both practical necessity and mystical conviction.

On the practical side, the Cage had a carrying capacity of five thousand people, and care had been taken from the very beginning not to overpopulate it. At the age of sixteen just about everybody left the Cage for temporary life elsewhere. Few of them came back for more than a decade at a time, and many never came back at all. It didn't matter: A Catcher was a Catcher for life; even those who never came back never really left, and every one of them took Catchcage with them.

Either by death or permanent migration, about six per-cent of the population left Catchcage every year. Roughly half of their replacements were Catchers coming home for a few years. The rest were the fruits of the Lottery, the children of Catchcage. Every year a new generation of one hundred and fifty children was conceived artificially from genetic ma-terial contributed by the Bios, the winners of the Lottery, and the genetic relics of URdon Wee, the patron saint of the Cage.

But the Bios were only the winners of the Lottery; the children were the children of URdon Wee. They were the children of the Cage, and the Cage as a whole raised and watched over them. Every adult Catcher was a co-parent to every child; every other child under the age of sixteen was their brother and sister and would be so for life. And beyond.

Year after year, while the children of the Cage were returning from going to see the end of the sky, the Bios were announced, and the babies who had been produced from their genetic donations during the year were revealed. Catchers visited the artificial wombs like pilgrims going to a shrine, and when the children who had survived their rites of passage returned, the wombs were emptied and the newest generation of Catchers was brought into the world.

It was a sacred time, a celebration of the great illusion, mingling birth and death, triumph and despair. No one who was not a Catcher and a follower of URdon Wee really under-stood its true significance. To Earthside, it was just one more lunatic ritual, and even within the League it was widely mis-understood. Nobody in Catchcage really cared. All that mat-tered was the Children and what they would become.

What they would become was determined by Going to See the End of the Sky. From that ordeal the Exceptional emerged. Push and Chancey were Exceptional People already. They were the first set of twins born in the Cage, and even if they were not, they would have been cherished everywhere in the Cage for the brilliant orange redness of their hair. Redheads were no rarity in the Cage; early Corporation psychologists were of the opinion that redheads took to the sky better and so sent up as many as possible, but Push and Chancey's hair was the vivid orange-red of URdon Wee. It was taken as a special indication of cosmic favor, and they were looked on everywhere as omens of good fortune and a reminder that nothing ever stays lost.

Nevertheless, they were about to depart without air, food, or water on an eighty-thousand-mile journey that would last six days, a trial that would involve their dying and their rebirth. Beyar watched the long, empty distance between the Cage and the moon, and remembered his own trip.

Beyar came out of the Little Death slowly. The kidneycar was still well outside the LUNAC Gates, and he had plenty of time. He let his heart rate increase by three beats every minute, but he made his respiration lag a bit to give his Re-breather a chance to catch up. The Re-breathers were good for four days, and a Catcher at full rest in the Little Death could make it last a week, but a sudden change in his oxygen rate might made him giddy, and he wanted to avoid it.

He worked his muscles from toes to head, just as he had been doing for three days, but the contraction-hold-release his body had been automatically practicing since he went into the Little Death increased in intensity and frequency. He'd have a good deal of scrambling to do before long, and he didn't want the residuals of three days inactivity to cramp him up once the Scouring Robot opened his pod. It took him twenty minutes to work his way back to normal, and when he finally began to move, his skinsuit was stiffer than he was.

The suit was a marvel of technology, but it was designed for hard work in unpressurized environments, and it required at least occasional movement to keep it supple. Three days of only minute shifts in position had left the thin, transparent skin as stiff as cold leather. For OBees laying up structure or. Catchers in the Catchround or Loonies working Outside on the moon, it was no more uncomfortable than a second skin three quarters of an inch thick, but on a Catcher laying in a kidneycar for three days it felt as if a glove had been stretched over him and shrunk. It was going to take a good ten minutes of the most strenuous exercise the kidneycar would allow without going off course to loosen it up. The only thing on his side was that the Little Death had kept waste processing to a minimum, and there was not a lot of excess thickness to the skin to get in the way.

There was no need to check the pressurizing layer of the suit; if it had failed during his hibernation, he'd already be dead, but he checked it anyway. It was in the least danger while he was immobile, but tough as it was, it would require careful movement inside the kidneycar. A snag on one of the rough chunks of ore still stuck to the inside of the pod could theoretically pierce it. The hole would not have to be a big one for his flesh to push out through and burst like a balloon. A rip the size of his palm would cause him to expand until he burst, and even the Little Death would not be able to keep him from being sprayed over the inside of the pod like a coat of wet paint. If a suit ruptured anywhere between the Moon and the Catchround, the remains were sent home in a bottle, if they were sent at all.

He touched the lump under his arm to check his rations. The skinsuit kept him from feeling it, except for a buzzing provided by sensors in the fingertips of the suit, but he could tell its size from inside better than from without, anyway. There was still plenty left. The Feeders were designed to meet the weekly energy needs of people doing heavy work under emergency conditions; they were more than enough for the minimal energy usage of the Little Death. Everything seemed abundant—air, water, food. There was more than enough to get back; all he had to do was survive the Scouring Robot. He would have to get the stiffness out of his suit to do that. He was still doing his routine of twists, tucks, and short rolls when the kidneycar went through the first gate.

The trajectory was a little off, and the field seemed to whack the kidneycar on one side harder than the other. The sudden jolt caught him in a weightless tuck and twirled him into the far wall. He caromed off immediately and hit the Nearside wall as well before he pinwheeled and regained control. He breathed a little sigh of relief that he hadn't split his suit on one of the rough outcroppings and settled down on the floor of the pod to wait for the next nine Gates. It did not occur to him that he had lost his orientation until the Scouring Robot cracked the pod, and then it was almost too late.

Except for the stinging buzz of so many pressure sensors being struck at once, the impact had not damaged the suit, and he was confident he was still in good shape. The gravity on the moon was not much, one-twentieth Earth's, but it was still a good deal more than on some levels of Catchcage, and it provided enough information for him to know down from up. What he didn't know was back from front.

It was a life-or-death difference. The Scouring Robot always began to clean a pod from the end farthest away from the accelerator. It cracked the pod, lifted the top shell, and turned to hang it on an overhead rack before it scoured debris from the bottom half. The usual strategy was to crouch in the front third of the pod and bolt for daylight as soon as it was cracked. A Catcher who was quick could be over the lip of the bottom shell and gone long before the Scouring Robot turned back and began grinding the clumps of debris from it.

But even the slowest Catchers had a reasonably good chance if they stayed at the front end and didn't panic. Hanging the pod lid took only a second or two, but a Catcher could be sure of another four or five seconds as the machine slid the lid toward the back of the kidneycar and put it into position to be lifted and hung. The scouring took even longer, and a Catcher had another thirty seconds before the blades and burrs worked their way down to the front end.

At the other end it was a different story. There were only two choices, the Scramble and the Long Run. Neither of them was very good. Those who opted for the Scramble positioned themselves under the lid while it was balanced at the back end of the shell and tried to scramble up the side and over the lip before the Scouring Robot could swing away, hang the top shell, and swing back. For most it was a bad choice. Anyone disoriented enough to be in the wrong end had probably been banged up and tossed around a good bit coming through the Gates, and they weren't likely to get over the lip before the robot turned back.

The Long Run was not much better. As soon as the robot swung back and its arms began their whirling assault on the clumps of debris still sticking to the inside, the shell shook and vibrated to sift the dust down to the bottom middle of the pod where it could be swept into the dust snake in one pass. The scouring raised a fog of debris, and the unsure footing and poor visibility made a successful dash for the far end of the shell a bad bet. At least half of those who came back Skyshocked had been forced to make the Long Run. None of those who did ever forgot it.

Beyar tensed himself and waited for the light, but it broke over him from the wrong direction, and everything seemed suddenly confused. The upper shell slid forward instead of back, blocking the way out. Everything seemed backward, and even the realization that he was in the wrong end of the pod did not suddenly put things right. The walls around him looked strange and distorted. He struggled to reorient himself, to decide between the Scramble and the Run, but when he looked over his shoulder, the pod twisted away from him at impossible angles, and the front wall of the shell seemed miles away.

He closed his eyes and forced himself to take a long, deep breath. When he opened them again, things had returned to their proper shape, but time seemed twisted and deformed. The lid lifted up and away with amazing slowness. The long, languid curve of its arc toward the rack fascinated him, and he could not stop watching it and make himself move one way or the other. The dreamlike slowness of the robot made him feel as if he had forever to decide. Time seemed to stretch and stretch and stretch. When it finally stretched to the breaking point, the robot was already turning back, and he had only one choice left.

He chose the Run, and everything snapped back to normal. He let himself slide down the wall and hit the bottom already running. Every time his foot hit, the pressure sensors raised the tingle on his skin to a buzz that was almost painful, and his legs ached before he had gone two steps. He felt like his feet were being held fast to the bottom every time he tried to lift them. The pod gave a shudder that almost toppled him as the arms of the robot banged down onto the sides, but it was nothing compared to the vibrations that ran through the metal when the scouring began.

At first the floor seemed to be sliding rapidly back and forth beneath his feet, but in a moment it seemed to disappear entirely as the vibrations overwhelmed the pressure sensors in the soles of his suit. It made him feel like he was running on nothing at all. The whirling arms of the robot closed in behind him, and the vibrations ran up his legs, canceling out the pressure sensors. The cloud of debris thrown forward by the scouring rolled past him, and he could not shake the impression that he was suddenly waist-deep in dirty, gray-brown water.

His legs kept moving, but he could no longer see or feel the bottom of the pod, and he half ran, half swam toward the safety of the far end. Dust and vibrations rose up the surface of his suit; the illusion of dirty water swirled everywhere around him, rolled over him and submerged him. He could no longer tell whether he was running or drowning. He did not

*feel the clump of debris when his foot hit it, and he did not
realize that he had fallen even when he hit.*

The impact was lost in the flood of vibrations that
drowned the suit's sensors. He had a vague impression of
tumbling or rolling, but he was not sure when he came to rest
or where. He lay still on the bottom of the pod for precious
seconds, trying to make some sense of where he was. But all he
could feel for certain was the terror. The dust flooded past him
in thicker and thicker currents. The burrs of the robot's
scouring arms were so close that he could almost feel them
beginning to tear into his suit. They roared and slowed,
roared and slowed, like a great beast toying with him before it
devoured him. He waited for the terrible pain. He was not
afraid of what would follow it, but he was terrified of the
pain itself.

When he heard the voice of URdon Wee, he thought it
was welcoming him to the Otherworld. The fear left him and
he felt a great peacefulness. URdon Wee's voice was gentle and
soothing, just as he remembered it from earliest childhood. The
sound of silent, blissful laughter still echoed beneath everything
it said. The words were familiar. "Nothing is what it seems,
Beyar. There is nothing to fear. You are the Center around
which everything forms."

It was all he needed to reorient himself. As they always
did, the words made perfect sense of everything. He recognized
the roar and retreat of the scouring arms for what it was. The
machine was simply grinding away at the stubborn clump of
debris he had tripped over. When it was finished, it would
move on to the rest of the shell. He would be gone by then, he
was certain of it. The robot itself would give him all the
information he needed to get out. He stopped running from it
and let it advise him.

He forced his heart to slow and let his senses open. What
he had needed to know was there all the time; fear had
obscured it. Even within the chaos of vibrations that roared

*through the suit there was a pattern, once he listened for it.
The vibrations were strongest from the front of his suit. It
meant he was lying facedown. He felt for the current again.
It was greater near his feet than at his head; the arms were
moving toward him from behind. It meant he had fallen
straight forward, apparently tumbling as he went.*

*He was probably closer to his goal than he had hoped,
but he still could not see, and the sensors of his suit were still
too overloaded for him to run. Without the blinding panic
that had gripped him, the answer was obvious. He crawled
forward until the wall began to slope uphill. Then he pushed
himself to his feet and reached up. His fingers hooked over the
rim of the wall. Behind him, the vibrations of the scouring
arms rose to a sudden peak as the last piece of debris crumbled
and dissolved. They would be moving rapidly up the wall
behind him, but he was not worried. He pulled himself up
and threw one leg over the top of the wall.*

*He looked back down into the shell as he eased his body
over. The huge whirring blades and stiff bristles of the
scouring arms were right behind him with no debris to slow
them, but they held no terror for him. He saw their beauty
and wondered how he could have seen anything else. He
waited until they were almost upon him, then he rolled over
the lip and dropped.*

Beyar gave one last look at the moon. It was time to go
up to the Catchround. Push and Chancey were probably already
there, and there would be little enough time for good-byes.
He turned away reluctantly from the Nearside Window. The
fact that *he* had survived the Long Run did not mean the
twins would. Two people had never gone in the same pod
before; two people could only get in each other's way. The
attempt would have been suicidal for anybody else, but the
Cage's only set of twins never did anything alone, and he
knew they would never go separately. He only hoped they
would come back together.

The reflection of something behind him moved in the

glass like a shadow. He noticed the eyes before he noticed anything else: dark, cruel eyes with a fanatic's gleam. The man behind the eyes was big; big enough to pass for a member of the Fist, if he had had a uniform, but he wore only the rough coverall of an OBee. He leaned against one of the pillars supporting the gallery above them as if he were simply looking out at the moon, but Beyar knew he was not. He could feel the eyes watching him, and he tried not to meet them in the glass. He looked through the glass toward the moon again. It looked somehow more ominous than before. When he let his focus shift back, the image of the man was gone.

Beyar searched for it right and left along the glass, but he did not turn to look for the man himself. It seemed too dangerous a thing to do, though he could not have said why. He felt a sudden sharp concern for Push and Chancey, as if the man had left him only to go after them. He turned away and hurried toward the zero gravity of the Upshoot, which would take him to the Catchway.

Partway there he realized he would have to stop for his suit, there would be no time to come back down for it. But if he stopped, the man was certain to get there ahead of him. Things seemed to be slipping past him out of control. He had the feeling of being overwhelmed again, of being drowned in dirty water to the roar of some danger just out of sight. His heart began to pound, but when he looked up toward the railing of the lower gallery, what he saw there made him feel safe. It was the smiling face of URdon Wee. It was a smile he had seen before, and it did not seem at all strange to him that it was the smile of a man who had died more than two decades before.

CHAPTER
TWO

URdon Wee was the original Skyshocker, the first of the lunatic saints of Catchcage, and the founder of the Catchcage religion, which held that all things can be, and are, transmuted into all other things; that death is only a temporary change of state, not a dissolution of matter or a permanent extinction of awareness; and that everything is an expression of an ultimately joyous intelligence. Or, as URdon Wee put it, "Nothing is what it seems," "Nothing stays lost," and "God is always laughing."

URdon Wee was a small, redheaded chemist named Donald Wheeler, who came up even before the first settlers. Like most of the original scientists, he was drawn by the promise of the Torch. The energy recovered from the incoming kidneycars by the Gates not only powered the smelter, it also ran a small torch with the highest continuous temperature ever achieved by mankind.

The high temperatures of the Torch promised insights into the very secrets of matter itself that were an irresistible lure to physicists and chemists alike. At the very least, the temperatures were expected to make possible experiments in plasma technology far beyond anything that could be achieved on Earth. But URdon Wee did not come for the least; he came for the ultimate, the key to the relationship between matter and energy. In a sense, he came for the Philosophers' Stone, the secret process the medieval alchemists had been searching for in their vain attempts to turn lead into gold.

URdon Wee was not attracted by anything as trivial as the ability to turn lead into gold. With an incredible expenditure of energy, and at the cost of a billion dollars an ounce, that trick had been accomplished as early as 1980, and a great deal was already known about the boundary state between matter and energy from early experiments with extreme temperatures on Earth. But those temperatures had been fleeting, from billionths of a second to a few minutes at best.

The Torch, however, promised hours, days, even weeks at the highest intensities of temperature. Experiments that had not even been considered on Earth were possible in Catchcage, and from those experiments might come an understanding of the transitional process that converted matter into energy and energy into matter.

To the Corporation that knowledge promised only more profitable techniques for producing energy. To a chemist like Donald Wheeler, who had studied the history of his profession all the way back to the alchemists, they promised the secrets of creation itself. He understood what the alchemists had understood and what had escaped even the avarice of the Corporation: The power to transmute energy into matter and back again was the ultimate power of creation and re-creation. Like the Philosophers' Stone, it meant nothing short of immortality.

The fact that Donald Wheeler was a history buff and an amateur alchemist was a matter of anything but coincidence to the Skyshockers; it was a matter of destiny. But it was not as unlikely a set of credentials as they liked to pretend. Science had been adding a metaphysical dimension since the dawn of the new century, anyway, and Donald Wheeler was simply a continuing step in the process. The limit of twentieth-century science had been that it saw with only one eye, and thus saw only the surface of things, missing significance in the pursuit of mechanics.

When Donald Wheeler became URdon Wee, he saw the interrelatedness of all things and the underlying process of energy, of which all things are merely illusory forms. To the enlightened understanding of URdon Wee, matter, the basic stuff of reality, was nothing more than a beat phenomenon created where passing forces overlap. Even to Science, beat phenomena were commonplace; the darkened shadow formed where two shadows overlap, the play of light on water, and the pattern created by the intersecting lines of a moiré pattern were all beat phenomena. All beat phenomena have no substance; they are artifacts of interaction, created by the overlap of forces. They are, in short, illusion.

To the Skyshockers, the first beat phenomenon is the physical world itself, the second is death, the third is the illusion of personal existence. It was URdon Wee's insistence on referring to the illusion of death as "The Great Joke" that made scientists from Earthside refer to the religion of the Skyshockers scornfully as Weeism, or Regional Laughing Zen. They were equally skeptical of URdon Wee's enlightenment, and the circumstances surrounding it did little to change their opinions.

URdon Wee, in one of the religion's ubiquitous contradictions, came to his enlightenment not like a Catcher but like an OBee, that is, through sex and violence. The story of URdon Wee's enlightenment always begins with the words "Nothing is what it seems." The Skyshocker explanation of this statement, in its shortest form, holds that URdon Wee meant both that everything is something different than it appears and that nothing is just what it seems to be, nothing. Nothingness does not exist. Nonbeing does not exist. Loss of perception does not exist. "Nothing stays lost."

Perception, according to URdon Wee, is only the interaction of the perceiving force and the force perceived. The interface between these two, where the ultimate awareness curves back on itself, is reality. But all reality is only a beat phenomenon created where the Ultimate Perceiver perceives itself. What seems like death, then, is only a temporary state in which the force unbends, becomes completely itself, and enjoys, for a moment, unlimited perception before rebending over itself again and creating some new reality. The nothingness of nonbeing, the end of perception, then, is nothing more than an inexpressible perception that is without limits and therefore cannot be understood in limited terms.

As URdon Wee put it before he received enlightenment, "The infinite cannot, by definition, be expressed in finite terms." Which led to its corollary, "All perception is a limited distortion of the unlimited," which led inevitably to "All perception is ultimately wrong, or everything is an illusion." In other words, "Nothing is what it seems."

This chain of conclusions was translated into enlightenment for Donald Wheeler by a woman's kiss, an OBee's fist, and a swallow of sunrise.

Nothing is what it seems. Many of the original scientists of Catchcage were conducting tests with the Torch while the Original Builders were still constructing Catchcage. The Catchers lived in the completed portions of the Cage while the OBees lived in the jumble of converted cargo containers and dormitories known as Hardcore. Despite the seeming difference in their backgrounds, attitudes, and interests, some members of both groups got together for mutual entertainment far more often than the psychological engineers of the Corporation had ever anticipated.

The creation of chemicals to change perception was well advanced by the time Catchcage was being built, and a number of those who volunteered for work at the Torch dabbled in pharmacology as frequently as they practiced chemistry. Because the Philosophers' Stone is a substance that transmutes *everything*, Donald Wheeler was as active in this pursuit as anyone in the Cage, and it was not surprising that he headed a small group of creative scientists he named the Alchemists.

The OBees had a symbiotic relationship with the Alchemists. Whenever the Alchemists invented something new that might or might not alter human perception, they naturally need some guinea pig to test it on. To their credit, they were very straighforward about their concoctions, telling the OBees exactly what thrills and spills each new chemical might provide and warning them that they had absolutely no idea what the ultimate consequences of taking such a pill, powder, or potion might be. The OBees, being OBees, inevitably took whatever was offered, and from time to time some of them succumbed as the result of such experiments. These fatalities were regretted more by the Alchemists than by the OBees, who were used to death and did not expect to live out the week in any case, the mortality rate of early construction being what it was.

Skyshocker theology is ultimately silent on how URdon Wee discovered the Philosophers' Stone, although secular legend holds that it was the first room-temperature plasma, a gaseous form of matter or haze of energy Donald Wheeler had transmuted from the two basic nucleoproteins found in every human cell. Whatever its source, Donald Wheeler embarked for Hardcore with a small beaker of what looked like crimson haze, in search of an experimental subject.

Like most of the Alchemists in search of a guinea pig, Donald Wheeler ended up at Grandy's, a place of recreation and respite for the weary souls of Hardcore. Grandy was just that—grand. She was gorgeous, bright, and pragmatic, and she was the first, though far from the last, woman to get rich in the League. She was a woman everybody wanted but nobody could get, except on her terms and for her purposes, and then very infrequently. She provided other young women and men of less virtue and craftiness with a way of getting together without the kind of tangling alliances that make for bloodshed in such cramped quarters. She was well respected and well paid for her mediations, and she was both the most desirable and least attainable woman in the League.

Immediately prior to the moment of his enlightenment, URdon Wee was defending the scientific principle that all events in the natural world are the result of measurable forces and can be reduced to quantities and ultimately to number. He was holding a beaker of sunset-colored haze and had seemingly reduced Grandy to a point of no rebuttal with his argument when she grabbed him by both ears and kissed him with such passion and skill that Skyshockers insist the contents of the beaker began to glow with heat and had to be set down on the long table that passed for a bar. Certainly it aroused the envy of every man in Grandy's Place of Respite and Recreation for Weary OBees.

When she let him go, Grandy said, "Now, let's see you reduce *that* to a known and measurable quantity." Whether Donald Wheeler would have been able to do so is doubtful, but it will never be known because, before he could compose himself, an OBee named Back Toss Hool, whose unrequited passion for Grandy had squeezed him beyond the limits of endurance, stepped roaring up to him out of the crowd and punched him squarely in the face, breaking his nose and scattering his wits. "Yeah," said the OBee, "let's see you reduce *that* to a known and measurable quantity."

Donald Wheeler said nothing but sat down abruptly on the nearest chairlike object, which happened to be Grandy's lap. Grandy, in an attempt to revive the Alchemist, gave him a long drink from the beaker, and the rest is history, or, in Catchcage, religion.

Whether it was Grandy's kiss, the OBee's blow, or the contents of the beaker is not known, but Donald Wheeler was on the instant transformed into URdon Wee. He later interpreted the incident by saying that the overlap of all three forces was necessary to create the beat phenomenon of his enlightenment. Grandy's kiss was certainly more than the sum of its parts, and the OBee's punch was equally incapable of being expressed completely in numerical terms. URdon Wee said that he understood these two points completely, even before the contents of the beaker took effect. However, it was the sudden transmutation of everything in the room that made the real breakthrough.

The contents of Donald Wheeler's beaker allowed him to see the entire universe as a flux of overlapping energy patterns that formed matter wherever they overlapped. This perception also rendered him capable of several significant abilities, not the least of which was an absolute freedom from the terrors of mortality. And from that instant on, he became the first of the Skyshockers.

He received his holy name when Grandy, in an effort to ascertain if he was suffering from a concussion, asked him what his name was, and he answered, "Ur . . . Don Whee . . ." But he could not for the life of him think of the rest of it, to the great hilarity of the OBees, who thereafter called him URdon the Wee. Skyshockers generally treated the disrespectful reference to his size with a smile, as URdon Wee had done. But among OBees converted to the form of the Skyshocker religion practiced secretly in Hardcore, saying it without the proper tone of reverence was worth a broken arm at the minimum.

URdon Wee's beaker became the sacramental vessel of a religion that swept Catchcage and much of Hardcore. Its success cannot be explained simply as the invention of the ultimate brain-distorter for which a clever chemist with a background in alchemy provided a bogus theological justification. Neither the OBees nor a good many of the Catchers were strangers to the altered states of consciousness available through chemistry. They were clearly not people who had never experienced a transcendent state or one in which their normal processing of information was radically changed. The swallowing of URdon's Sunrise allowed not a distortion of ordinary perception, but a radically new way of perceiving and conceptualizing the universe.

The new perception automatically separated the Sky-shockers from the rest of humankind and especially from nonbelievers in Hardcore and the rest of the League. The radically new intelligence it produced seemed like madness to everyone else, especially when it turned out that although one exposure brought enlightenment, two usually brought death, or as URdon put it, a temporary change of state. For some, even one swallow of the Sunrise was fatal. Even so, it spread throughout the League.

Eventually the Corporation banned its use. Skyshockers ignored the ban. The Fist enforced it. The Skyshockers resisted. For a moment the League teetered on the brink of a holy war the Skyshockers had no chance of winning. It was not at all what URdon Wee intended, and twenty years before Beyar was born, on the twenty-seventh day of the second lunar month, URdon Wee assembled the core of his followers on the Catchround. He told them what he had been telling them for ten years. "Nothing is what it seems. Nothing stays lost. God is always laughing." Then he told them one thing more. "I am getting lost," he said. "And I am taking the Sunrise with me."

Then he stepped into an empty kidneycar and pulled the lid down over him. His followers pleaded to know where he was going. URdon Wee cracked the pod a moment. It was already moving toward the accelerator. There was a twinkle in his eyes. "Where else would I take the Sunrise," he said. "To the End of the Sky."

"But what are we supposed to do?" they shouted.

"Get lost too," he said. Then he pulled the kidneycar shut, and the accelerator shot him toward the moon. The kidneycar broke open going through the first of the LUNAC Gates, flinging URdon Wee toward the lunar surface. His body was never recovered.

The rest of the Catchers took him at his word. The religion officially disbanded, and the Fist withdrew from Catchcage. But, true to URdon Wee's words, "Nothing stays lost," and on the first anniversary of URdon Wee's death the children of Catchcage began Going to See the End of the Sky.

It was one of the things that made URdon Wee smile as he watched Beyar hurrying toward the Upshoot.

CHAPTER

THREE

Chancey paced impatiently back and forth along the window that looked out into the Catchround. Her skin-suit was sealed up to the chin, but she had yet to peel the transparent hood up over her head and down tight against her face. There was no need; the Watchdeck was fully pressurized. Only out on the deck of the Catchround would she need its protection. The torso of her suit was a brilliant green that set off the redness of her hair. Normally her hair was brushed up and away from her head in a short, fiery halo, but now she wore it pulled tight against her head to fit more snugly into the hood. "Where's Beyar?" she said. She looked at Push as if he were intentionally hiding Beyar to make them late.

Push grinned as if her suspicions were correct. "He's not late," he said. They had spent the morning together, and Beyar had left them only a half hour before. "I don't know why you're so impatient." He was already a size larger than Chancey, but he had the same red hair, the same high cheekbones, and the same blue eyes, bright with anticipation. They were as identical as two people could be and not be of the same sex. Even at twelve it was already clear that Push was going to be a strong young man, although not as big as Beyar, and Chancey already had the grace and maturity of a young woman.

Chancey turned and looked out at the other children piling into the kidneycars that bobbed like corks through the guiderails of the Catchround. "Half of them are gone already," she complained.

"It's not a race," he said, "and we're going last, anyway."

Chancey turned back toward him. "I know," she said. "It's already too late to go first." For somebody who wanted to become an Exceptional Person, first and last were the best positions. The first off got the most attention going, the last back got the greatest welcome home again. She knew all the reasons why they had chosen to go last instead of first, but she had not anticipated the waiting.

Push knew that without being told, just as he knew a great many things about Chancey without her saying anything. "It's not *when* you go," he said, "it's *how*." He gave her a conspiratorial grin. She nodded, but he knew what she was thinking. "Beyar won't try to stop us," he said.

Chancey looked doubtful. "No, but he'll *want* to." He knew what she meant. All adults were their co-parents and all children their brothers and sisters, but there was a special bond between them and Beyar. They were all frozen stock, and the biology they shared had brought them together from the beginning. One of the things that kept Catchers forever part of Catchcage was the special provisions of the Lottery. Whenever a Catcher came of age, they donated a sample of genetic material to be frozen as their entry in the Lottery for as long as the Lottery was run.

It was a kind of immortality; a Catcher long gone out of the illusion of the world might still win the Lottery and contribute the frozen stock from which one of the next generation would be cloned. A winner could even choose whether the offspring made from their contribution would be male or female, and while it was still a small uncurling ball of cells, a spurt of male hormone or female into the artificial womb would see to it that their wishes were carried out. Every year five or ten of the winners did not currently live in Catchcage, and one or two no longer lived anywhere, but it did not happen often that the winner was one of the originals who had known URdon Wee.

Most of the children had a Bio who had contributed to their genetic makeup along with URdon Wee, and although the Bio was not their parent in the sense of a parent Earthside, or even elsewhere in the League, they enjoyed a special relationship with their offspring. Those whose Bios were gone generally formed a special relationship with one of the thousands of co-parents or with one of the two thousand or so children and young adults who qualified as their older brothers and sisters. For Push and Chancey it was Beyar.

Because of a series of coincidences that would have made anyone else in the League suspect that the Lottery was fixed, there was no one else it could have been but Beyar. They were the closest thing to biological brothers and sisters that existed in the Cage. In thirty years only one person had won the Lottery twice, and all three were made from the same winner. By the time she won the first time, there were about 9,000 people, living or dead, in the Lottery.

The odds were about the same four years later when she won again, but as cynics from other parts of the League were quick to point out, since there were 150 winners every year, the odds against being one were only about 60 to 1, and the odds against winning twice only about 3,600 to 1. Statisticians, in fact, argued that the truly remarkable thing was that it had happened only once in thirty odd years, especially in the early years when fewer people were eligible.

But what made everybody but the Catchers suspicious was not that the winner both times had been dead for twenty years, but that it was none other than the woman most responsible for URdon Wee's enlightenment, Grandy herself. The Catchers, when confronted with the coincidence, said only, "God is always laughing." Nevertheless, they thought so much of it that they voted unanimously that the new off-spring should be twins in honor of the uniqueness of the event.

For Push and Chancey there was no question that Beyar would have to be the one to seal them in for their trip to see the End of the Sky, and yet both of them knew it would be Beyar who suffered most if their plan failed. They would be beyond suffering.

Chancey scowled, as if it were something Beyar had already done. "He'll think it's his fault, you know."

Push knew she was right. If they failed to return, Beyar would always believe it was something *he* had done wrong or failed to do. "Don't worry," he said, "nothing will go wrong."

"I know," she said.

It was what she didn't say that worried Push. He knew she felt a kind of dread about what was going to happen, and yet he himself felt certain that everything was going to turn out all right. It was not the premonitions that bothered him, they had always had an extra sense about how things would turn out; it was the fact that they differed. When Chancey had a feeling about something, he usually felt the same way, and for them to feel differently about the outcome of anything as important as Going to See the End of the Sky was a major cause for concern. It would have been easier to chalk it up to nerves on Chancey's part, but he knew better. "Besides," he said, "Beyar would understand." He shrugged as if it didn't really matter. "You can't be Exceptional without taking risks."

He was perfectly right about that, and Chancey knew it. To be Special a child needed only to survive; to be Outstanding required surviving unusually difficult circumstances, but to be Exceptional was to do something so radically different from what had been done before that it changed the *way* people went to see the End of the Sky. Beyar had made the Long Run, which had made him Outstanding, but it was what he had done at the Accelerator that had made him Exceptional.

He had done the unthinkable, and they were sure he would understand what they were going to do.

Chancey looked back out the window. She watched older children securing the shells of the kidneycars for their specialbrothers and sisters. The kidneycars picked up speed just beyond the curve and started into the Accelerator. She thought about the long journey in the dark. "Do you ever think about her?" she said wistfully.

Push frowned. It was a question she had only asked him once before, while they were waiting for Beyar to come back from the end of the sky. "Grandy?" he said. She looked at him over her shoulder as if it were a stupid question. He nodded. "Sometimes."

She looked away again. "What do you think she was like?" It was an impossible question. The only answers they had were legends and a few holos. Push shrugged.

"Like URdon Wee," he said.

"Really like," she said.

Push shrugged. He watched Beyar's reflection close in on them from behind across Watchdeck. "Ask Beyar," he said. It was something he'd been saying to her since they were able to talk.

Beyar cocked his head. "Ask Beyar what?"

Chancey turned away from the window with a smile. She ran over and hugged Beyar. "Where were you?" she said. "We've been waiting for hours. Everybody's gone. We thought we were going to have to close up ourselves," she said.

Beyar laughed. "I went for my suit," he said. He did not mention the man in the Nearside Window or URdon Wee. "I thought you were going last."

"We are."

Beyar looked out the window at the knots of children still on the deck of the Catchround. "You've got days yet."

Push laughed. "She wants to be last but leave first." Beyar smiled. Patience was never Chancey's strength. She was all action and enthusiasm, a field of crackling energy in constant discharge.

Chancey pouted. "I've waited a quarter of a century for this," she said indignantly.

Beyar raised an eyebrow. "You're only twelve," he said.

"I don't care," she said, "it feels like a quarter of a century."

Beyar put a hand on her shoulder. "It'll feel like a full century before you two come back," he said. Even Beyar was not sure whether he meant that it would seem like it to them or to him. Chancey gave Push a look that said she knew Beyar would spend the whole time worrying about them. Beyar changed the subject. "What were you going to ask me?"

Chancey looked away in embarrassment. "Oh, I don't know. Nothing, really." Beyar tried to keep the disappointment out of his face, but the twins both felt it and knew where it came from. No matter how close he was to them, there was always a barrier he could not cross into the world they shared only with each other. It was nothing intentional, it was just that they seemed to know each other's thoughts so well that there seemed to be a constant conversation going on between them he could never take part in, a dialogue he would be forever deaf to. It made him feel separate and alone in a way he was sure the twins never felt.

The twins knew how he felt even though they knew there was nothing they could do about it. They did not intentionally exclude him, and they felt closer to him than any other human being, except each other. Chancey felt a twinge of sorrow for the uncrossable gulf between them whenever she saw it. She asked the question like a bridge. "I wanted to know what Push thought she was like."

Beyar said the same thing as Push, but he had no idea who she meant. "Who?"

It made Chancey feel even further from him at a time

when she wanted to feel so close. She had half hoped he would *know*. "Grandy," she said finally.

Beyar nodded as if it were a question he asked himself some times. Chancey was glad of that. "A lot like you," he said. Chancey smiled and turned away toward the window. Beyar came up beside her and stood with his arm around her shoulder and Push's as they watched the crowd dwindle. They said nothing else for a long time.

CHAPTER
FOUR

When there were only about ten Catchers left waiting for pods, Beyar gave their shoulders a squeeze. "Time to get you two into your kidneycars," he said.

The twins cocked their heads toward him. "Cars?" they said in unison.

Beyar shrugged as if it had been worth a try. He knew there would be no arguing them out of going in one car, and he said nothing. They knew his arguments already. They were too young, hardly twelve; in another year they'd be bigger, stronger, smarter. Nobody knew what effect two people trying to work the kinks out after three days in the Little Death would have on the balance of the kidneycar. There wasn't room enough to get out. Two people would only get in each other's way. Having to think about somebody else would distract them from saving themselves. It was no argument at all to tell them nobody had ever even tried it before. That was the reason they were doing it: It guaranteed them an Outstanding at the very least, and they all knew it.

He knew their arguments without needing to hear them. They were the same age he had been when he went. Two bodies moving in unison were more likely to balance the kidneycar than unbalance it. They were not two people, anyway, but one person in two bodies. They wouldn't get in each other's way because they always anticipated each other's thoughts. They'd be more distracted wondering how the other was making out in a separate pod. They had the right to make their attempt just as he had; they had the same heritage to uphold.

"*Car*, then" he said. They smiled at one another, and he gave each of them a hug in turn. There was an awkward moment while they dug out their Leavings. It was a tradition. Anyone Going to See the End of the Sky made out a note the night before assigning everything they thought of as theirs to be given to the special people in their lives if they didn't come back.

The Leavings could be anything from a special place to sit to some little piece of home art or some prized possession. They were given to the specialbrother or sister selected to close the pod lid over them and were given back to the survivors when they returned. No one knew how you would have given out your things if you came back, and it was considered bad form to ask a survivor what had been written. The Leavings were kept sealed and returned the same way; nobody wanted to risk the terrible luck that came from opening a Catcher's Leavings before they were back safe and sound.

The twins handed their Leavings to Beyar with a smile. "Nothing's what it seems," they said. "Nothing stays lost," he answered. They grinned as if it were just a silly formality over a message they would never have to make real use of. He kissed them both good-bye. They pulled their hoods over their heads and smoothed the masks tight against their faces. He checked them without seeming to, and they let him without seeming to notice that he was doing it. Then he pulled his own hood on and they went out onto the Catchway.

Everyone was gone by the time they got to the deck of the Catchround. It gave Beyar an eerie feeling as he bent to pick up a pair of podwrenches. He chalked it up to nervousness when Push picked one up as well. Two empty kidneycars went by before he hooked one with the podwrench and then secured it to the guiderail with the lower hook on its shaft. He took the other podwrench and banged the buttons open. Push helped him lift the lid and stuck his wrench in to prop it open until he and Chancey climbed in.

Beyar rested his hand on the lip of the pod to steady it. It was covered with a thin coating of dust that made the sensors in his fingertips buzz as if they had touched something wet. For a moment it felt like blood and his own trip to see the End of the Sky came rushing back again.

Beyar pushed himself up on his hands and knees and shook his head. The dust came up to his elbows. The fall was not a long one, and the slight gravity had softened the part of the fall that the mound of dust under the tracks did not. The Scouring Robot no longer had any interest in him, and he picked himself up slowly and began to jog toward the far curve of the track where the loaded cars paused before the Button-up Robot sent them on their way to the Accelerator.

It was an easy run, and he took it in long bounding strides that were more a matter of exuberance than necessity. He expected to have to wait, anyway. One out of five kidneycars went up empty, for one reason or another, and the Corporation considered it a reasonably good average, high enough to keep the smelter going, low enough to justify charging as if three out of five went up unloaded. He climbed the low maintenance-platform beside the track without expecting an empty pod to be waiting for him. He was surprised that the first pod by had nothing in it.

He put his hand on the rim and started to pull himself up, but there was a tingling buzz from his palm that indicated something wet. He looked to see what it was, but the maroon glaze he saw made no sense to him. He held his palm up in front of him and touched it with his finger. He looked into the pod. The inside seemed to have been freshly painted. The sudden realization sickened him.

His hand and the pod were both covered with blood, and it meant that whoever had come down in that pod had not made it. He tried to think of who had left that far ahead of him, but it could have been anyone. It could have been him. The narrowness of his escape made his knees suddenly weak, and he almost put a hand on the kidneycar to steady himself. He jerked it back just before it touched the blood again. He looked at the hand again and shivered as the car began to move toward the Button-up.

He jumped down from the platform and fell on his hands and knees, trying to rub off the blood in the dust. But the sensors continued to tingle, as if it only got wetter the more he wiped. He rubbed his palms on his thighs, but it only made the sensors there tingle as well. He felt as if the blood, the blood of one of his brothers or sisters, would never come off, as if it had seeped through the suit and was permanently staining his hands.

He looked up and saw someone running across from the the Scouring Robot, and he knew he should climb back up on the platform and get in the pod before he caused a major backup and got somebody else killed, but he could not do it. The only other hope he had was that two cars would come up empty in a row, and it was too faint a hope to catch hold of. He could not stay where he was, and he could not go on if it meant climbing into that pod. He did the only thing left to do, and it made him an Exceptional. He broke the rules.

Actually there was only one rule in Catchcage: "Make it work." There were no rules at all in Going to See the End of the Sky. Everybody knew there were no rules, and yet even Catchers had unrecognized assumptions about what could be done in the way of tampering with machinery that belonged to the Corporation. What Beyar did changed assumptions about what could be done. It was the kind of thing that separated Catchers from everybody else. An Obee in the same situation simply would have fought any new arrival for the next empty kidneycar that came along. But that was unthinkable to a

Catcher. The girl running toward him was his sister, and anyone who came after her would be the same. Instead, he made his own kidneycar.

Near the end of the maintenance platform, just before the loading ramp for Button-up Robot, there was a Tally Computer that made the final decision about whether to shunt empty cars off onto the recycling circle for another chance at being filled or to let them continue to the Button-up Robot and then the Accelerator. If the side track was full, all cars went on to the Accelerator, empty or not. Beyar looked at the Tally Computer and then at the mounds of dust he had buried his hands in and thought the unthinkable.

He ran to the back of the Tally Robot and lifted its maintenance panel. Then he picked up a double handful of dust and grit and forced it into the machine. There was a series of flashes and a cascade of sparks, and when the fireworks were finished, so was the Tally Computer. Without the Tally Computer to shunt cars off onto the side track, every car that came along went on to launch.

Half of them were empty, but after the malfunction of the Tally Robot backed up the line, the loading stopped and nothing but empty cars came along the tracks. Everyone after Beyar could take their pick of empty cars. Beyar let a half dozen of his brothers and sisters go ahead of him before he finally climbed into an empty pod. He had done something revolutionary and he knew it. He had fulfilled what was expected of him. But even as he put himself into the Little Death, he thought of the blood that still lingered on his hands.

Beyar lifted his hand and saw that it was only dust, but it felt like blood nevertheless, and he had the urge to pull Push and Chancey back out of the pod before it was too late. But there was no hope of that. Both Push and Chancey were scrappers, and although he might, with a little bloodshed, have forced one of them out of the pod against their will, big as he was, he was no match for both of them. So he said nothing, for fear of making his fear theirs and putting them at a disadvantage, and turned to buttoning them up.

He lifted the lid and waited for Push to remove the podwrench and toss it out, but instead Push held on to it and brought it back inside the kidneycar with him. Beyar cocked his head, and Push and Chancey gave him a wink and a final smile before the lid banged shut. Push gave a little wave of the podwrench, and Beyar knew that Outstanding was not going to be good enough for them and the podwrench was going to have something to do with making them Exceptional. He was afraid to wonder what.

He thought for a moment of not buttoning them up, but he knew it would only delay them at best. As soon as he left the Catchround, they would be back with somebody else to button them up, and the buttoning-up was crucial. A strong seal would take the Scouring Robot a little extra time to get each button undone, and the twins would have that much longer to orient themselves properly. A badly buttoned car could split open when it hit the first LUNAC Gate, dumping out everything inside to go whirling away toward impact on the moon.

He turned the snaps to lock the shells together and began banging them with the podwrench to make them harder to open. He unhooked the car and let it float free, but even after it started to move he was not satisfied that the buttons were as tight as they could be. He ran alongside the kidneycar, hitting the buttons a third time each and then a fourth. But the fourth time he missed and hit the side of the pod. Chancey must have thought it was a signal because she banged back twice. He was not sure whether it meant "Good-bye" or "We're going to be okay" or "See you in a while" or maybe just "We love you." But her banging had a hollow ring that he thought would haunt him for the rest of his life if they did not come back.

He ran alongside the kidneycar on the deck for as long as he could before it began to accelerate, and he couldn't keep up. He sprinted for the Little Deck beside the opening of the accelerator, but they were gone before he reached it. He looked out to where the kidneycar dwindled toward the moon. At first it was a dot, and then a speck, and when it vanished, he was afraid it was gone forever.

CHAPTER
FIVE

They came out of the Little Death almost simultaneously. The suits glowed faintly in the dark, they had not been exposed to light since launch, and they had been radiating back what they had absorbed in storage for almost three days. There was not much left. They did not need much light to recharge, but there was none at all inside the kidneycar. Push looked over at Chancey. Her skin seemed pale and waxy in the faint light. She smiled.

They worked themselves slowly toward movement, increasing their heart rate, respiration, blood pressure. When they were ready, they canceled the magnetic strips that had held them in place and floated free. Beyar's fears about getting in each other's way when they moved were groundless. They moved like different parts of the same person; balanced, coordinated, graceful. They turned and stretched like delicate beings of light in a void. Their dance was almost finished when Push said, "They say the First Gate always comes early," he said, "We'd better get—"

They hit the first gate like the surface of the moon. It set them bouncing off the walls. They collided twice before Push grabbed Chancey and managed to stabilize them. One of them was upside down. There would be no way to tell which until they could feel lunar gravity. Chancey slumped limply against him, her head lolled, and her eyes were closed. They went through three more gates before she opened them. She blinked and shook her head. The motion made her wince. Push studied her pupils; they looked all right, but there was not enough light to be sure. "I don't know about fast," Chancey said, "but they *do* come up hard!"

Push nodded. "Too hard." The LUNAC Gates had to handle less variation in mass than the gates outside Catchcage, but their magnetic fields still varied widely depending on what was about to pass through them. Not many kidneycars came back from Catchcage unloaded, but it *did* happen, and allowances had been made for that kind of error after the first added a sizable crater to the moonscape and took three Loonies with it.

There was no time for LUNAC to control their field strength, so each gate had to read the incoming mass and react accordingly. They were programmed to err on the side of too much resistance rather than too little. From time to time they misread things. When the kidneycars were empty, it didn't much matter. It mattered considerably to Push and Chancey.

"You all right?" he said. Chancey nodded. She seemed all right, but when the next gate bumped them, he could see pain in her eyes.

"I'm Flash," she said. When a fully loaded kidneycar went through the gates at Catchcage, it made a flash; the saying meant everything was as it should be.

Push looked unconvinced. "What way's front?" he said. It was a ridiculous question; after the tumbling they'd done, Push had no more idea than she did.

"Whatever way we're facing." She was right. Even if she was wrong, it was better than being undecided. And as far as Push was concerned, it didn't really matter. He looked for the podwrench. It lay like a distorted question mark on the bottom of the car just beyond reach. It had apparently come loose when they hit the gate. He retrieved it in two short steps. "Lucky we didn't hit it while we were bouncing around," he said.

They felt the bump of another gate. It was a very light bump. "Which one was that?"

Push hefted the podwrench. "Must be the next to last, or this would still be floating." He was wrong by one. They waited for another jolt. Instead, the lid opened and the far end of the car filled with artificial light.

The unexpectedness stunned them for a moment, but they did not panic. They were in the wrong end, but they were ready. Front or back, they would scramble up over the lip and out. They waited for the Scouring Robot to slide the lid forward and lift it. As soon as it rose, they started to scramble up the side.

Push pulled himself up and threw a leg over the lip. Chancey was right beside him when he started, but, halfway up, her arms seemed to collapse and her feet slid back down the side. She hung there as if trying to clear her head. Her arms bent at the elbows as she tried to pull up again, but it was no use. Her feet clambered against the side.

She was still trying to pull herself up when the robot hung the lid and turned back. The burrs began to whirl and the arms came for Push. "Drop," he shouted. There was no point. If she couldn't climb, she certainly wouldn't make the Long Run, but she let go and slid down into the car.

She sat in the bottom, trying to make the car stop spinning. She had a moment or two. The Scouring Robot would start with the nearest clump of debris, and that would be Push. Only after he dropped to the ground would it begin to work its way down the sides toward her.

But Push had already begun the unthinkable. He did what no one had ever thought to do, even those who were trapped and knew they had nothing to lose. He attacked the robot itself. He came leaping off the lip of the car with the podwrench in his hand and scrambled right up between the robot's arms onto the main unit. The robot had no head, but Push kept beating on the topmost part of it until he could figure out where the vulnerable part of it was.

He found it mainly by luck, and the luck almost killed him. The Scouring Robot interpreted him as a clump of debris that had splashed out onto it and acted accordingly. A chunk of debris could work its way down into the robot's moving parts while it was working, causing a costly breakdown. That made cleaning itself a priority function. The arms swung up toward Push.

He was too busy banging away at it to notice until the burrs were almost in his face. He ducked sideways and they missed him, but the bar of the arm caught him near the top of the head and toppled him backward. He hit heavily, flat on his back, and lay still. The Scouring Robot, cleared of debris, returned to its primary task. The burrs and brushes started their steady progress down the inside wall toward Chancey.

She watched with a mixture of fascination and horror as it began its routine. Her head was clear, but she still felt weak, and her legs buckled twice as she tried to stand. It was about halfway down the side before she managed to get up, but the vibrations were already overwhelming her suit, and the dust was billowing down across her, making it impossible to see. She turned and started toward the far end, but she hadn't gone three steps before she fell again.

Push watched the robot swing back toward the kidneycar. He wanted to get up but he couldn't get his breath. He kept trying to breathe in, but his chest just wouldn't inflate. He'd been winded before and knew exactly what was wrong. His diaphragm was spasmed. He had to relax, let it reshape itself and reestablish its rhythm. He seemed to have been lying there for days already, and his mind kept telling him to get up before it was too late, but his body held his breath and wouldn't give it back.

He put the heel of his hand on top of his diaphragm and

pressed down in short, rapid strokes. The air seemed to pop back into him with a gasp. He gulped in two more breaths, and the diaphragm started to spasm again. He forced himself to take slow, moderate breaths. In a moment he could breathe; in another he could stand. He looked around for the pod-wrench.

Chancey struggled to her knees and looked over her shoulder. The thick cloud suddenly thinned and swirled toward her, and in the opening she could see the whirling blades. They were almost on top of her and she scrambled forward. She had no idea how far the end of the car was, and she had no real hope of making it. Her only hope was to stay ahead of the blades long enough for Push to help her.

Push scooped up the podwrench; clouds of dust boiled up out of the shell. He pounded on the back of the robot, but it paid no attention to him until he jumped up and slapped one of the hooks over its lowest arm. The vibrating of the shells slowed for a minute, then revved up.

Push hung on, dangling from the podwrench and kicking the sides of the robot with his feet. The burrs stopped, the blades retracted, the arms lifted, and the robot turned away to clean itself. There was no other way for it to interpret the situation than as a piece of hanging debris caught in its lowest arm mechanism. In their wildest dreams its designers had never thought of somebody attacking it with a podwrench. The idea was unheard of even among the Catchers.

When the arms were fully retracted and about to turn on themselves, Push dropped to the ground. He batted the bottom of the podwrench to unhook it, and it spun around the arm and dropped free. The machine turned away from its distraction.

But it did not go immediately for Chancey. Interruptions for self-cleaning happened too infrequently for it to be worth keeping track of where in the cleaning process the robot had been when it stopped. It was cheaper and easier just to have it start over. The burrs and brushes started again at the top of the back end of the pod. Push didn't give it a chance to go much farther.

He searched the back and sides for the opening to the main power unit. Warnings all over the panel told him it couldn't be opened while the machine was in motion, and he banged the thin crack of the door's outline until he had dented it enough to get the tip of the podwrench under it. He gave it two sharp pries, and it popped open.

He had bent it out and hammered it down by the time the arms had worked their way halfway across the bottom of the shell. The dust was getting thick again, and he knew it must mean that the robot was back where it had been when he had distracted it. How far beyond that Chancey was, he had no idea. There was no time to figure things out; he picked a pair of terminals at random and laid the podwrench across them. The flash knocked him backward just as Chancey dropped to the ground at the far end of the car.

She was on her feet before he was, and she staggered over to him. He was sitting up shaking his hands, as if they were on fire, when she got to him. She could see he was all right, and she flopped down beside him and lay there trying to catch her breath. He looked her over; she seemed all right. She nodded that she was before he could ask.

Push looked at the palms of his hands. They were burned, almost charred through in places, and full of cracks and blisters he would have to be careful not to break open. He'd come a lot closer to rupturing his suit than he wanted to think about. The panel was still sputtering and showering sparks out in a continuous stream. The Scouring Robot was slumped forward into the pod as if somebody had stabbed it in the back. He looked at his sister. She smiled. "Exceptional!" she said.

Push nodded. Undoubtedly she was right. The attack had been a whole series of things nobody had ever even thought of doing before. He had succeeded beyond their wildest expectations. When he had taken the podwrench along, he had expected only to wreck the Tally Computer as Beyar had done.

But even that would have been Exceptional. Beyar's attack on Corporation property had been spontaneous; that had been remarkable. But their attack would have been premeditated, and that was revolutionary. Wrecking the Scouring Robot was the stuff legends are made of. He felt as if URdon Wee had laid his hand upon him, as if he were standing at a crossroad of destiny. He exulted in his moment. He thought no other instant in his life would ever compare to it. He was wrong.

CHAPTER
SIX

Chancey took one last deep breath and started to get up. "Time to go home," she said. She put out her hand to help him up, but he only showed her his palms. They made her gasp. The skin of the suit was all bubbled and blistered, and they both knew what would happen if just one of the blisters broke. He curved his hands in, afraid the contact might open the cracks on his palms, and she grabbed his forearm and pulled him up.

They helped each other across the uneven terrain to the Button-up Robot. Push kept trying to hurry them forward, but Chancey held them back, afraid that if he stumbled, just putting a hand down to stop his fall, could pop the bubbles on his palms and suck him out into the vacuum.

It didn't matter; there were no pods going out. The loading robot was no longer loading because the Scouring Robot had broken down, and nothing else was being processed.

The Tally Computer was shunting cars off onto the recycling loop and not letting any through to the accelerator. Nothing was leaving. It left Push and Chancey with a dilemma: They had beaten the Scouring Robot, but they had no way back. It was something they hadn't counted on, and they stood on the loading platform just in front of the Button-up Robot, watching the kidneycars come forward and then shunt off to the left and the recycling track at the last moment. They got the idea almost simultaneously, but it was Chancey who acted.

She grabbed the podwrench from Push and bounded across the platform and down over the other side. The kidneycars went down a slight hill at the beginning of the recycling track, to give them enough momentum to travel the long, flat stretch of track that carried them up onto the main oval.

Chancey hooked the side of the kidneycar with the first hook of the podwrench and then rocked it to the side. It didn't move a lot, but the distance was shortened enough for her to catch the bigger hook on the outer side of the track. The car did not stop moving immediately, but the friction slowed it down to a bare crawl. The car behind it came down the little hill at full momentum and piled into it. It shifted the first car almost sideways in the track, and they were afraid for a minute that the podwrench was going to come loose, but it didn't.

Both cars scraped slowly along the track, but not fast enough to avoid the third car coming down the little hill. Its momentum was less than the two it hit, so it didn't knock into them very hard, but it, too, jammed up in the track. The fourth hit the third, the fifth hit the fourth, and when the sixth car came along to be shunted off on to the recycling track, Chancey was back on the platform with Push, waiting to board it.

The Button-up Robot was faced with a decision for which it had not been programmed. With the Scouring Robot broken, it should have shunted all kidneycars onto the recycling track until the problem was fixed. However, the Button-up Robot had no instructions for what to do if the recycling track was full or disabled. So it had to decide what to do on the basis of general principles. It had two choices: stop the traffic on the track and risk collisions from incoming cars, or start letting the cars through uncleaned for a long round trip to Catchcage and back.

There was a large enough track and enough stacking facilities to accommodate a three-day train of incoming cars from Catchcage. They could, with a few crews of Loonies, even be untracked manually and stacked if it became necessary, but there were no crews to take the burden of that decision from the Button-up Robot, and its overriding program in times of crisis was to pass the cars through to the Accelerator. Shutting down the line meant shutting down the Accelerator, and since it was cheaper to let a few dozen cars, or even a few hundred, go through empty than to shut everything down, it started passing cars, even unscoured ones, on through to the Accelerator.

Push and Chancey took the first car it let go through before it could receive other instructions. But the Button-up Robot was confused; even though it had made a decision, it was hesitant, as if it were not comfortable with its choice and wanted further instructions.

The presence of Push and Chancey inside the kidneycar was not what made it hesitate. One of its functions was to inspect the work of the Scouring Robot, and if it found a car with excessive debris, to shunt it off onto a sidetrack that would take it back for rescouring. The outside of the car Push and Chancey had boarded had obvious splatters of debris and should have been sent back. But the kidneycars were beginning to back up along the platform, and the Button-up Robot was forced to make a decision. It chose launch.

The car bumped its way into the inner mechanism of the Button-up Robot and stopped. There was a long delay before they felt the vibrations of the first button being twisted shut and then another long delay. Chancey cocked her head at Push. He knew the question. There was no good reason for the delay. Once the Button-up Robot had decided to pass them to the Accelerator, that should have been the end of its hesitation. He shrugged.

The car seemed to waver forward a little and stop, then waver back a little and stop. "Loonies?" she said.

Push shook his head. "No, if they were overriding it from LUNAC Central, it wouldn't be hesitating." But he had no other explanation. "Maybe it's afraid," he said.

It was patently impossible. There were some robots who did the equivalent of independent thinking, but if the Corporation thought there was even a remote possibility that they were developing emotions, they'd have all been so much scrap. And if a robot as ordinary as the Button-up Robot was developing a personality, the League was in big trouble. "What of?" she said.

Push smiled "Being fired?" The kidneycar jerked forward. "It must have heard me," he said. They waited for the last button to be snapped shut. The car began to pick up speed. "Better brace for the Dip."

Chancey spread-eagled herself against the floor of the car. It was only a few seconds from the Button-up Robot to the sharp decline where the kidneycar separated from the track of the Accelerator. The G-forces there would be tremendous, and even with the protection of the suits and the car itself, it would be rough, and he was not sure how much Chancey's head could take. Suddenly everything seemed to drop out from under them.

CHAPTER
SEVEN

O n Third Day, Beyar, like everyone else in Catchcage, stood watching the holos. The three tiers of balcony beyond the holos were jammed with Catchers looking down onto an almost life-size image of the Scouring Robot. Three-dimensional images of what was happening at LUNAC were everywhere in the Cage, but the largest were in the Great Hall, where five twenty-foot spheres arced across the space in front of the Nearside Window.

Between the larger spheres and the balconies, an overlapping series of eight-foot spheres displayed an overview of the entire area from the LUNAC Gates to the end of the Accelerator. Catchers could follow the path of each kidneycar as it landed, and the larger spheres gave a life-size close-up of the action on the ground.

As a kidneycar came through each of the LUNAC Gates, it appeared full-size in the first of the larger spheres. When it passed up onto the platform of the Scouring Robot, it filled the middle three. The fourth covered the Button-up Robot and the fifth, the final stage of the Accelerator.

When a child's image passed out of the larger spheres, anyone with a special interest in them could still follow their progress on personal holos that gave a close-up of anything that could be seen on the overview display. The crowd that packed the space between the larger holos and the Nearside Window seemed to be made up entirely of small groups knotted around personal holos. At least one in each group clutched the Leavings of some specialbrother or sister.

Catchers who followed the children in general, or who simply preferred a ground-level view and more life-size action, jammed the space that stretched from the smaller holos back under the balconies. Once the unloading process started, three-dimensional figures would be moving in every sphere in the Great Hall.

Almost nothing would be going on in the rest of Catchcage. Nothing ever went on during the Wee Pause. The Wee Pause lasted two hours, and during it, almost all work in Catchcage stopped; for two hours nothing would come through the Gates to be guided within the Catchround or unloaded at the Dumper. Nothing would be processed, sorted, stored, or recorded. Work still went on within the smelter, but most of that was automatic, and what monitoring had to be done was usually done between glances at some smaller version of what was going on at the Scouring Robot and the Button-up platform.

Skyshockers insisted that the Wee Pause was entirely due to the miraculous powers of URdon Wee acting from his change in state. Even those who did not believe in the more or less holy ghost of URdon Wee had to admit that it certainly was not the Corporation that stopped the Accelerator at the precise moment the children of Catchcage began their journey and started it again two hours later. Corporation did everything to stop that gap in production year after year, but year after year it failed.

At first it was always some new part of the Accelerator that would break down, a short in the Scouring Robot, an inexplicable drop in the magnetic fields of the Accelerator track, a mysterious malfunction of the Button-up Robot that miraculously cleared itself up after a two-hour gap had been left in the normally unbroken train of kidneycars that stretched across space between the Accelerator and Catchcage.

But from the year Beyar was born until the year he went to see the End of the Sky, the moment the first kidneycar left Catchcage, the Tally Computer spontaneously started shunting every car, empty or not, off onto the recycling track. The first year it happened, the Corporation dismissed it as just one more in a seemingly endless number of ways to disrupt the smooth functioning of the Accelerator. When it happened two years in a row, they did something about it: They reprogrammed the Tally Computer byte by byte.

The job took a team of Earthside logicians eight months to complete. In the fifth month they found the hidden loop that had caused the Tally Computer to sidetrack everything temporarily. They were sure it wouldn't have kicked in again the next time, but they kept working. Before they were finished, they found two more, but when they were done, there wasn't a bit that hadn't been tested for necessity and newly inserted.

People in the League laughed that it would have taken half as many Catchers eight *weeks* to do the job. They were probably right; the best minds in the field had come Up over the years, and even the best of what was left Earthside were hopeless amateurs by comparison. Half the people who had *invented* the field in which Spencer LeGrange's Logic Team were now the "experts" were still alive somewhere in the League, and time had done nothing to dull their wits. More than a few of them were Catchers, and some, if the truth were known, had drunk the Sunrise once with URdon Wee.

The Corporation was not about to put the Tally Computer in the hands of Catchers or anybody else in the League. Even Loonie technicians who had operated it for years were kept away from it, and when it was finished, only the handpicked crew from Earthside was allowed to repair it or maintain it. Every command LUNAC Central put into it had to go Earthside first and be put in from there. It was awkward and inefficient, but Spencer LeGrange meant business. A two-hour gap in production over the silliness of some long disbanded religion was more than Spencer LeGrange was going to put up with, and he wanted Catchcage to know it.

Everybody Earthside waited confidently for the twenty-seventh day of the Second Lunar. In the Grand Sphere the smart money was on the Corporation, not so much because they expected it to succeed as because so many of the disbanded followers of URdon Wee were willing to give such outrageous odds that the Corporation wouldn't.

Granders, of course, couldn't resist any kind of a bet, and almost any of them would take whatever side nobody else wanted just to get a wager going. The OBees, who had survived outrageously long odds just by being alive, were constitutionally unable to resist a gamble where the odds were finally in their favor. It was estimated that half the wealth of the League was set to change hands in the minute after the first kidneycar left for the End of the Sky.

The instant it did, the Tally Computer started shunting off every car that came along onto the recycling track. It kept doing so for two hours, despite everything the Logic Team could do. When it was good and ready, it went back to its old routine.

Spencer LeGrange was furious. His retaliation was swift. He ordered the Tally Computer replaced with a completely new one, constructed and programmed entirely Earthside. He made the lunar Accelerator off-limits to everyone without his personal clearance, and he ordered that everybody on the moon be replaced before the year was out with someone who had been born and raised Earthside.

Twenty-four hours after his third command was made public in the League, two thirds of the Loonies had changed their identities and disappeared into the habitats. Only six applied for return Earthside.

Spencer LeGrange didn't care; he replaced the lot of them and kept the loyal third on temporarily to train them.

It was a disaster from the outset. There is nothing more inept than somebody fresh Up from Earthside, and Spencer Le-Grange sent them Up in wholesale lots. They died in wholesale lots. They perished separately, but they did it with such startling rapidity that the effect was almost the same as if they had died in a single natural disaster.

In two months the moon was critically understaffed, and the Accelerator was operating at less than thirty-percent efficiency even on its best days. The solution was obvious: Spencer LeGrange would have to grant general amnesty to those who had fled into the League. All of his advisers encouraged him to do so immediately, and Spencer LeGrange admitted he was willing to listen—just as soon as the new Tally Computer was installed.

In the meantime he sent a new wave of technicians to work the Accelerator. The moment they landed, the Accelerator spontaneously shut down. Nobody who wasn't from Earthside had been near it since Skyday unless they were under the constant surveillance of somebody whose loyalty was above question. There was no way it could have been sabotaged. And yet it not only would not work, but every screen connected with it flashed the same message. The message had only one word: "Enough!"

The Accelerator stayed closed for almost a week. It was the longest shutdown in the history of the Accelerator, and the losses of revenue within the League, as well as Earthside, grew to staggering proportions. Spencer LeGrange would have capitulated by the third day if only a way could have been found for him to save face, but public relations miracles like that do not come overnight.

He had to wait until the eighth day before a bright young executive at CORPQ, the Corporation's headquarters in the League, pointed out that, in fact, the two-hour shutdown had never really cost the Corporation money, anyway, because in the two hours that followed it, the full cars that had been shunted aside during the shutdown were cycled back into the Accelerator and fired off to Catchcage.

When they arrived three days later, the facility at Catchcage functioned at one hundred percent of capacity for the only times in the history of the Accelerator. Nearly the entire population of Catchcage turned out without additional pay to handle the overload. The effect on the Torch of having such a constant stream of maximum energy could not be immediately calculated, but it was estimated that the research benefits alone were worth more than had been lost during the annual shutdown.

It may not have been entirely true, but it was plausible enough to get Spencer LeGrange off the hook, and he ordered the immediate withdrawal of the newest wave of replacements. In addition, he announced a complete amnesty for any former employees who would return, and a bonus for those who reported to work within twenty-four hours. No questions would be asked about their absence, no retaliation would be made against them, and they would be paid for the time of their absence out of their sick-time and vacation-time allotments.

The moment the new recruits left the moon, the Accelerator spontaneously started again and didn't stop until the next time the children of Catchcage went to see the End of the Sky. Most of the staff of LUNAC Central returned to their jobs, and things went on as before, with the exception of the day before the new Tally Computer was due to land.

Exactly twenty-four hours before the shipment was due to arrive, the monitors at LUNAC central associated with the Accelerator began to flash the same message, "NO!" The message flashed with increasing frequency until the new computer's announced time of arrival. When the replacement computer did not arrive, the messages stopped.

Officially, the Corporation ignored the entire incident, but privately Spencer LeGrange was enraged. However, the LeGrange Corporation had not come to dominate the politics and economy of the planet under the direction of a fool, and Spencer LeGrange bided his time and waited for an opening. When Beyar disabled the Tally Computer he had the excuse to replace it he had awaited so long. Almost immediately a much newer and more secure version was shipped to the moon and installed, and the Accelerator was back under the complete control of the Corporation. Spencer LeGrange waited impatiently for the next Skyday. When it came, the Tally Computer no longer automatically shunted all cars onto the recycling track.

Instead, it shunted full cars onto the recycling track and sent the empty ones along to Catchcage where they would be only a minimal distraction from the true business of Third Day, watching the arrival of the kidneycars at LUNAC. The Accelerator never actually stopped, and the full cars went to Catchcage in a body at the end of the two-hour interruption, so the Corporation didn't actually lose anything.

In fact, it was better off than it had been before. It had gained all the energy the empty cars discharged at the Catchcage Gates, and it could still claim that the new computer had succeeded in stopping The Wee Pause. URdon Wee's ghost seemed to be offering Spencer LeGrange an olive branch, and the head of the Corporation took it.

For the third year in a row the Tally Computer had separated the full from the empty for two hours, and three days later, the empty kidneycars had begun arriving in the Catchround. They had been coming in for almost an hour and a quarter when Push and Chancey's kidneycar popped through the first of the LUNAC Gates.

Beyar watched it enter the first of the five large spheres from the middle of the first tier. He stood against the rail clutching the twins' Leavings like a link between them. He frowned. The intensity of the flash meant that the magnetic field of the gate was much too high, and the way the car seemed to shudder all the way through the gate could only mean that the twins were taking a pounding inside it.

They were sure to be disoriented, and it seemed to take them longer to pass through the remaining gates than it had for them to get to the moon, and it had taken *forever* for them to get there. What everyone said was true, waiting was worse than going. It made him wonder how the twins had felt standing there waiting for him, whether it was easier to wait knowing what it was like or in blissful ignorance. It probably didn't matter; the wait was hard either way.

Cheers and laughter and sighs of relief greeted the opening of every new kidneycar, but by the time Push and Chancey's pod reached the platform in front of the Scouring Robot, everyone seemed to be holding their breath. For the first time in anyone's memory, every child had survived both the trip and the Scouring Robot. No one mentioned it; there was still the trip back with all its dangers, but everywhere there was the unspoken feeling that if only all of them could survive the Scouring Robot, they would all come back safely.

When the cover was lifted, everything fell silent. Even the small groups rooting one or another of the last five on to safety did it with gestures instead of sound. There was a murmur of relief when Push popped out of the back end of the pod and straddled it as the robot turned. Beyar could see down into the pod as clearly as if he were hovering above it on the moon. His heart sank when he saw Chancey's arms raise her partway to the lip and then give out.

Everyone on the balconies gasped as Chancey slid down into the pod, and those on ground level who could not see why Push was hesitating let out groans as the robot turned back toward the pod. Everything seem to careen toward disaster. Beyar shouted for Chancey to start her run as if she could hear him, but his voice was drowned in the cheer that went up when Push shot up onto the robot and started bashing it with the podwrench. Even before it was certain that they would get away, there were bursts of astonished laughter that such a thing could be done.

Beyar squeezed the railing in front of him, the twins'

Leavings crumpled in his hand. He leaned over it shouting, but what he said was drowned in the din of other voices shouting encouragement or screaming. The intensity of the noise dropped a level when the Robot knocked Push to the ground, and the crowd near the window seemed to surge forward as if they could help him up.

Those in the balcony could not see what Push was doing behind the robot when he did get to his feet, and they were too busy screaming for Chancey as she scrambled through the dust cloud to pay much attention to him. But the crowd nearer the window had a clear view of what he was doing, and they shouted themselves hoarse from the moment he pried open the power panel. The flash of the main power panel shorting out drew everybody's attention back to Push as Chancey dropped to the ground.

Everybody seemed to be congratulating everybody else at once, and the din did not subside until the twins got to the Button-up. There was a universal groan of disappointment as people realized that no kidneycars were being launched and the most Exceptional pair in the history of the ritual were going to be stranded on the moon. Arguments began immediately about what the effect of having to be rescued would be on their standing, and the possibility that they might even fall into the hands of the Corporation. All Beyar cared about was that they were alive.

There was a general lull as the twins stood on the Button-up platform, but a wave of excitement spread through the crowd again as more and more people realized what Chancey was doing on the recycling track. When she succeeded, another shout of astonishment and joy went up, and there was general cheering until the twins disappeared into the kidney-car.

There was a slight pause of concern when the kidneycar seemed stalled inside the Button-up Robot, but before the speculations could gather much steam, the kidneycar reappeared and went flying down the Accelerator track toward launch. The crowd breathed a collective sigh of relief when the car shot out over the surface of the moon and rose steadily up out of the area covered by the holospheres.

Beyar raised his eyes from the spheres to the Window beyond them, as if he intended to watch the kidneycar make its three-day journey back, but all he could see was the reflection of the balconies and the crowd. He started to turn away, but the shape of the face off to his right, one face in the sea of faces too far away to be seen clearly, drew him back to the window. He turned and stepped up on the middle rail to see over the crowd.

He only caught sight of the man for a moment, but he recognized him instantly as the man who had been watching him before. For the briefest second their eyes met, and he felt a chill run through him. Then the man was gone, and someone was tugging at him to get down from the rail before he fell.

When he stood on the floor again, waiting for the crowd to melt back to the work that would occupy them until the kidneycars came home again on Last Day, the dark eyes still seemed to stare at him from the long wolfish face. The intense hatred seemed to still flare out toward him. He turned and walked away in the opposite direction, wondering what it meant. Only when he started to put the Leavings back in his pocket did he realize that they were open.

He folded them shut again immediately, without looking at them, but it seemed a terrible omen to him nevertheless.

CHAPTER
EIGHT

Grandy watched the holo of the children inside the kidneycar. She looked remarkably good for a woman who had been dead for almost a quarter of a century. It was one of the things she liked about dying: you didn't age much after that. She was thirty-three when she died, but she had looked twenty-five. Now, on her worst days, she looked twenty-seven. Death had been good to her. Dying had been hard.

She stood staring out of the Nearside Window at the end of the sky. The LUNAC Gates twinkled even against the bright surface of the moon. The first one was always the brightest. Every time it sparkled with the energy of another kidneycar discharging its energy of momentum into its magnetic field, it made her think of her husband. She could not get used to being a widow. Even when URdon Wee had left, she had been certain she would see him again. He had promised her she would be with him again, and soon. Now he was gone.

It was hard to believe. But she knew it was true. She had seen the holoscan made by the monitor at the first LUNAC Gate. There was no doubt about it. The kidneycar had split apart going through the gate, and he had come tumbling out almost into the monitor. She remembered watching him go spinning by it, wondering why he didn't reach out and grab it to stop himself from falling into the moon. But all she would ever have for explanation was his blissfully silly grin of total amusement at what was happening to him.

They were still looking for his point of impact on the lunar surface, but it didn't matter. There wouldn't be much to recover—certainly not enough to identify him—and if there was, the Skyshockers would see to it that the evidence disappeared. Some of them seemed almost happy to have a martyr, even if it was for a religion that had been disbanded by its founder's own command. URdon Wee would have found it enormously amusing. A large part of her really believed that he still found it so. Somewhere he was laughing at the Great Joke. Nothing is what it seems. Nothing stays lost. God is always laughing.

It was true. She had drunk the Sunrise twice with URdon Wee. The illusory nature of the world was as much a certainty to her as it was to him, and yet she was going to miss him. For all their enlightenment, he was still Donald Wheeler to her and always would be. She felt the dull ache of his loss flare into pain again. "Nothing stays lost," she told herself. It didn't really help. Even if he came back, even if he came back as Donald Wheeler exactly as he was, he was not back now, and now was where she was.

She thought of that first kiss, the "Kiss of the Enlightenment." They had laughed so often over the seriousness so many of his followers attached to it. The first time he had tried to explain it all to her, she had called him a lunatic. All he had said was, "There are no lunatics, only unrecognized saints." She'd laughed at that too.

But it really had been a kiss of enlightenment, her enlightenment, even though she did not realize it right away. It was from the moment of that kiss that she had loved Donald Wheeler. Even when she had thought he was crazy,

*she had loved him. Even after she had shared his
enlightenment, she still loved him in the ordinary way, if it
was ordinary to love someone as the single and only right
person out of all the billions alive and all the trillions who
had ever lived.*

*She had not believed in the idea of true love before the
moment of that kiss. She had never considered it even remotely
possible that people might be destined for one another. All that
had seemed a romanticized justification for sex. She had
understood sex, and destiny had nothing to do with it.*

*She had arranged the environment for enough of it to
take place to know that it was just like any other business, an
exchange of services for which both parties were willing to pay
her a finder's fee. It was an exchange of affection, perhaps; a
trading of pleasures; an emotional solace for hard times and
the threat of imminent death in a place where death was
always imminent; but it was not destiny. She had been certain
of that.*

And then there was the Kiss of the Enlightenment.

*Not that she had known on the instant that Donald
Wheeler was the one true love of her life. That had come
later. But she knew it as she looked out the Nearside
Window, and it was the most painful thing she had ever
known.*

*The tears made it impossible to see the End of the Sky.
She turned away from the window. Dreem Shalleen was
waiting for her. She hardly saw her long enough to recognize
her. She saw only a blur of scarlet-and-indigo hair, and after
the flash, the ebony-outlined lips parted to say something she
never got to hear. She never saw the electric cane, even when
its points touched her chest with the voltage of her death.*

*But she felt it. Her chest seemed to explode with pain all
the way up into her shoulders, all the way down into her
abdomen. It was like she had split open from her throat to her
navel, just cracked apart, and fire was flowing out of the
fissure. It lasted a long, long time. The complete measure of*

*the universe was the dimensions of that pain. It encompassed
everything, was everything. She, herself, was absolutely gone.
The pain occupied every cubic centimeter of her volume. It left
no room for her. She vanished into the dark.*

The children were as familiar to her as if they had been
her own. There was no need to ask: They were the children
of her vision, and the children of URdon Wee's vision, but
she asked, anyway. "These are the children?"

"You *know* they are, Grandy." URdon Wee shook his
head in exasperation. "Why do you always ask me things
when you know what I know before I do?"

Grandy smiled. "I like to hear you make saintly
statements," she said.

URdon Wee smiled. It made him look like a little boy.
"There *are* no saints," he said solemnly, "only unrecognized
lunatics."

It was Grandy's turn to laugh.

URdon Wee pointed to the figures. They were just
beginning to move out of the posture of the Little Death.
"Those were undoubtedly acts of Revolution," he said proudly.

"The stuff legends are made of," Grandy said. She seemed
enormously proud of both of them too. She nodded toward
Chancey. "I don't think there'll be another like her along this
century."

"One will be more than enough," Wee said. "Are you
ready?"

Grandy looked at them for a long moment, like a mother
looking at her sleeping children. "All right," she said finally.
"Crack the pod and spill them out into Eternity."

CHAPTER
NINE

The days did not pass quickly for Beyar. Everywhere in the Cage there was an atmosphere of barely repressed joy, and yet he could not escape a feeling of inexplicable ominousness. Two nights in a row he had dreamed of the man he thought of as the Watcher, both times waking in a cold sweat to the feeling of those dark, gleaming eyes watching him.

The first night he even got up and went to the wallfront and cleared it and looked out into the courtyard formed by the other dormiciles in his "leaf" of the clover, but there was nothing to see except the white birch trees and the fountain. But when he went back to bed, his mind wouldn't shut off, and it took him a long time to get back to sleep. He kept thinking about Push and Chancey, going over little things he remembered about them as if he were never going to see them again until, an hour before his clover was due up at the Catchround, he fell asleep.

The second night he had gone out through the courtyard down to the central garden, but the courtyards of the other three "leaves" were empty as well, and there was no one in what he could see of the gardenyards of the other two clovers. It was very early morning, but nobody had work until after noon in his set of dormiciles, and there should have been half a dozen dormiciles in the three tiers of his leaf with clear front walls sending beacons of light out into the courtyard.

Somewhere in the clover there should have been sanctuaries full of the brothers and sisters he had gone to see the End of the Sky with, staying up all night mixing Farfliers and talking. Somewhere there should have been laughter and music echoing out into the courtyard and welcoming brothers and sisters in, or at least a pair of lovers in the gardenyard, Dancing the Dove.

But there wasn't a single one. Every wallfront in the clover was clouded over, and even in the next leaf over, nobody was up. Everything seemed unnaturally deserted and dead. It made him feel like he was the only one left in the Cage, except for the Watcher, who pursued him relentlessly through the uninhabited courtyards and lanes.

And when it turned out that that was a dream as well, he got out of bed and threw himself on one of the sittables and watched foot-high brothers and sisters Dancing the Dove on the holopad in the center of his room until he fell asleep and woke up with a start and a stiff neck and a hangover of dread that got sharper with the realization that it was finally Last Day.

It was still early, but the courtyard was bustling and when he went and stood in his wallfront, half a dozen voices invited him to go down to the Wombs and have a last look at the Fruits of the Lottery. But he just smiled weakly and waved them on their way and went back inside and tried to get the sour taste out of his mouth.

He caught another hour of fitful sleep before he started down to the Nearside Window. On the way he stopped in at the Wombs and took a look at the new brothers and sisters floating serenely in the fluid, waiting to be brought into the world once the Children of this year were back from the End of the Sky.

It always made him feel good to come down to the

Wombs and put his hand against the glass where some new brother slept his liquid sleep, waiting to be awakened into the world of the Cage and the League. Sometimes he and Push and Chancey would come and sit for hours without saying a word, just watching the babies grow through the glass. No matter how many people were there, there was a tranquillity to the Wombs that couldn't be found anywhere else in the League.

It was a place of beautiful memories to him. It was where all young Catchers were first taught the Breath, and the exercises that made possible the Little Death, and it was the first place he had seen URdon Wee.

He sat down and let the peacefulness of the place seep into him. Then he practiced the exercises of the Little Death, and the slow waking, as if by going through it he might make it easier somehow for Push and Chancey when they came out of it later in the day.

Somehow he lost track of time, and the fact that he was the only one still there did not make him realize that everyone else had gone down to the Nearside Window to watch the kidneycars come in. When he got there, there were no spaces left up along the rail, and he had to go down on the floor between the spheres and the window. Half a dozen of the cars were already in the Catchround, and people were watching cars come through the first two or three Gates and then rushing to the Upshoots to be in the Catchround when their specialbrother or sister's pod came in.

Beyar had plenty of time before Push and Chancey's pod came in. They were the last off, and they would be the last back. He would watch them come in through the first three gates and then pop up to the Catchround and bang the buttons open on their kidneycar and help them out. Then he would give them their Leavings back, and they'd all come down laughing and watch the Fruits of the Lottery brought into the world and named.

There was absolutely no reason why it should be any

other way. Those who didn't make it always died in the Scouring Robot or the first LUNAC Gate. But the LUNAC Gates were run by the Corporation, and they always put the first Gate up near maximum to squeeze as much energy out of the empty kidneycars as they could.

At Catchcage the best experts in the League would match the magnetic fields of each gate with the velocity of the incoming car to bring it gliding into the Catchround with hardly a bump. Nobody'd been lost in the Catchcage Gates since he was five, and there was almost no reason to worry.

He put the idea out of his mind and enjoyed the festival. Brothers came by and joked with him, sisters flirted, and there was a general atmosphere of being alive in the best of times that lifted him out of his mood and made him forget the vague dissatisfaction that tugged at the back of his mind.

The number of people on the floor had dwindled by the time Push and Chancey came in. There was a trickle of people to the Upshoots to greet the last of the children home, and a lot of Catchcage was already up in the Catchround waiting for the triumphant return of the twins. It was a remarkable day, an historic day. The first totally joyous homecoming in the history of the ritual. Not one child lost. Seventeen Outstanding children, and not only two Exceptionals, but also two in the same pod.

The Cage was still buzzing about what Push and Chancey had done. There was no higher thing to do than to do the unthinkable, and both had done revolutionary things, things no one had even considered before. Attacking the Scouring Robot and then outwitting the Tally Computer! Even the unprecedented act of going two in a car paled to insignificance beside it. The twins would return to a well-deserved lionizing.

Beyar knew what it was like to return triumphant, and he smiled to himself whenever he thought of it happening to Push and Chancey. The depression that had gripped him for three days left him completely, and he looked forward to their return with the same joy that was flooding the Cage.

He watched the last four kidneycars come almost all the way through the Gates before he looked out for the twin's pod. A cheer went up from the crowd still standing on the second and third balconies when the car approached the first gate. The place was alive with excitement.

Beyar looked out the window and waited for the flash that would tell him they were in the First Gate. He glanced over his shoulder at the first holosphere to watch them go into the Gate. The next to last car was already in the Catch-round, and all five spheres carried the image of the twins' car as it came into the First Gate.

But just beyond the first sphere, as the twins' car started to nose through it, Beyar caught sight of the Watcher. His eyes drew Beyar's attention from the sphere. They seemed to burn with a dark, cruel secret. Beyar felt the hair on the back of his neck rise, and the cry that went up from the crowd snapped his attention back to the sphere. It was a cry of horror and despair. And Beyar saw the reason for it immediately. As the kidneycar came through the field it was beginning to crack, and as it emerged on the Cage side of the Gate, the pod opened like a mouth and split in two.

Larger that life in the holospheres, two bodies tumbled out. The larger one seemed to catch for a second on something near the lip of the lid before it ripped free. It made a half tumble forward before it exploded in a spray of blood. The smaller figure made two complete tumbling turns before it vanished like a soap bubble bursting. In an instant they were gone. The debris of the kidneycar tumbled endlessly through the five spheres, but there was nothing left of the twins. On the far side of the first sphere the dark-eyed man was laughing.

CHAPTER

TEN

Back Toss Hool looked only at the gold fist in the middle of Nohfro Pock's bald and bullet-shaped head. It was a Catcher technique. By focusing on a point, everything else was out of focus and had to be recognized as part of a larger pattern. Nuances of behavior that were lost in the ordinary attention to detail stood out brightly in the blur of peripheral vision.

Pock searched Hool's eyes but found only the fires of fanaticism. He leaned back on the airecline; his electric cane floated on the cushion of air beside him within easy reach. He had only been in command of the Fist, the LeGrange Police in the League, for a year, and he was still finding out where his enemies lay. Commanders had perished before by assassination from the ranks beneath, as he well knew, but they were seldom attacked by their informers, and the nearness of his cane was no more than reasonable caution.

Hool was one of his best Ears, certainly his best in Catchcage. But he was anything but trustworthy. Like everybody in the League, he had his own interests at stake. Those interests were not as complex or devious as they would be in somebody from the Grand Sphere, but Hool's motivations were surprisingly complex for an OBee. Undoubtedly his

years in the Cage accounted for the ascendance of intrigue
over brawn, but age might have had something to do with
it. It was hard to tell a Catcher's age; people everywhere in
the League seemed to age more slowly than those from Earthside.

In any case, he looked far from weak. Like most OBees,
he was big, almost as big as Pock, and age had not quite
begun to bend him yet, although it was beginning to show
in the lines of his face and the hair at his temples. There was
also a certain leanness to his features that made him seem
more cerebral than the usual OBee. Still, he had a good bit
of the OBee straightforwardness when he spoke.

"URdon the Wee is moving," he said.

"URdon Wee is dead." It wasn't the first time they had
had the disagreement. Pock only did it to annoy Hool into
revealing more than he wanted. He was only occasionally
successful. Still, he would have had no success at all with a
Grander. That was the advantage of dealing with religious
fanatics: They might be harder to understand, but dogma
made at least parts of what they were doing predictable. "The
Fist has no interest in ghosts."

There was an edge of rage in Hool's voice, but it was
directed at URdon Wee rather than Pock. Pock was aware of
Hool's history as a former disciple of URdon Wee and took
no notice of the anger other than as a possible tool to pry
Hool open with. Hool was adamant. "No ghost, no saint, no
lunatic! One *man*!" He held up a lone finger. "And everything
he does lays up structure on your destruction."

Pock smiled to himself at the construction metaphor.
Laying up structure was an OBee term for building the framework of the habitats, and it showed Hool's roots as one of
the Original Builders. If he was really First Wave—one of
the construction workers sent up to build Catchcage—he
would have to be in his sixties, but he certainly didn't look
it. But then, every OBee over the age of thirty claimed to
have built Catchcage or drunk the Sunrise once with URdon

Wee. He added the fuel of sarcasm to Hool's rage. "And what is the ghost of URdon Wee using these days for our destruction?"

Hool took the question at face value; his answer was direct and truthful. "Children," he said.

Pock raised an eyebrow. He had been in the League a long time, with most of it spent in the Grand Sphere where everything was a plot within a plot, but he was a long way from having heard everything. Every day brought some new twist on an already snarled complexity. "Buying or selling?" he said. It was a calculated insult. Such things went on routinely Earthside, but they were the exception rather than the rule in the League, and the insinuation that such things could be done with children in Catchcage was sure to bring a Catcher to fighting stance.

The flames of Hool's rage crackled toward Pock as he expected. "Fool!" It was what anyone from Earthside was called everywhere in the League, but Hool clearly meant it as more than an insult to Pock's origin. "These are the children of Wee's Vision!" His voice rang with prophecy. "Catchcage will grow the children, and the children will grow the Revolution!"

The word made Pock frown. The brief but bloody insurrection that had brought him to power as the head of the Fist and cost his predecessor his life was only a little more than a year old, and nobody in the Corporation used the word aloud. Pock had more reason than most to pay attention to it. The flames of Revolution were always burning in Hardcore and Catchcage, but even though they never could ignite the League as a whole, a flare-up could be enough to cost the head of the Fist his life. "When?" he demanded.

Hool's scowl said that the answer was obvious. "When they're grown." He made a decade sound like minutes.

Pock shook his head in exasperation. "The Fist don't pay for prophecy," he said.

"It *will* pay!" For Hool, however much he hated URdon

Wee, Wee's Vision was certainty. He pointed a finger at Pock. "*You'll* pay!" Pock's hand edged toward his cane. He glanced to see if it was set for stun or kill. ". . . if it's not stopped *now*!"

Pock shifted closer to the cane, keeping his eyes on Hool. Hool looked at the cane and then at Pock. His voice was full of scorn. "You think *that* will help you?" He gave a snort of derision. "*Guns* won't even help you, if you don't act *now*!"

Pock winced. The mere mention of a handgun was enough to start a riot almost anywhere in the League. It was the use of a handgun that had led to the insurrection that had raised his rank to gold, but it was the use of the same handgun that had led the Corporation to approve his assassination of his predecessor. They were banned forever from the League as part of the settlement of the uprising, and he didn't like the way Hool mentioned them as if they were part of the prophecy. "Is this more of your crackpot religion?"

Hool's voice made Pock look at his cane again. "It is not *my* religion. *I* do not follow URdon the Wee."

Back Toss Hool waited for Dreem Shalleen to return. The homecile was hers, a vertical two-slice in the center of a middle "leaf," with two wallfronts looking out across the gardenyard into the widerlane beyond. He sat in the top slice looking out through the wallfront at the traffic coming out of the clover opposite. It was almost shiftchange at the Torch, and Techs were hurrying for the Downshoots. In half an hour another flurry of traffic would be flowing in or past on the widerlane to clovers farther up the steep, cone-shaped valley.

He liked the view; he liked the engineering that let each concentric terrace blend into the ones above and below it so that they looked like one long narrowing funnel of a valley. He liked the way the three-leafed housing clovers seemed randomly arranged on the terraces when he knew they were fitted to the inch for maximum usage. He liked the way the gardenyards and the trees in each court seemed to blend together into one hillside forest instead of looking like potted plants stuffed in around the housing.

There was nothing like it in Hardcore, where everything was narrow passageways and sharp turns, a thrown-together collection of old storage containers converted into rooms and big oblong dormitories converted into halls. A vista in Hardcore was somewhere you could see the roof without feeling like you could reach up and touch it.

He liked the newness of Catchcage as well; even after two years everything seemed as if it had been finished yesterday. Everything in Hardcore smelled old, tense, bloody. He liked the fact that he'd laid up structure on the Cage as well, even if OBees weren't given preference for settling.

He didn't even mind his work up in the Catchround. It wasn't nearly as exciting or as well paid as laying up structure, but it would do until construction began on Henson's Tube, and he might even get some work laying up structure on the satellite modules Catchcage was rapidly beginning to need. And in the meantime it was better than living in Hardcore. Dreem made it almost perfect.

It was true—she was not Grandy—but he'd mostly gotten over that infatuation, except when he heard she'd joined URdon the Wee's followers. He'd gone back to Hardcore that night and started a punch-up that broke both his hands and left a dozen OBees and two young Blues from the Fist "unbroke but largely battered." He still couldn't believe she'd sunk that low. URdon the Wee! He'd hated that little Chemie from the first time he'd seen him, and he regretted every time he thought of it that he'd let him off with one punch instead of brainbashing him when he had the chance.

Not that it really mattered. His love affair with Grandy had been all one-sided, anyway. Dreem had helped him see that, even before they'd become lovers. He'd known her for almost three years, since they'd Danced the Dove at Grandy's the first week she'd come Up to work on the Torch. Nobody made much out of the difference between Construction

*and Technical then, but that was before a real population had
settled in, with its hierarchies and prejudices.*

*Dreem still didn't seem to care that there was that social
gap between them, and even he only thought about it when
some Corporation flunkie offered to give him direction to the
Outstation for Hardcore. The fact that Dreem loved him and
admired him made him forget what transplanted Fools
thought.*

*He looked for the scarlet and indigo of Dreem's hair
bobbing along the widerlane from the Upshoot on the terrace
below, but he couldn't find her. He didn't give her lateness
much thought. An hour later he was still waiting, but he was
giving things a lot of thought. Most of it was jealousy and
paranoia and a nagging fear that her admiration for him
wasn't genuine after all. An hour after that, he was giving
some serious thought to going out looking for her, but he
couldn't decide whether to bash her, whoever she was with, or
both of them. He'd have just gone and made up his mind
when he found her, but there were over a hundred and fifty
clovers in the valley with ten to twenty homeciles in each, and
he had no idea which one she might be laid up in.*

*Finally he gave up waiting and started suiting up for
the sixhour he was scheduled for up in the Catchround. She
finally came in when he was halfway dressed. He was in a
rage by then. She didn't even seem to notice; she was just
bubbling over with excitement. The crimson star she always
sprayed on over her left eye was smudged, and the ebony
lipline was worn away in the middle of her lower lip as if she
had been biting it, the way she always did in the midst of an
ecstasy. He didn't wait for an explanation; he just hit her
and walked out.*

*He punched out his boss on the Catchround, too, and
went back to Hardcore, but after a week he missed her and
finally left a message for her when he knew she'd be out. She
left one for him that told him to come back at exactly six and
they'd talk. When he came, the wallway was half open, and*

he stepped through it, still trying to think of what he was going to say, but he didn't get to open his mouth. Something as hard as a podwrench hit him flush in the mouth and knocked him backward out the door.

There was blood all over the front of him, and his lip and nose were one continuous lump, but he got up and staggered through the door again. She was sitting on the airecline waiting for him. She had her star over the wrong eye, but it didn't hide the bruise very well, and there was still some swelling on that side of her mouth. "Now," she said, "talk."

He tried but it was muffled and halting, and he had to keep wiping the blood away with the back of his hand. All in all, it was a good bit short of convincing, because every time he started to talk about it, the rage came up and made him inarticulate. She finally held up her hand. "You didn't even let me explain," she said. He tried to justify it but she shook her head. "No, listen. You want to come back?" He nodded. "I'm changed," she said. "You want to change with me, okay. If not . . ." She nodded toward the widerlane.

He gave it thought; she'd met him at the door like a Hardcore wife, not like some upper-class Tech, and a woman like that was not going to be easy to replace. He wanted her and missed her, but there was still the matter of who she was with. He made a compromise with himself: If she gave him who it was, he would go and bash him bloody and forget her part in it. She didn't give him a chance to ask.

"I want you to come with me." She got up, as if the argument were settled and the negotiations complete. She started for the door. He just looked at her, and she seemed flustered for a minute, as if she'd forgotten that he didn't know anything about what had so overwhelmed her life. She answered the question he hadn't asked. "To see URdon Wee, of course." He couldn't bear the sound of the joy in her voice.

"You followed him once," Pock said.

"I drank the Sunrise once with URdon the Wee." He

said it as if he had only gone through the motions for reasons of his own.

Pock scoffed. "Everybody in Catchcage claims that."

Hool ignored the insinuation that he was a liar. "I know his vision," he said. "My life is to make that vision fail!"

Back Toss Hool set the beaker back down on the table. It passed right through it and crashed to the floor. The Sunrise splattered everywhere, obscuring everything in an expanding cloud of reds, oranges, and golds. He could see things only vaguely through the rising crimson mist, and the objects he saw seemed tinged with green fire. The walls of Wee's four-slice had vanished; the walls of the Cage had dissolved as well. The mist thinned, and he could see all around him frozen moments like bubbles in an infinite froth.

He understood instantly and totally the significance of what he saw. Crackling cords of white light twined through and between the event bubbles connecting them into what he knew were realities. Each individual in an event bubble was connected to himself in other bubbles by cords of white light that twined together, both entering and leaving the event. How they exited and where they went next depended on the interaction of the light within the event.

The thickness of each cord, the strength of its energy, depended upon the individual's Will; the momentum of previous events entered each new event through the cords of all the individuals involved in it and emerged from it based on the composite force of all Wills acting within the moment. He knew the key to it all was that a single individual, if he chose the exact moment, could change the direction of events, could alter the flow of energy that connected them, no matter how many others were involved.

One man, if he waited for the precise event in which all competing energies canceled one another, could change the flow of energy from millions, could alter its direction and its ultimate outcome. It was the knowledge he had been searching for, the knowledge that gave URdon Wee his power. The only

*other thing he needed to know was which moments could be
changed, which ones were so delicately balanced that the Will
of Back Toss Hool could make the difference, which moments
in the Vision of URdon Wee were vulnerable to change.*

*The instant he asked himself the question, he began to
careen along the cord that united the events of URdon Wee's
Vision. A bubble containing Hardcore came hurtling toward
him, growing larger and larger until it was all he could see.
He twisted from side to side, trying to get away before it could
hit him, but there was no escape.*

*But when it collided with him, he simply passed right
through it. It did not vanish; he could see it moving by him
above and below and on both sides. He was within it, passing
through its walls, through its cubicles, across its main
corridor, through Main Bay, through another series of wide
corridors and narrow passageways.*

*And then suddenly he was in a long, low corridor whose
blue-and-yellow walls converged to a point in the distance. He
had the overwhelming feeling that Dreem Shalleen waited for
him at the end of that corridor, and he recognized that it was
one of the moments when his Will could irrevocably alter the
Vision of URdon Wee.*

*But it was replaced in a flash with a homecile in the
Cage; he was crouching in a wash & flush, holding a noose
made of beta cord, and beyond him there was a boy with his
back turned.*

*Then the boy was gone, and he was watching the river of
energy flowing between the discharge points of the Torch. The
yellow bubble of an Insertion Vehicle hovered just outside the
energy reaching into it with mechanical arms.*

*There was a brilliant flash, and he was standing in
Fist Headquarters at the foot of an enormous holoball in
which the head of Spencer LeGrange glared down at him. A
tall, bald, bullet-headed man in a Gold uniform stood next to
him. The man had been badly beaten.*

There were people all around him, mostly young, and he

could see himself standing among them, rather than feeling as
if he was there. Near him, a gorgeous woman with one eye
swollen shut stood next to a white-haired young man with a
cruel smile. There was a beautiful young redheaded girl in
emerald green and a young man with an impish smile and
brilliant orange-red hair who looked exactly like her. And
before Spencer LeGrange could open his mouth, they all
jammed their fists into the air and shouted, "Live Free or
Die!" and he knew it was the triumph of Wee's Revolution,
the moment he must prevent at all costs.

And then he was outside Hardcore again, hanging in the
void, watching it shrink away into the distance. When he
looked back along the cord, he saw the bubble of another
habitat roaring toward him. It was a long cylinder much
larger than Catchcage and Hardcore put together, and he
knew from the plans he had seen that it must be Henson's
Tube. But it couldn't be, because the Tube hadn't even been
started.

It, too, hurtled toward him until it crashed into him
and he passed through it. But this time he did not pass
through dingy compartments and tight, dim corridors; instead,
he soared down the center of the cylinder, and what he saw
made the view looking down into the Valley in Catchcage seem
trivial.

The walls curved up around him and overhead; three
wide strips of land with lakes and trees and small cities
alternated with three narrower, oblong windows running
almost the length of the tube and filling it with light. Above
him, a blur of land whirled beyond small, puffy clouds.
Below there were rolling hills, winding roads, and clusters of
buildings with tall, cylindrical towers.

He looked down the length of the cylinder just in time to
see the non-o-rail capsule before it hit him. But it passed
through him, too, and the seats flashed by him on either side,
the passengers looking out the window as if they were trying to

see something under the capsule. When it had passed him, he looked back after it and saw what they were looking at.

A young boy stood on the rail underneath the capsule. He took a long look down at the walls of the Tube rotating away from him and jumped. Hool watched him fall and fall and fall, but just before he hit, he sprouted wings and soared up the curve of the wall into a perfect landing. He knew as he watched that if only he could alter that fall, the Vision of URdon Wee would also be changed.

The mountain that formed the endcap of the tube rushed toward him, and he passed through it, out of the bubble of that event and into the void between. When he looked back the way the habitat had come, he saw another and two more behind it so far away that at first he mistook them for stars. The nearest one was a wheel with an inner rim of glass and a tread of stones. It was a little smaller then Henson's Tube, but even the huge, circular mirror that was suspended above its center was much bigger than Catchcage.

He no longer flinched when he roared along the cord into the bubble and crashed into the habitat. He was just a shadow of light as Wee had said, and he had always been so, without his being aware of it. The simple, limited way he had always understood and experienced things seemed strange and alien to him. He passed through the rim of the wheel.

There was a blur of water around him and then greenery flashing past, and when he looked down, he saw, at the bottom of a wide V of terraces packed with weeping willow trees, a canal that flowed into the distance where the clear shell of the roof and green stretch of the land both curved upward until they seemed to meet. Wide, flat boats filled with people traveled along it, and around and past them smaller pointed ovals with one or two passengers darted.

But almost before he could see them, he passed out the other side of the rim. He looked up at the great mirror, bright with the glare of the sun, and passed into the banked mirrors of the hub and out again and into the far rim. He plunged *head downward into the far arc of the canal. Along the banks, office buildings had replaced the trees; the stacks of glass did not reflect him as he passed. No one saw him fall, except for an android, which looked, in some way he could not fathom, like the Scouring Robot. The android looked up and smiled knowingly at him before it dwindled out of sight.*

Almost before the first had gone, another bubble with a second wheel roared toward him. It dwarfed Henson's Tube, and Catchcage could have fit in two of the spheres that circled around it like little moons. But he did not crash into it as he had the others. Instead, it passed below him and he could see down through the glass inner rim.

It looked like a circular tube divided into different-colored segments that contained a variety of Earth environments from polar cold and ocean depth to dry desert and continuous surf. Some of the segments were environments that hadn't been found on Earth in a century, and others had never been found there at all and never would be.

As it passed, the bigger wheel spun out a trail of Earthsiders, a different type from each segment, yet each with the face of Back Toss Hool. But when they were strung out across the sky in an almost endless line, as one, they peeled off their faces to reveal, uniformly, the face of URdon Wee.

Hool stretched his head up and away from the Vision with a strangled snarl. His rage lit up the dark of space like a green flame and threw him forward toward the next bubble and its satellite. At first he thought he was careening into the moon, but he realized at the last instant that it had no craters and all around its equator was a mountain range of metal. It could only be an enormous habitat.

Even though he passed through it, he felt its impact like the door of destiny slamming in his face. A blur of gray swept over him as he passed through the inner ring of mountains and burst into the hollow core of the Grand Sphere.

The sight of so vast a landscape left him awed. He had never imagined that such a habitat would be built and that so many people would live in the League. Hundreds of times as many people as he had ever seen streamed out of the foothills of the lower hemisphere toward enormous complexes at either end of a broad highway he had not imagined could exist in the League.

It was as if someone had taken the earth and turned it inside out, and all the people in it seemed of one mind, seemed to be rushing unanimously toward the sound of gunfire and the destruction of the Corporation. He knew it immediately to be the Revolution of URdon Wee's Vision, and he longed to put a stop to it, to change it. He yearned for some hint as to what he could do.

But before he could find a key, he passed into what had seemed a thin belt of sparkling gold-and-silver grains in the very center of the sphere. It was only as he began to pass through it that he realized that it was a ring of ions focused and projected by the mountains and the solar wind.

He could feel his passage into the Ring like nothing else in his Vision. It made him tingle and gave him the feeling of being both without substance and substantial at the same time. While it buzzed around him he felt that he was the Ring and not himself, and that his whole perception of himself as a single and unconnected being was totally false.

But when he passed out of the far side of the Ring into the sphere again, the feeling was swallowed up by his rage that all that he had seen would fall under the direction of the Will of URdon Wee. He understood that what he had seen in the habitats was merely the highlights of Wee's Vision, a series of crucial events that would occur as the Vision moved toward completion. What he had seen was the potential history of a Revolution that would free the League, that would turn mankind's back on the Earth and direct it outward toward the stars.

But what tormented him most was an absolute certainty that among those stars mankind would find its eventual annihilation. If Wee's Revolution came to pass, it would be the crossroad where mankind made an irrevocable turn down the road to extinction.

Only an equal certainty that he could stop that chain of events kept him from despair. If only he could do the right thing at one of the crucial points in that chain of events, Wee's Revolution would fail, and mankind would never venture out to meet its destruction.

He had no idea what that action was, but he clung to the hope that he would discover it if only he waited, that it would be revealed to him outside the Sphere. But when he hovered again in the emptiness of space, waiting for it to change into something else, the Grand Sphere remained the Grand Sphere. Nothing was revealed to him, and he looked away from it in despair.

But when he looked in the direction in which the habitats had disappeared, he saw that they had returned and were in orbit around Catchcage. And from Catchcage a long stream of children flowed down to the moon and back, and a second stream of older children, who grew toward adulthood even as they came, flowed steadily out of Catchcage and into each of the other habitats and even down to Earth itself.

As soon as he saw them he knew that among them was the key to canceling the Vision of URdon Wee. He knew that it was his destiny to oppose URdon Wee, and he felt a certainty that his hatred for Wee had been an unconscious recognition of their unalterably opposed destinies. He knew, without doubt, that a single moment would come when he could prevent Wee's Vision from coming true, and he knew that no matter how many times he failed, he would know that moment when it came.

The Children of the Cage streamed out and out. Hool watched them come, the seeds of mankind's destruction, waiting for what, he did not know, until he saw it. Toward the middle of the procession three of the children seemed surrounded by a white light that isolated them even in the midst of the crowd.

The first was a young girl who grew as he watched her into a beautiful young woman. The second was a boy who seemed to change his shape continually. Their face, though one was undeniably feminine and the other undeniably masculine, was clearly the same face, Grandy's face. The third child was a little older and much bigger. As he came, he grew into a huge, bearded bear of a man, but young or old, his face was the face of URdon Wee.

He watched them go, part of the continual stream that flowed back and forth between the habitats, and he knew that somewhere in the Cage, or in Henson's Tube, Hardcore, or the Grand Sphere, his moment would come, and those three children would be at the center of it. And he saw also what would happen if his moment escaped him. The three children came to the Grand Sphere, and together they opened it like an egg. Inside it was the face of URdon Wee. The face was smiling at him.

The sound Hool made was partway between a howl and a scream. It filled the emptiness of space with a green fire that burned him without consuming him.

He did not say why he wanted Wee's vision to fail, and Pock did not press him. It didn't matter to Pock; he had learned long since that friends make weaker allies than strangers who share the same enemies. It didn't matter to him *how* Hool did it, either, but he wanted to know. "And the children?"

"Kill them." It was an unthinkable thing for a Catcher to say. "No children. No vision."

The logic was irrefutable; the only question was why his best Ear in Catchcage was coming to him with it. "You need the help of the Fist to kill a child?" he said. He put as much contempt into his voice as he could without provoking Hool to violence.

"*Three* children," Hool corrected.

Pock looked at him scornfully. "Well, of course, since you're outnumbered..." The mockery in his voice would have been enough to bring an ordinary OBee to blows, but it had no effect on Hool. "Would a dozen Blues be enough, or would you need more experienced men?"

"I need you to *find* them." Hool hissed the words between his teeth.

Pock shook his head in mock wonder. "Amazing," he said, "an Ear who needs an Ear." Hool did not look amused. Pock shrugged. "Done," he said finally. "Do you know where they were last?"

Hool glowered at him. "I know where they are *now*!" Pock looked puzzled. "I want to know where they are *later*, after they're dead."

Pock wondered for a moment if Hool's religious fanaticism had not passed all the way over into insanity. "You'll have to ask URdon Wee about that." Hool ignored the wit. Pock shrugged to himself; subtlety was always wasted on OBees. It was why he preferred dealing with Granders, even if every sentence they spoke had at least five contradictory meanings.

"You know what I mean," Hool snapped, "when they're Twiceborn."

Pock looked incredulous. "You expect Wee to resurrect them?"

Hool looked at him as if he thought Pock were the crazy one. "Do you expect him to leave them lost?"

Pock gave the man a long, hard look. He was a good Ear, but a crazy man was of no use to anybody. The interview was a waste of time. When his best Ear risked his cover by showing up at the Fist's headquarters in the Grand Sphere and demanding to see the commander, Pock expected something of substance. He had gotten nothing but fairy tales. "If we hear of any ghosts, you'll be the first to know," he said. He nodded toward the door.

When Hool did not move toward it, Pock sat up. His hand fell naturally on the cane. Hool made an obvious effort to control his rage. "They won't be ghosts," he said. He held out his hand. The tiny holodisc in his palm became a small sphere of light; the light became a young boy about twelve with bright orange hair. The sphere glowed again and became a beautiful young girl on the brink of womanhood. The girl dissolved into an older man-size boy. There was an obvious family resemblance to them all. "The children of URdon Wee," he said. He tossed the disc on the airecline.

Pock felt a sudden uncanny chill. It made him angry to think that Hool's superstitious nonsense might be getting to him. *"That's* the Revolution?" He laughed.

Hool's voice was deadly serious. "They will be," he said, "they *will* be."

CHAPTER
ELEVEN

Beyar stood stunned at the Nearside Window. He seemed outside of himself, outside of time, as if the accident had yet to occur and if only he could do something differently, it would be all right. If this time he did not look away from the sphere of the holoscan into the eyes of the Watcher, the pod would come through the gate whole. Or if he could just go back and handle their Leavings more gently, they would not have opened, and nothing would have happened.

He kept looking out the window, expecting their car to come bursting through the gate at any minute. The distance between the Cage and the End of the Sky seemed utterly empty, the moon desolate and the sky endlessly dark and deep. He looked back at the five spheres; the First Gate still hovered in them and then it, too, vanished, leaving nothing but glowing balls of light. And then the light disappeared as well, as if there was nothing left to see and never would be.

His partbrothers and specialsisters flocked around him crying and trying to console him. But there was nothing to say, except what they said, "Nothing stays lost." But the idea seemed to bounce off him, and after a while he could not even hear it, nor feel the hands that reached out to touch him and take some of his grief. But the grief was not even his yet. It would become his over the next few days, and it would stay his all his life, but at the moment he felt only numbness and an overriding sense of unreality. He felt like a holoscan, a moving three-dimensional figure of light without weight or density or effect.

He was dimly aware of the wailing and the groans of bitter disappointment in the background, the cries of negation, the refusals to believe it could happen, *had* happened. Stunned faces went by his, leaned close, said things, and drifted away, but he was unable to recognize them or comprehend what they had said. The crowd moved sluggishly toward its appointed places. The beginning of the ritual turned stunned grief to solemnity; occasionally there was an outcry as someone who had been in the Downshoot when it happened, and had not heard, was told of the tragedy.

But it all seemed unrelated to him. He did not even seem to be there. He was a great emptiness that, by sudden misfortune, had suddenly become aware of itself.

Soon everyone was down from the Catchround. The children were all triumphantly returned, except for two. The complete despair that had been everywhere began to be diluted by the presence of so many alive, so many who had gone to see the End of the Sky and returned as new people. Children who had gone off and come back as adults.

Slowly the stunned shook their despair and remembered what the ritual was all about: the dance of birth and death, the illusion of loss, the Great Joke of death, the Vision of URdon Wee. They began to put aside their natural grief, to wash it away with the truths URdon Wee had left them.

The balls of light grew again to full size, and a man appeared in the middle one and then in all the others. He said what he was supposed to say. "Some of the best have been lost. Two of the finest Exceptional people have gone to see the End of the Sky. Push and Chancey. Let us remember, as we remember them, that nothing stays lost." The man's voice rose. All voices in the hall spoke it in unison, "Nothing stays lost."

"Here," said the man, sweeping his arms to encompass the other spheres, "are the lost, *found*." The spheres filled one by one with the first Fruits of the Lottery. The New Generation. And one by one, as they appeared, the man read their names and welcomed them. The first taken from the Wombs were given the names of those lost the year before, just as Push and Chancey's names would be given to the first two born the next year. All Catchcage cheered after each name. And those who knew the names from when they were lost cheered loudest, to hear the names returned. And the cheering went on until the last was named.

And then the crowd broke up and went to get their suits and meet again in the Catchround. Later there would be dancing and laughter, but within the hour the continual stream of loaded kidneycars would pour into the Catchround, and everyone would work together to empty them and send them on their way, empty again.

Beyar went as well and did his portion of the work, let himself be absorbed by the work, became the work so that he did not have to think or feel or remember. The work took his mind as it took his body, and for a while he had the relief of forgetfulness.

But finally the cars stopped coming in full, the work trailed off, the crowd in the Catchround melted away to celebrations and special remembrances, and Beyar was left alone with his grief. He worked on with the regular crew for a while, and no one stopped him, but eventually someone came and put a hand on his shoulder and told him it was time to go, and he went.

At first he went to the Downshoot, but he could not bear the thought of his dormicile. The courtyard would be full of laughter, there would be countless offers to join the revelers, and he would have to smile and pretend that a giant part of him had not vanished. He wanted to be alone, and at first he stayed in the Downshoot as far as the Great Hall, but when he got out, the Nearside Window seemed so dark and empty that he could not look at it. He wondered if he would ever be able to look out of it again. He turned away and got into the Upshoot and rose almost to the Catchround again before the one place he could be alone came to him, and he went to the Wombs.

He sat on the airecline where he always sat with Push and Chancey and tried to let the serenity and the silence seep into him, but all he could feel was the emptiness. The Wombs that had once glowed with life were all empty, and their emptiness only added to his own. It made him ache, and it seemed as if the babies had not been born but had vanished, had evaporated like Push and Chancey, leaving behind only glowing, empty balls of light.

He sat for a long time waiting for the emptiness to go away, for the certainty that it was all illusion, anyway, to flood him with joy for the wonderful illusion they had created. But all he could feel was the emptiness and the guilt. Somehow it all seemed his fault. He felt he should have stopped them from going together in one car, but the fact that they were in one pod had not been the reason the kidneycar had split apart. He felt he should have buttoned them up better, but it was the Button-up Robot that had failed for some reason to fasten them securely. It had happened before. It would happen again. Going to See the End of the Sky had to have a price, or it would be worth nothing. He understood that. But it seemed his fault, anyway.

Softly Beyar began to cry. He looked at the empty Wombs, and the tears became sobs that grew until they hurt his chest and burned his throat and still would not stop. He cried for all that Push and Chancey could have been, and then he cried for that they *had* been, which was gone, and then he cried, as he had secretly cried all along, for himself. And for himself he cried hardest of all.

He let the pain and the grief take him, and when it was

done, when he had no more tears, he opened the Leavings and spread them on his knee. They both said the same thing. "We, Chancey and Push, leave to Beyar our seat in front of the Wombs, where we will be found again, to think of us and remember 'Nothing stays lost!'"

CHAPTER
TWELVE

URdon Wee touched three icons on the top row and the kidneycar turned on its side. He touched the fourth and it cracked open, spilling the twins out into the dark. He pressed another and the pod turned back. The Button-up Robot fastened it and sent it on its way.

In the chamber under the Button-up Robot the twins floated slowly downward through a crimson mist. Their skin-suits reacted to the sudden presence of an atmosphere and took in the mist like ordinary air. Grandy reluctantly touched the icon that would put them the rest of the way under. Sound above and below the level of hearing scrambled their brain waves like a burst of static. They touched the bottom of the container unconscious. She touched an icon shaped like an arrow, and the chamber packed around them and moved through the long tunnel under the Accelerator. When it stopped, it was in the same underground room with Grandy and URdon Wee.

They were not the first children to end up there, and they would not be the last. Every Skyshocker in the League had spent at least a few moments there, whether they were dropped out of the Scouring Robot or the infield or the Button-up, or whether they were plucked from one of the kidneycars hurtling toward the moon or hurtling back. Nor were they the first to be given the dream of their death or the dream of the Revolution.

URdon Wee had no hesitation about creating that illusion. To him everything was an illusion, and the rational explanation that he snatched them out of reality and created a new one for them with a diluted form of the Sunrise was no more real to him than the probability that they had died and were transformed. What mattered was the fact that they literally would be living in a new reality. The mechanical explanation of how he induced the trances in them and programmed their vision with subliminal sound was only a physical explanation for a spiritual event. To him they were only illusions within the illusion he was following.

If someone had told him that what he was doing was a fraud, he would have laughed and told them, "*Every*thing's an illusion." The world, what we do in it, what is done to us. Only *assumption* separates dream from reality. And besides, when it was time to drink the Sunrise, they would die, even in physical terms, a death and still transcend it. What he did was only a promise of the rebirth to come when they were old enough to choose it of their own free will.

In the meantime secret training was necessary that could not be accomplished in any other way. And in the long run what he did was what he was destined to do in the current version of the world, where all acts were shaped by the illusions of space and time. On other planes, with other dimensions, all deaths were real. And all resurrections.

He touched another icon and the jamming of their brain waves stopped. He could have begun their dream immediately, but there were still things to be learned about their character. The way they had dealt with obstacles on the surface was remarkable, but there was still the question of what they would do with problems that simple action could not solve. Undoubtedly they had the necessary courage, and they had the initiative and the originality. But there were more tests to pass. He waited to see if they would realize their dilemma and how they would handle it.

Grandy watched the holoscan of what was going on inside the chamber with an intense concentration. She nodded encouragement when the twins began to unravel their situation. That it was an illusion that they were traveling back to the Cage without enough air made no difference. Belief made the difference between reality and illusion. Belief shaped the perception of events and generated other events.

The twins would act no differently if they were actually traveling through space. The fact that they existed at all was an illusion. She knew that as well as URdon Wee. The world was ultimately nothing more than the dance of electrons; no physical thing was more than a temporary configuration in that dance. All existence was a beat phenomenon, a temporary overlapping of the illusion of space and the illusion of time.

Still, their illusion fascinated her. She had watched them all their lives, waited patiently and impatiently for them to come, and now they were before her; now they were about to become more than three-dimensional ghosts in her world. She had waited a long time for them to hatch into her world, and finally it was about to happen.

She looked at URdon Wee; he began the whispering— subtle, subliminal sounds too low to be heard, too strong to be resisted. Deep in the mind where the voice of the self chatters continually, a new voice spoke, a voice that had already spoken hour after hour, day after day, while they were still in the Wombs. And the voice made them see the pod opening, made them feel the inevitable tumble forward, made them understand the sudden imminence of their death.

The voice tumbled them into the void, and they died.

The chamber tumbled them into the room. They fell limp to the floor. He and Grandy raised them up, laid them on aireclines, and waited for their eyes to open into the new world. They did not have to wait long.

Chancey woke first, and her face was filled with joy at

the sight of Grandy. Grandy's voice was husky when she spoke the words of the ritual. "Welcome to the World, Chancey of the Cage, who-has-died-the-Little-Death-and-the-Big. Welcome to the World, Chancey Twiceborn."

Chancey reached up and put her arms around Grandy's neck. Grandy hugged her. Chancey's voice was on the verge of tears. "Oh, I hoped it would be you. I used to dream of you every night."

Grandy held her close. "I know," she said, "I was *there*. All dreams are one dream."

"I *knew* it wouldn't be the end." Her voice was filled with joy and excitement.

Grandy smiled at her innocence. "It never is," she said. "Not this time, not the next." She thought of her own first resurrection.

Grandy woke to a dim light in a low room in Hardcore. Her eyes fluttered briefly but saw nothing. The pain in her chest was gone, but she was afraid to look. She felt her chest with her hand, but there was neither wound nor blood, and her hand did not pass through her body as she had expected. She was certain she had died; what she had experienced was real beyond a shadow of a doubt. And yet she was neither dead nor the substanceless hologram she had envisioned herself to be in the next illusion.

She could move, and yet she had no inclination to move. She was perfectly at peace the way she was. She kept her eyes closed, she told herself, because it was restful. But in truth she kept them closed because she was afraid that Donald would not be there and the afterlife would turn out worse than death.

His voice put all fears aside. "Welcome to the World, Grandy Wheeler, who-has-died-the-Little-Death-and-the-Big, Welcome to the World, Grandy Twiceborn."

When she opened her eyes, he kissed her, and all things were right. He helped her to sit up. She looked around the room; she recognized the white bulkhead, the peeling paint, the metal walls of Hardcore. She shook her head. "Who would have thought it," she said.

URdon Wee smiled. "Thought what?"

"That Paradise would turn out to be Hardcore."

Their laughter made it Paradise. As it always had.

URdon Wee's voice was deep and resonant. "Welcome to the World, Push of the Cage, who-has-died-the-Little-Death-and-the-Big. Welcome to the World, Push Twiceborn." Chancey turned her head and her joy was complete.

Push sat up and stared openmouthed around the room. When he saw Chancey, he smiled as if he had known all along that she would be there. He looked at Grandy, at the room with its tons of equipment, then looked back at URdon Wee. "So this is death," he said.

URdon Wee shook his head. "No, your death is over," he said. "At least your first death is."

"Death is the opposite of *birth*," Grandy said, "not the opposite of life."

Wee put his hand on Push's shoulder. "It's a rite of passage," he said, "like Going to See the End of the Sky. The person who begins the journey is not the person who returns."

It was true; even if they had returned to the Cage, they would have been changed; were changed already from the moment the pod opened on the moon, perhaps before. Just the going had made them different. Push thought of all the people he had seen go; all of them had returned different, some more confident, more certain, some more withdrawn, more aloof, some more serene, some more erratic, but none had returned the same as they left. Even Beyar.

The thought of Beyar filled him with a deep sadness. Chancey felt it too. It brought tears to her eyes. Grandy stroked her head.

"We've waited a long time for you here," URdon Wee said. "You have important things to do," he said. "Both of you."

Push looked around the room, wondering what he could do there. "Here?" he said.

URdon Wee laughed. "No," Wee said, "your destinies are much too large for so small a stage as this."

Push waited for more of an answer, and when it did not come, he asked. "Where, then?"

"In the League," he said. "In Hardcore and Henson's Tube and eventually in the Grand Sphere." He looked specifically at Chancey. "And even Earthside."

"Will we see Beyar again?" Chancey asked. The tears that could not be seen in her eyes could be heard in her voice.

Grandy smoothed her hair. "Yes," she said gently, "you *will* see Beyar again." Chancey brightened. She was afraid to ask the rest of her question. Grandy smiled. "And he will see *you*."

"Will he be able to touch us?" Push said.

URdon Wee smiled. "We can touch you," he said.

"Yes, but you're . . . we're . . ." Push shifted uncomfortably.

"Dead?" He struggled to suppress a chuckle.

"Well, no, but . . ." Push struggled for a way to express it. "Beyar hasn't died," he said finally.

"He *will*." It was a surprisingly reassuring statement.

CHAPTER
THIRTEEN

The voice startled him. "You didn't think I'd leave them lost, did you?" Beyar looked up. URdon Wee smiled at him. The smile made him feel safe and warm, as it always had. He felt suddenly ashamed of his tears. "There's no need," URdon Wee said. "Even Grandy cried when *I* died. She cried for herself. Because even if nothing stays lost, it's lost for now."

Beyar bit his lip to keep from crying again. URdon Wee smiled. "You know, if I hadn't died first, I would have cried when Grandy died." He nodded to Beyar to emphasize that it was the truth. "I'd have cried for me. That's part of everything too. Grief and death, despair and loss; it's all part of the beauty of the illusion. So you're entitled to as good a cry as you can have." Beyar nodded, and URdon Wee pointed to the Wombs. "There's a time to stop crying too," he said gently. "And this is it."

Beyar tried, but the tears welled up in his eyes when he thought of never seeing the twins again, never hearing them, never being able to give them a hug. "You'll be together with them before long," URdon Wee said. "They're with me, and although they're dead"—his eyes seemed to twinkle with some secret joke—"they're well and happy and waiting for you."

Beyar was afraid to hope. "You mean I can go to them?"

URdon Wee nodded. "Of course."

"How?"

URdon Wee laughed. "By going to see the End of the Sky, of course."

It was the same as saying "By dying." Nobody Beyar's age could last the trip. Beyar didn't care. "Can we go now?" he said.

URdon Wee raised a finger of warning. "There are obstacles." He pointed to the Womb in front of Beyar, and the face of the Watcher appeared in its hazy depths. "You recognize him," URdon Wee said. Beyar nodded. "That's Back Toss Hool, who helped bring me to my enlightenment. He drank the Sunrise with me once, long before you were born.

The table was small and round; Hool sat on one side, URdon Wee on the other; between them was a tall beaker of liquid the color of Sunrise. There were formalities to be taken care of. URdon Wee thought of how simple it would have been once. He would have said, "This will probably kill you, but if it doesn't, it'll melt your brain." And the OBee would have said, "How much do you take?" And whatever he said, the OBee would have belted down twice as much just to make sure. But that was before Wee himself had taken it, and before others had taken it.

In a very real way everyone who drank the Sunrise died. Although the form the change took was different in every person, the change itself was so abrupt and so revolutionary that no one who experienced it could be said to be the same person afterward. Superficial details remained the same, the person might look entirely the same, but inwardly they were changed. Their whole way of perceiving and interpreting the world was irreversibly altered.

Some were so radically changed that they could no longer be said to exist within the Great Illusion at all. They had fallen for the Great Joke and were laughing somewhere with God. He thought of Allohvar and Third-Degree Burns, of Jain of the Torch and Jain of the Catchround, of Wit-mon from Hardcore and Podwrench Bob. All gone to see the End of the Sky. Lost for the moment. For the moment, gone out of Catchcage and into the Vision of URdon Wee.

Hool would be different; he knew that, just as he had known what would happen to the others at their point of transition. They had had their part in the Great Illusion, Hool had his. Only the individual Visions of those who drank the Sunrise remained beyond URdon Wee. The outlines of what would be and the far-ranging consequences of important but seemingly trivial points along the way were clear to him. He knew things that would not happen for ten thousand years and would happen then only because of the Revolution. And the Revolution would happen only because of what was happening at the moment, and a dozen other moments that had already happened, and a dozen moments still to occur.

It was entirely up to URdon Wee who drank the Sunrise and when, and URdon Wee decided according to the pattern formed by the interaction of his Vision and the Moment. In the moment of his Vision URdon Wee had known everything, and whenever he reentered that Vision, he knew it again. But in the time between he knew only a rough outline. It was as if he saw the world with two different eyes. In one eye, the eye of his Vision, he saw all things simultaneously, from a cosmic perspective in which time, like space, was merely an illusion. Through the other eye he saw only the Moment, as it existed within the limitations of space and time.

In short, in the moments of his Vision he knew everything. In his Vision of the Moment, he forgot most of it. He did this, like God, for his own amusement, and the continual recognition of what he knew but had willingly forgotten never failed to keep him laughing. When those two overlapped and the event he knew to be coming finally occurred, he was delighted by the familiarity of it. Nothing

*delighted him like the realization that he was on the brink of
a Significant Moment. He was delighted when he looked at
Back Toss Hool.*

"Nothing is what it seems," he said to Hool.

"I am," said the OBee. "I'm the one you can't fool."

*Wee tried not to laugh. He knew what Back Toss Hool
was and what he would be, and neither of them was what he
seemed. Or what he thought he was.*

"Hold your hand out over the table," Wee said.

Hool gave an exasperated grunt. "More parables?" *he
said.* Wee nodded, and Hool held his hand out. It cast a
shadow on the smooth, white surface.

"That," said URdon Wee, "is what you are."

"A shadow?" Hool said. He scowled as if he thought
Wee was dismissing him as unimportant.

"A shadow made of light," Wee corrected. He held his
own hand out; its shadow ran parallel to Hool's. "That is
what I am," he said. "An action. A process. An event. A
shadow made of light." He moved his hand until his shadow
overlapped Hool's. Where they crossed, a darker shadow
formed, a shadow that had no existence of its own, a shadow
created solely by the interaction of one shadow and another.
"Do you know what that is?"

"A beat phenomenon," Hool said.

URdon Wee nodded. "Exactly," he said. "That is the
world."

*Hool moved his arm and the doubled shadow
disappeared.* "Your world," he said, "not mine."

URdon Wee laughed. "What you can't see, isn't
necessarily gone."

"Another Weeism," Hool scoffed. "I'm not like the rest,"
he said. "I can't be moved by a lot of words."

"You want to go to see the End of the Sky, then." *It was
hardly a question. The Sunrise was what Hool had been
pressing for since the day Dreem Shalleen had brought him in.
His continual skepticism was a constant source of amusement*

for Wee, and he really enjoyed their discussions. He would miss them, he thought, once Hool drank the Sunrise.

"Are you finally going to stop hoarding it?" To Hool the only thing Wee had that could produce a following was the Sunrise; everything else was clever fraud and platitudes. Enlightenment meant nothing to him.

"It will be the end of you," Wee said.

"It wasn't the end of you."

"It was the end of Donald Wheeler." Wee's voice still held a sense of wonder as strong as the moment of his Enlightenment.

"It won't be the end of Back Toss Hool."

It was all Wee could do to keep from laughing. "Some don't come back at all, you know," he said solemnly.

"Fools die every day," Hool said. "It's a small price to pay for Enlightment."

Wee ignored the sarcasm and gave the second warning. "One man goes on a journey, another comes back."

"Enough talk." It was a favorite OBee expression.

"Why?"

"Why what?"

"Why do you want to drink the Sunrise?"

"I want Enlightenment." When Wee raised an eyebrow, Hool amended it. "I want to know what you know."

URdon Wee shook his head. "If you overlap your shadow with your shadow, will you get mine?" Hool didn't want to hear the question any more than he wanted to hear the answer. Wee gave it to him, anyway. "You won't get my vision. Everybody's vision is different. You'll get your own."

There would be no good telling Hool that the Vision would be determined by the beat phenomenon of the moment— the overlapping of the taker's mental and emotional tendencies with what had happened to them the moment before they took the Sunrise and the effect of the Sunrise itself. There would be no good warning him that if he took it before he conquered the jealousy and rage in himself, they would distort everything he would see, everything he would learn. Hool would only be certain that Wee was just trying to put him off again.

It did not occur to URdon Wee not to give Back Toss Hool the Sunrise. He knew in a general way that he had already done it and would always do it, had to do it, *because that was the way the illusion was structured. He knew also that it was not the only illusion in which he made such a decision, but he had decided from the beginning to treat the illusion he was in as the only one until his purpose in it was accomplished. He wondered what it was like in the illusion where he and Hool were reversed, but he put the thought quickly aside. There would be time enough to explore alternatives when the present illusion was complete.*

Hool looked impatiently at the beaker. "My life. My death. My vision. My change." He looked at URdon Wee for confirmation that he had stated the terms of the bargain correctly. When Wee nodded, Hool reached for the beaker. "Done," he said.

Wee put a hand on his wrist as he lifted the beaker. "Wait," he said. He remembered that if Grandy and Dreem Shalleen were there, it would make a difference, but he did not remember what the difference would be. Hool jerked his hand away and lifted the beaker. As he drank, the wallfront unclouded, and Grandy and Dreem Shalleen came in. The first thing Hool saw, through the crimson haze of the Sunrise, was the way both Grandy and Dreem Shalleen looked at URdon Wee. The rest of his vision was tinged with fiery green. Wee recognized the look of rage and jealousy on Hool's face and remembered what the difference was and what its consequences would be.

"Back Toss Hool has spent every waking moment since then trying to destroy the truth of my Vision. Do you know why he's been watching you?" Beyar shook his head. "To kill you."

Beyar had felt as much. "Did he kill Push and Chancey?"

URdon Wee laughed, as if there was so much he could

not say. "No more than I did, although Push and Chancey wouldn't have had to die if Back Toss Hool didn't exist."

"I should have killed him myself," Beyar said. URdon Wee threw back his head and laughed.

"You might as well kill *me*," he said.

He took pity on Beyar's look of bewilderment. "*He's* part of my Vision, too, you know. Everything he does is what I've seen him do, what he *has* to do to play his part in the illusion." He shook his head at some private joke. "I tell you, Beyar, God is always laughing when he thinks of Back Toss Hool." But Back Toss Hool was still nothing Beyar could laugh about. URdon Wee seemed to find that enormously amusing. "You'll laugh at all this yourself, eventually," he said. Beyar still felt as if he would never laugh again, until he could see Push and Chancey.

"Do you know *why* Back Toss Hool wants to kill you?"

Beyar shrugged. Nothing he had ever done could account for it. "Because he's crazy?"

Wee shook his head, as if surprised that Beyar did not know better. "There *are* no lunatics, Beyar," he said, "only unrecognized saints."

Beyar could see only one other explanation, but it made no sense. "Because he hates me?" Wee nodded. Beyar frowned at the injustice of it. "But I've never *done* anything to him."

"It's not what you've done, Beyar of the Cage, it's what you *will* do." Beyar felt a rush of pride. It made him think of his return from Going to See the End of the Sky. "*You* are a child of my Vision, and Back Toss Hool lives to destroy that Vision. He will do anything to prevent that Vision from coming true."

Beyar saw the reasoning behind it. "And if I don't live to do what I do in your Vision, it can't come true?" URdon Wee smiled, pleased that Beyar had grasped the truth so quickly.

URdon Wee nodded. "Precisely! And he's waiting for you now, up on the Catchround."

"Then I'll stay down here until he's gone," Beyar said.

URdon Wee shook his head regretfully. "I'm afraid you won't get to see Push and Chancey if you do."

"Then I'll go," Beyar said, "but he won't get me."

URdon Wee laughed so hard, he could barely stand. "But, of course, he will, Beyar. That's what I'm here for."

Beyar looked incredulously at the lunatic saint. "You mean..."

"Exactly! I'm here to help him."

CHAPTER
FOURTEEN

Back Toss Hool disrupted the field of the wallfront and went through it without unclouding it. None of the revelers in the courtyard noticed. Beyar's dormicile was much smaller than Dreem's two-slice, or any of the other adult homeciles farther up the Valley. It was designed for single, young people between twelve and sixteen who had gone to see the End of the Sky but were not yet ready to leave the Cage and make their way in one of the other habitats for a decade or two.

Because the only responsibilities they had were two hours a day learning Theory from the holoscans and another two hours gaining practical experience in the Catchround or the Smelter or the Torch, Catchers of that age generally spent their time out in the courtyards or roaming the Cage, and the dormiciles were little more than bases of operation. They were temporary quarters, a place to live in passing, unlike the homeciles on the higher terraces of the Valley to which they would return after time abroad in other habitats in the League.

Beyar's slice was like all of the others. It was not small, but none of its space was wasted, and it offered few hiding places. The bed and a work surface took up the back wall;

head-high above them was a double storage bin running all
the way across. Two sitables and a Fooder claimed the wall
to the left of the wallfront.

And across a large holopad, along the right wall, was a
bigger sitable; the walls of the wash & flush screened it from
the door, and it offered a comfortable place for Hool to wait.
But from there he could not cut off the boy's retreat, and he
passed it up in favor of the only real place to hide, the wash
& flush itself.

He was lucky; the partitions of energy that made up its
walls were blacked, as if it were in use. If they had been
down instead, he would have had nowhere to hide at all, and
he was thankful for the carelessness of children in a hurry to
get somewhere. It never occurred to him for a moment that
URdon Wee had left it that way on purpose just for him.

The enclosure was not large, but it filled the space between the sitable and the wallfront. The bed, the work surface,
and two of the sitables were beyond it, and if the boy went
straight to any of them, Hool would be able to cut off his
only exit. If he came to the wash & flush first, Hool could
hide behind the catchscreen of the mist-er and leap out at
him when he was fully in.

If there was a lot of blood, he could always use the mist-
er's mixture of forced air and water to clean both himself and
his worksuit before he made his escape. He folded the drop-
sink up into the wall and pulled the seat & flushfunnel out
and sat on it. The seat was designed for a much smaller body,
and it was not comfortable. The wait was longer than he
expected, but it was nothing to the more than thirty years he
had waited already.

Finally there was movement at the wallfront, and he
shifted silently to crouch closer to the catchscreen of the mist-
er. Behind him, at the bottom corner of the wall, a thin tube
crawled slowly through the blackened field. He listened for
someone to enter, waited for footsteps to cross in front of the

cabinet. But nothing came. He did not hear URdon Wee leave the dormicile.

He was used to false alarms. More than once he had thought it had come, the crucial turning point at which he could change everything. He had passed scores of Significant Moments, balance points in the unfolding of Wee's Vision. But they were never *His* moment, never the one moment, where things *would* change, and *his* vision, *his* future, would replace Wee's.

And yet each one had *felt* like His moment.

Time after time he had felt the change, the subtle shift in reality that marked a balance point on which the momentum of Wee's Vision turned, a moment in time when the just right action could kick Wee's Vision off its course and send it spinning off into the chaos of unfulfilled possibilities. Moments that *might* be Back Toss Hool's moment.

That was his agony: that it was so easy to be mistaken. He knew only fragments, things remembered from the distant and half-forgotten dream of his Vision, things retained imprecisely from its intermittent return. Echoes of the Sunrise still circulated in his blood, and its unpredictable floods sometimes tinged even ordinary moments with an aura of the cosmic.

There was a vague hiss, like the escaping of an all but imperceptible gas, and Hool smiled. He had heard it dozens of times before, whenever he crossed into the orbit of a moment that *could* be changed. He waited for other changes, subtle shifts in the texture of reality that marked a Significant Moment.

His Vision seemed to rise around him like a crimson mist. The hiss became a whisper, as if an unheard voice was speaking to him from another dimension. He did not recognize the voice URdon Wee had left behind. For him it was the voice of his own vision, and with it came the knowledge that his wait was in vain. The boy would not come there.

He felt the keenness of his disappointment settle into his

bones, and he waited for the eerie specialness of the moment to drain away. The whisper dwindled, and he waited for time to return to its ordinary passage, and the mist the color of sunrise to settle and leave him stranded in the emptiness of another missed opportunity.

Instead, the mist deepened and the whisper rose again filling him with certainty. He did not know where the boy *was*, but he knew where the boy *would be*. He knew exactly where their paths would intersect, and he knew exactly what he would do when they did.

He moved slowly toward the wallfront. There was no need to hurry. They would meet inevitably in the midst of *his* Moment. With perfect timing, inevitable destiny was already drawing them both toward the Catchround.

CHAPTER
FIFTEEN

The Catchround was all but empty. Few loaded kidney-cars were coming in, and even fewer were expected for more than a day. At LUNAC the Scouring Robot was back in operation, but Catchcage was still receiving the cars shipped the day Push and Chancey had gone to see the End of the Sky. The backlog that had been built up before Push and Chancey ruined the Scouring Robot had been exhausted, and the kidneycars backed up on the holding track had to be rationed for fear of running out and having to shut down the Accelerator altogether.

LUNAC Mine had been ordered to slow production, and every available Loonie had been assigned to cleaning the cars by hand until the Scouring Robot was repaired. One out of five that came in needed a thorough scouring, but what the Robot had done in minutes took human crews half an hour or more. It had been a losing battle for more than a day before the Robot was finally repaired. And for the last six hours before it was back in operation, all but the worst cars were being shunted through uncleaned in hopes of keeping the Accelerator running.

With so few loaded cars coming through the gates, power to the Torch had dropped off drastically, and many of the

Techs there were being sent home early. Nobody complained,
Last Day celebrations were raging everywhere, and all but a
few rabid scientists with long-term experiments ran for the
Upshoots to get to them. None of the Techs came as high as
the Wombs, let alone the Catchround, and Beyar saw no one
in the Upshoot. No one saw URdon Wee. Even on the Watchdeck no one saw him. There was almost no one *to* see him.

Out in the Catchround only one man was hooking the
occasional kidneycar out of the Round, checking the consis-
tency of its contents and shunting it into one of the nine
offshoots for emptying in different parts of the smelter. LU-
NAC labeled each load on a scale from one to nine, and each
grade emptied into a different level of the smelter. Fine grade
or "dust" went into the longest channel and emptied into the
bottom of the smelter. "Crud," or impacted dust, went into
shorter channels that led to the body of the smelter, and
"hardpack" was tipped almost immediately into the Dumper
at the top.

Half a dozen other workers lounged in small groups
scattered across the apron of the Catchround, talking and
laughing. None of them paid any attention to what was happening beyond them. Beyar had been doubtful about getting
into one of the cars without being stopped, but a half dozen
empties were tethered with podwrenches just short of the last
offshoot, waiting to be sent off to the Button-up when they
made an even dozen. The first was out of sight of the podhandler, and nobody else was concerned with that part of the
Round. Back Toss Hool was nowhere in sight.

He turned to URdon Wee to find out why, but Wee only
smiled. "He's where he's supposed to be," he said. "As are
we all."

Beyar did not want to seem reluctant, but he was not
sure whether he should go immediately or if Wee had something more to tell him. Wee put a hand on his shoulder. "Push
and Chancey are waiting for you," he said, "at the End of
the Sky."

Beyar nodded. He did not ask where Back Toss Hool was waiting. Wee took his hand and placed two small discs in his palm. Beyar cocked his head. "Nose filters," Wee said. "They'll help you breathe better," he said.

Beyar pressed them into his nostrils, and Wee pulled the hood of Beyar's skinsuit up over his head for him as Beyar had done for Push and Chancey. It made Beyar think of the last few moments he had seen them, and the tears crept into the corners of his eyes. He took a deep breath to fight them back, and everything seemed tinged suddenly with a crimson haze. He felt as if he were entering a dream. URdon Wee winked at him. "Get lost," he said. Beyar started for the Catchround. He did not look back until he was on the walkway at the edge of the apron, and when he did, URdon Wee was gone.

The quickest way to the kidneycars would have been straight across the apron, but there was a group of podhandlers in the way. He walked along the front of the Watchdeck almost to its far end before he went forward. All the way he felt as if he was not actually there doing the walking. He felt aloof, strangely removed from himself. A crimson mist seemed to be rising from the apron of the Catchround.

He picked up a podwrench and made his way back toward the tethered pods, skirting the edge of the apron. No one noticed him, or if they did, they assumed he was back up trying to drown his feelings in work. One Last Day or another, at least half of them had done the same thing, and they understood. If he had looked in their direction, they would have looked away almost universally, but none of them seemed aware that he was there. He wondered if it was because they couldn't see him clearly in the haze. He stood near the first kidneycar for a minute, idly touching it here and there with his podwrench. The stack was up to eight.

The pod was cracked, and it would only take a second to lift the lid and climb inside. He gave one last look around the apron; Hool was nowhere in sight. He raised the lid and scrambled inside. He quickly lowered the upper part of the shell over him. Just before it closed, he saw Hool walking toward the pod from the other end of the Catchround. His heart raced. He pulled the lid down more and watched Hool through a hairline crack.

But Hool did not come directly for the pod as he had feared. He looked around the Catchround and back up at the Watchdeck and frowned, as if he couldn't understand why Beyar wasn't there. When he came near the podhandler, he stopped and talked. After a few minutes Hool hooked the next kidneycar to come floating around the bend, and the podhandler walked away, waving his thanks. Beyar breathed easier. Hool would not have gone to the trouble of finding cover if he did not expect a long wait, and he would not be waiting if he already knew where Beyar was.

He watched Hool catch two empties in a row and walk them toward the end of the line, but he lost sight of him as he worked them into position. He felt partly relieved; only two more and his trip would begin. He did not think about how it would end. URdon Wee had assured him he would see Push and Chancey again, and he believed it. But Wee had also said that Hool was there to kill him and Wee was there to help. But Wee's eternal smile had said "Nothing is what it seems" and seemed to counsel him not to worry.

Motion caught his eye, and he saw Hool banging the buttons on the pod next to him. He must have been coming up the line, getting ready to send them all off. Beyar crouched in the bottom of the pod. He was less afraid to die than he was that Hool would stop him. There was no reason to worry; Hool had no reason to lift the lid and look inside.

The crack between the halves of the pod widened an inch, and then another. He expected it to be flung up at any moment, and Hool's podwrench to come crashing down on him. But the top lid stopped rising no more than a hand's width from the bottom. In a moment Hool's face appeared in the crack. A slant of light cut into the darkness of the pod, but Beyar was outside of it and he was sure Hool could not see him. Still, Hool's eyes met his across the darkness. It made him suck in his breath, and the crimson mist rose between them. Hool's face turned away from the opening. Its smile was ruthless and cruel and eerily satisfied, as if Hool had seen him, after all.

The lid bounced shut. The light ceased. He felt the vibrations of Hool banging the buttons closed. He hit them again and again, as if making sure they would not be easily opened. It made no sense. If Hool knew he was there, he would want them *unfastened* so that Beyar would be spilled out with the first buffeting of the Gates. He felt the podwrench hook the car and the gentle motion of the kidneycar being moved forward. In a moment it would be swung out into the main channel for the Button-up Robot.

But the car did not turn left. Instead, it hesitated and bobbled a moment, before the back end swung the wrong way. It could only mean that Hool knew he was there and was swinging the kidneycar into the last offshoot and a one-way trip to the bottom of the Smelter. He understood, as the kidneycar bobbled along in the narrow channel, why Hool had fastened the buttons so tightly: He had not wanted Beyar to get out until the Dumper at the bottom opened the snaps and pitched him into the molten glow of the Smelter.

He felt the kidneycar come to the end of the channel and slant forward and down, and he knew he was headed for the dustdumper. It was a slow, steady descent, as slow as the realization that he would not survive. His breath was coming thick and fast, and he forced himself to take long, slow, deep breaths. The pod edged downward. Beyar thought he heard whispering, a voice that seemed to be inside his head and yet seemed too far away to be heard. Even with his eyes closed he could see the mist. He thought it was the heat.

He knew how the Smelter worked—he had seen all parts of it—and he knew the temperature would rise until the metal of the pod itself began to expand to loosen the load. The suit would keep him conscious even through that, and he would still be aware when the pod hit the last pause block and opened to topple him out. But the suit would not protect him in the Smelter itself. It, too, would incinerate, and there would be nothing left of him but the shadow his life had left in a few people's minds. No one would even know what happened to him. He simply would have vanished without a trace.

He doubted that anyone on the apron of the Catchround would remember even seeing him near one of the pods before it was sent down to the Smelter. And if they did, it only meant his death would probably be explained as an accident or a suicide. No one would suspect murder. He had no hope that anyone would realize what must have happened to him in time to enter the walkway along the channel at one of the pause blocks and get him out. He expected no last second miracle. He did not get one.

The temperature rose steadily as the pod slid down the slanting channel to the dustdumper. Even the suit could not keep him from feeling it, and the closer the pod got, the harder it was to breathe. Even Wee's filters did not help much, and he felt like he was suffocating before he felt the burning.

The crimson mist seemed to be congealing around him, and the whisper inside his head was almost audible when he felt the pod bump to a stop at the last pause block. He imagined URdon Wee scrambling through the access shaft and running along the walkway toward the pod. He could almost hear him banging away at the buttons and feel him fling open the pod to drag him out to safety.

But it was just a dream, and he woke from it afraid. The pod began to move downward again, and the full impact of his situation struck him. No one could help him; no one even knew he was there. He was going to die. The certainty of that fact filled him with momentary horror.

In the last fifty feet of the descent the burning was intense. He felt as if the suit were melting into his skin, but he did not let himself dwell on the pain. There were greater pains to torment him if he let them: the fact that he would never see Push and Chancey again; the fact that he had failed URdon Wee; the impact his death would have on URdon Wee's vision.

He felt the pod drop sharply from the last pause block to curb of the podstop. There was a bump that tossed him forward when it stopped. The seam of the pod cracked open. A plane of incredibly hot whiteness cut into the pod and widened until the lid was well up and the back of the lower half had lifted up to spill him out into the burning mist of the Smelter. He had only a brief moment of flight. The crimson mist vanished in the white mist of the heat. He fell into it like falling into the sun.

His last feeling was a blast of heat so strong that it seemed numbingly cold. He felt neither his suit nor his flesh melt away. There was just brightness and heat and pain. He thought only how beautiful it was in its way and how glad he was that he had been given such a beautiful way to die. His next to last thought was a certainty that he, too, would not be lost forever. His last thought was of Push and Chancey.

CHAPTER
SIXTEEN

Beyar dreamed in his death. But they were dreams without memories, and when he awoke from his death, there was nothing left of his dream except a vague feeling that he had had one. The first thing that he heard after his death was the voice of URdon Wee. The voice said, "Welcome to the World, Beyar of the Cage, who-has-died-the-Little-Death-and-the-Big. Welcome to the World, Beyar Twiceborn."

The first thing that he saw when he opened his eyes were the faces of Push and Chancey. Nothing in his life had made him happier than that moment in his death.

URdon Wee and Grandy smiled benevolently as the twins hugged him back to the world. They were all three laughing and crying at the same time and trying to say things which were, and had always been, unsayable. Finally they helped Beyar up off the airecline and held him up while he tried to stand. His legs felt weak and rubbery, as if he had gone to the End of the Sky without the Little Death to keep them supple while he slept. "Where . . ." he said finally.

There was no need to let him finish. URdon Wee smiled, as if there could be no other answer. "End of the Sky, of course."

Beyar smiled. It was exactly where he was supposed to be. But he wouldn't have cared if it *wasn't*, as long as Push and Chancey were there. He asked the second obvious question. "How?"

URdon Wee cocked his head. "Does it matter?"

It didn't, except for curiosity. Beyar shook his head. "No," he said slowly. There was an unspoken *but* at the end, and Wee heard it.

"You'll know the *how* when you drink the Sunrise," he said. He seemed to be laughing at some private joke he would eventually let Beyar in on. "Of course, all hows are meaningless once you drink the Sunrise, but you *will* know."

"There's a long time before they drink the Sunrise," Grandy said.

Beyar looked at her shyly. Like the twins, he idolized her, and he had wondered about her all his life. He was surprised how little she had changed from the holos of her they had seen. It did not occur to him that only the living age. She came over to Beyar and hugged him, as if she had waited all his life to do it. "The important thing is that you're finally here again."

Beyar looked bewildered. "Again?" he said.

"You were here four years ago," she said.

Beyar frowned. Literally the End of the Sky was the moon, but when people said someone who had died had gone to see the End of the Sky, it had never occurred to Beyar that they might literally mean the moon. And yet that seemed to be exactly what Grandy meant. Beyar was afraid the question would sound foolish but he asked it, anyway. "People go to LUNAC when they die?" His voice was incredulous.

Grandy laughed. She looked meaningfully at URdon Wee. "Not everyone," she said. "Some go to Hardcore."

Wee smiled. "Some even drink the Sunrise there."

Grandy smiled as she remembered.

Grandy looked around at the chaos of the Main Floor with pride. It was the biggest open space in Hardcore, and

*probably the smartest business deal in the short history of the
League. She had bought the long, double-hulled cone of metal
for a hundredth of its value. It had been the catchfunnel from
the original mass catcher the Cage had replaced. Hardly two
years before it had been catching the last fifty-pound packets of
moondust thrown up by the little Accelerator on the moon, to
be smelted in the solar furnace. With Spencer LeGrange's new
accelerator at LUNAC complete and the big metal kidneycars
replacing the little fiberglass bundles of moondirt, the three
mass catchers were obsolete. Two had gone for scrap, and
Grandy had bought the third with her life savings, all the
favors that were owed her, and a secret loan from the
Corporation based on a third of the profits Grandy's Place
would turn selling just about anything the Corporation made
illegal everywhere else.*

*The wire mesh at the mouth of the funnel, which had
burst the small packages of moondirt into moondust, had made
a perfect framework for laying up structure, and the mouth of
the funnel had been sealed with a wall in no time. Off-duty
OBees, working in return for lifetime memberships, had done
the work, and the cost of renovation had been minimal. She
looked around at the scattering of metal platforms welded to
the inside of the mesh of the Widewall and the steel of the
Sidewalls like shelves. They were crammed with customers,
sitting or lying on the slabs or coming and going on the maze
of ramps and ladders that connected them. Their movements
made the entire place seem alive at times, and Grandy never
tired of looking at it.*

*She had ample opportunity; Grandy's Place never closed.
Work on Catchcage never stopped, and the crews of OBees that
continually left and arrived in Hardcore always needed some
recreation before they slept. Something of interest could always
be found at Grandy's, and the men and women of Hardcore
seldom passed a week without visiting it. On the large, open
floor where Grandy dispensed bottles, tubes, pipes, injection
bulbs, and assorted pills, potions, salves, and cylinders of*

"home air," two dozen couples Danced the Dove until they were ready to take a Squeeze.

She looked down into the middle section of the funnel to see how many were empty. On the far wall, which separated the public portion of the funnel from the storage and production facilities for just about everything on Grandy's menu, were three columns of circles that served as clocks for each of the eighty small, horizontal Squeezes where couples who had come to an agreement and had the resources could retire for privacy. About six were completely red, and another ten or so were in their last quadrant of green and would be unoccupied and up for rent again in ten minutes.

Traffic was light on the series of ladders that ran up the middle of each bank of compartments and connected the narrow walkways that ran along the bottom of each squeeze. It was considerably heavier in the five Uprises that divided the compartments into stacks. Half a dozen couples, too unsteady to hazard the ladders, rose in the transparent columns to their horizontal havens. Grandy smiled. If there was a better business in space, it had yet to open.

In the tip of the cone, beyond another wall, was Grandy's private apartment where few people had ever been, and no one ever went uninvited. Two of the biggest and nastiest OBees she could find guarded the door, and two more guarded them. She liked her privacy as much as she liked her work, and she spent as much time out on the Main Floor as she did alone. It pleased her to arrange for so many people to have the opportunity to make each other happy, and it pleased her even more to do it at a profit. "Doing well by doing good," she said to herself as she watched the Widewall doing its continually changing dance.

About halfway up the Inner Sidewall, two customers with less inhibitions than most were exploring each others virtues, and Grandy looked back toward the Stacks to see if there was a Squeeze they could be encouraged to occupy. She was surprised to see Donald Wheeler making his way down the ladders on the last stack. It was not that he hadn't been a frequent visitor to Grandy's Place, even when it had had less lavish quarters, but she had not seen him since their last discussion of metaphysics had ended in his drinking the beaker of crimson mist. he had brought with him.

She hadn't seen him in almost five months, but what she had heard said he had weirded considerably during his absence. She thought it was a shame if he had. In a place where everybody was strange, Donald Wheeler was unique. Where everyone else exhibited eccentricities of behavior, Donald Wheeler exhibited only eccentricities of thought. Of all the men in Hardcore and the Cage, he was the only one who was more interested in arguing the meaning of life with Grandy than getting her into one of the Squeezes.

Not, she was sure, that the thought never entered his mind. She'd have been disappointed if it didn't, but it was not the only thought in his mind, or even the foremost. She did not like the idea of his having changed. He had a naive honesty she would be sorry to see gone, and a childlike sense of wonder about things she would miss even more.

With misgivings she watched him come toward her. She hadn't kissed him just to make a point. Somewhere in the back of her mind, without admitting it to herself, she had saved him a place in her future, and if that was a mistake, she didn't want to know about it.

He waved to her from the end of the Stacks. He didn't look much different except for a huge, knowing smile, as if he were the sole possessor of some cosmic joke. She waved back, and he danced his way across Main Floor, falling in perfectly with the rhythm of whoever came across his path. Dancing the Dove was as individual as lovemaking, and as various, and she was surprised to see that he could do it.

It came easy to her, but in all the times he had come to Grandy's Place, Donald Wheeler had never done anything but talk, except for the occasional bit of recreation in the Squeezes, and those liaisons were almost never ones he initiated.

It was true that if words had been movement, Donald Wheeler would have been able to do the Dove with the best, and his conversation had all the subtlety of the Glide and at least as much passion as the Scatter. But the Dove had to be danced, and Donald Wheeler's body had never seemed to her as graceful as his mind. She was surprised to see him move as effortlessly as he used to talk.

"Long time gone," she said when he finally reached her.

Wee smiled. "Nothing stays lost forever." He seemed infinitely less serious than he once had, but it didn't seem to have ruined him. He looked as if he had a great joke to tell her. She wondered what it was.

"Did you go Down?" She knew he hadn't been Earthside, but it was the standard Hardcore greeting for somebody you hadn't seen in a while. It was a kind of gallows humor. Laying up structure was dangerous business, and for most OBees space was a one-way trip and usually a short one. Only Execs went both Up and Down.

Wee shrugged. "Every place I go is Here."

Grandy laughed. He sounded completely serious, but even he didn't seem to take it seriously. "You haven't been to Main Floor in . . ." She let the time hang. She didn't want him to know that she knew it was almost five months to the day, but she did know, and it surprised her that she had kept count.

"I never left," he said. He seemed to really believe it.

She shrugged it off. "Well, I haven't seen you."

"What you don't see isn't necessarily gone," he said.

"It isn't necessarily here, either."

Wee threw back his head and laughed. Things seemed to delight him in a way they had not done before. She liked that. But there was a kind of irony to everything he said that was disconcerting, as if he knew how it all came out and saw everything from its ultimate perspective. She could see why people would think he had weirded out. Before, he had been eccentric in the way genius is eccentric; now he was unmistakably mystical. She understood how that might upset people who had known him. It did not upset her. "You're changed," *she said.*

Wee laughed again, as if what she'd said was hilarious beyond her imagining. "You changed me," he said.

"Me?" she said. But she was not entirely surprised. She remembered the kiss, Hool's punch, the beaker of crimson haze she had made him drink to revive him. She remembered the long, rapturous ramblings that followed it, as if all the secrets of the universe were flooding into his mind at once and kept ramming into each other, trying to get out his mouth.

Wee leaned forward and kissed her. It was startlingly out of character for him and astoundingly good. It sent a chill through her, as if she were crossing a point in her life beyond which nothing could ever be the same again. The loneliness she had hidden from herself for so long seemed to surface in a rush. The emptiness that all her good fortune hadn't filled, the unadmitted longing for completion, the need her cynicism hadn't been able to destroy; all broke through at once and overwhelmed her. She felt as if she were falling.

"Now let's see you reduce that to a known and measurable quantity," he said.

Grandy recognized her own words, but they seemed to be full of so much more meaning than she had put into them that she felt as if their significance could continue unfolding all the rest of her life. She shook her head to clear herself of the spell she seemed to be falling under. "I heard you'd become a saint," she said.

"Or a lunatic?" he asked.

She nodded, unsure of what she felt, what she ought to say. She had not felt so little in control of things since she was a child. Her life seemed to be careening toward some unforeseeable impact, and she had no idea what it was, only that it was gaining momentum. She tried to break free of its pull. "You were that before," she said.

Wee smiled. "There are no lunatics," he said, "only unrecognized saints."

"No saints, you mean. Only recognized lunatics." She wanted not to believe that something mystical possessed him and was in the act of possessing her, but the cynicism that usually came easy to her seemed hollow and foolish. It frightened her, and the fear put a sharpness into her voice she did not intend. "Why are you back?"

"For your birthday," he said. It sounded like he meant the day of her birth instead of its anniversary. "I brought you a present," he said.

Grandy raised an eyebrow. Men had been bringing her presents since she was thirteen, but none of them had ever bought her with one. Men a hundred times richer than Donald Wheeler would ever be had brought her presents other women would have killed for, but she had sent them back, their strings as untouched as their ribbons. She could tell by the look in his eye that Donald Wheeler's present was more dangerous than anything she'd ever been given. "What?" she said.

Wee raised a small crimson vial. There was a twinkle in his eye. She recognized the contents immediately. "The Sunrise," he said.

She was afraid of it without knowing why, and she tried to turn it aside with ridicule. She knew what it meant to him.

"Enlightenment!" she said. She shook her head disdainfully, as if he were some OBee trying to bribe her with her own wares. "I have gallons of enlightenment." She waved a hand at an assortment of bottles, flasks, and cylinders. "I sell enlightenment."

Wee only smiled, as if everything that was to pass between them was already a memory to him. The vial seemed to glow, as if he had captured live energy and bottled it up. It was like nothing she sold and she knew it, but she was not going to admit it, not to him, not to herself. "You don't even know what it is," she snapped. Wee only smiled as if he knew what everything was and wasn't. "Well, what is it then?"

She sounded like a child challenging another to answer, and it embarrassed her.

Wee seemed delighted with her anger. "It's the greatest of all gifts," he said. "Your death." He said it as if death were the greatest of all jokes.

"What are you talking about?!" She felt as if she knew and she was afraid to know.

"You have to go to know," Wee said.

"Go where?"

"To see the End of the Sky, of course."

She kept challenging him, but she was more unsure of herself every time she did it, and he seemed all the more certain that she would take it, as if she had already taken it as far as he was concerned. "And what will I find there? You?"

Wee laughed out loud. "Yourself, of course." He held out his hand to her, as if she had already taken it.

But she was still trying to resist, trying to treat him like just another male with an ulterior motive. "And do I get it before or after the Squeeze?" The sarcasm in her voice was meant to turn him to stone.

Wee turned the choice back on her. "Do you want to know the World according to passion or compassion?" He looked at her as if he already knew what she would choose.

She felt as if somebody's premonition were coming true and she was in the middle of it. Events seemed to blur toward some unexpected conclusion. She could not change the sweep of events, so she swam with the current. She grabbed his hand, as if it had been her idea. "All right," she said, "let's go." She looked in his eyes as if she were in control. "I'll show you the End of the Sky." Wee bit his lip to keep from laughing.

It made Grandy laugh out loud to think of it. Beyar looked at her blankly. "I'm sorry," she said. "After you're dead awhile you'll understand." Her voice was gentle and reassuring. "Then and now and tomorrow are all the same once you drink the Sunrise."

"And every place is Here," said URdon Wee. He put a hand on Beyar's shoulder. "But you three have a lot of every place to go between now and Sunrise." He made it sound like a game. "And there's a lot of training to do before you meet Back Toss Hool again."

Beyar frowned. "Again?" he said. The heat of the Smelter roared back over him.

"There's no joke without conflicting expectations," Wee said.

Grandy was more reassuring. "You'll be much better prepared the next time." Beyar remembered what he felt like when he thought he had failed URdon Wee's Vision. He wanted nothing more than another chance. Nothing had really been lost, and yet what had been done to him filled him with rage. Grandy stroked his cheek. "You'll have to burn that off before you meet him again, Beyar. It'll make you vulnerable to him." It sounded as much like a prophecy as a warning.

"We are all Back Toss Hool," Wee said. The secret irony of it made him chuckle to himself. "Besides, there *are* no villains, only unrecognized heroes."

But it was not something Beyar could forget so easily. Even being with Push and Chancey again did not make it entirely all right. Chancey put her arm around him. "We'll be together the next time," she said.

Grandy looked away, as if there were things she did not want to say. Chancey looked to URdon Wee. Wee smiled. "Back Toss Hool has *his* moments; *you* will have *yours*." But he did not say that their moments would be together.

CHAPTER
SEVENTEEN

They were safe at the End of the Sky. The only people who knew about the settlement were Loonies, and the Loonies were followers of URdon Wee. The only people on the moon who weren't followers of URdon Wee were the crews of unemployed OBees who came in to work during the sun cycle every two weeks, and few of *them* stayed for even a portion of the dark period unless the backlog of kidneycars loaded to go out during the shadow time was far below quota. OBees didn't like the moon; they found it primitive and boring, and they despised the incessant sameness of the gravity. The longer an OBee went without at least some time in zero-gravity, the crankier they got.

Since most could not find structural work, or they wouldn't have come to the moon even temporarily, they were already in a bad mood when they landed, and two weeks of twelve-hour shifts did little to improve their dispositions. As a result, there were not many places on LUNAC where new faces were welcome, and OBees kept to themselves, mostly in the Temporary Barracks where a certain amount of breakage and havoc were tolerated.

The true Loonie population consisted mostly of dust miners, the maintenance crew and technical staff for the Accelerator, a handful of scientists, a half dozen Corporation Execs who had committed some unforgivable transgression against the Corporation, and about three hundred service people who made frontier life more bearable.

There was a small tourist trade, mostly from within the League, but there just wasn't much to do on the moon, except work. Despite being the oldest settlement in space, LUNAC had remained relatively primitive. Its development had been mostly technical, and its settlers were closemouthed and clannish and decidedly unfriendly to strangers, and they were that way even before URdon Wee brought them the Sunrise and the secret of the End of the Sky.

Even in isolation the weeks went by quickly for Beyar and the twins. URdon Wee was there and gone, and they were almost entirely under Grandy's care. She seemed delighted to have them, and the twins and Beyar were even happier to be there. Even the work delighted them, and there was plenty of it. There were a dozen skills to master and not a great deal of time in which to do it. But they worked at it relentlessly, and most of the work was more like play to them.

The End of the Sky was not as large as the Cage, and because it was, for the most part, under LUNAC, it seemed bleak and cramped, and they missed the greenery of the Cage's courtyards and gardenyards. The only green at the End of the Sky was the Well, a deep shaft where the food was grown under a crown of intense lights.

The alternation of mirrors and plants down the walls of the shaft and the circulation of water through the hydroponics system made it bright and cheerful, and the landings at different levels had aireclines so they could double as work platforms for tending the plants and places to sit and enjoy the view. It was certainly not the Valley, but it was good enough, and they took their work there whenever they could.

Their favorite place was a small oblong platform next to one of the mirrors on the third tier down. It was just under a major platform, but it could only be reached by going down to a medium-size landing and then back up another ladder. Some of the plants extended in over the railing, and the whitish glow from the mirror gave it the effect of being a forest clearing in some high, steep mountain range.

When the plants were putting a lot of water vapor into the air, there was even a more or less vertical rainbow at the edge of the mirror. Chancey called it the End of the Rainbow, while Push held out for Rainbow Bridge. Beyar used either name, depending on which of the twins he was talking to, and called it simply Our Place when they were both there.

Beyar squinted at the mirror inside his facecase and fitted the plastic eye shield under his lids to keep the spray out of his eyes. He adjusted the nozzle of the spray to its finest line and added a drop of gray to the tan color already in the reservoir. He held the spray between his finger and thumb and began to draw in the final lines along the upper edge of his eyelid. The thin mist felt cool on his skin.

Six months before, he would never have believed how adept at it he would become. At first the mixture of fiberglass and rubbery gel kept clumping up on his skin, and all he could manage to do with two hours' work was make himself look diseased. The nozzle was always clogging, and he could never get the right color tones to change his face convincingly. By the middle of the second month he had mastered the tool, but it still took three hours instead of three minutes to change his appearance convincingly. Chancey said he could age naturally in the time it took him to add a few years to his skin with the Skyshocker facecase.

The small, flat case was a legend throughout the League, and people from Hardcore to the Grand Sphere believed it contained a hundred thousand complete disguises a Skyshocker could use to become anyone else in the world. In truth it contained only a few vials of basic color, an assortment of lenses, a few tufts of hair, and a small, flat spraying apparatus for laying down layers of fiberglass and resin on the skin. Deftly used, it could build up cheekbones or noses or foreheads that a little color could transform into a new face. Once dried, the fiberglass had the hardness of bone, and the resin had the resiliency of skin. It was an art few outside the Skyshockers had any master of, and it seemed magic to the rest of the League.

It still took Beyar too long, but he could age twenty years in as many minutes, and he was getting better all the time. Still, he was not nearly as good at it as Chancey. He turned away from the mirror and looked at her on the far side of the platform. She was on the airecline, practicing sitting like an old woman. She had the rounding of the shoulders down perfectly, and her movements had an understated stiffness that would have convinced the unobservant even without the face-ing.

There were not a great many old-looking women in the League. The vast majority of settlers had been young when they came up, and forty years of time had put less than twenty-five years of age on most of them. Still, if she ever went Earthside, she could have passed for Spencer LeGrange's mother. No one who had not seen her spray the changes onto her face would have believed she was not yet thirteen. She had chosen just the right shading to make her arms look thinner, and she had done an excellent job with the hands. The tendons stood up on the back of them with a realism that could have passed examination under a magnifying glass. She was working on a look of preoccupied vacancy when Grandy came in. When she looked up, her chin thrust out at exactly the angle it would have if she had spent sixty years standing up to the obstacles of life.

Grandy was delighted. "You've aged half a century," she said.

"Waiting for Beyar," Chancey teased.

Grandy looked at Beyar. He could have passed for Chancey's grandson, a twenty-five-year-old Corehard come to the moon to look for temporary work. "Your time's getting better," she said. "And that's very good eye work."

Beyar smiled. The refacing moved as fluidly as skin. When he spoke, his voice was deeper than she expected, and his sentences had the same belligerent pause at the end that marked OBee speech. "Don't mind Gran Hasselpeg," he said. "The steady gravity makes her cranky."

Chancey's voice had the cracks of age in it. "You mind who you're talking about, Bruise. I didn't raise you all these years for you to turn out a smart mouth like your father."

Grandy smiled. They were all still young enough to *become* other people rather than just pretending to be someone else. She had been pleasantly surprised at how quickly they had learned to feel the subtleties of character and to provide themselves with a complete history as they went along. The ability to improvise was crucial to a good Skyshocker, but it could also save their lives. She tried not to think about that.

"Where *is* my smart-mouthed father?" Beyar laughed.

Push stepped out of a section of railing and foliage that was neither. A hologram, backed by the reflective side of his Skyshocker's cape to give it depth and substance, had allowed him to blend into the background. Grandy was impressed. He was almost as good as Beyar at making himself invisible.

There was still a vague family resemblance to the three, but Push clearly did not look like Chancey's identical twin. His hair was thinning, and it was a sandy blond instead of red. His eyes were brown instead of blue, and they had dark circles under them that looked like they had come from long hours and hard nights. They were faintly bloodshot, as if he were recovering from a short, but recent, bout of carousing.

His face had the flatness of a man who had had high expectations when he was young but had reached forty as a failure. His arms had the kind of blurring definition that comes when the fat starts creeping back in even after decades of hard work, and they were covered with dark brown hair that was beginning to lighten toward gray.

"I'll make your mouth smart for you," he said. It had the ambiguity of someone who had spent a lot of time in the

Grand Sphere where nothing had only one meaning, but the way he raised his fist to his "son," with the back of it facing him, showed him to be an OBee at heart. Even OBee affection was always half threat.

All of them were naturally keen observers, but their perceptions had sharpened under Grandy's guidance. Things that they had noticed but never really thought about, the nuances that made the inhabitants of each habitat in the League different from the people anywhere else, were now concentrated on and consciously isolated. They had spent hours and hours studying holoscans of real OBees and Catchers and Granders doing ordinary things, analyzing them for the precise gesture that separates a Grander from a Tuber from Henson's Tube, or a Roundworm from the Little Wheel. They had come a long way in a relatively short time. They still had a long, long way to go.

"Excellent posture," she said to Push. Even with the rounded shoulders of the defeated, he still managed to make himself look almost as tall as Beyar. "What do you do to live?" There was no fixed answer, but whatever Push improvised, it should be convincing.

"Nothing," he said. "Living comes natural to a Hasselpeg." The mixture of OBee belligerence and Grander wit was perfectly in character.

"It's a good thing, too, Flush Hasselpeg," Chancey said. Her voice had fifty years of frustration and heartbreak in it. "You'd be dead if you had to *work* at it."

Beyar laughed. It was a young man's laugh, full of energy and the conviction that he would not fail as his father had. "Less gravity, Gran. The man's suffering from a Loonie night."

Push waved him to be quiet. "I carried *you* home," he said. Even Grandy believed they had spent a night carousing together for a minute.

Beyar shook his head in disbelief. "No, no. You *talked* about carrying me . . . the whole time I was carrying *you*."

Chancey shook her head. "You were both *crawling*," she said. "I saw you come in." She pointed a shaky finger at the door, as if they were still crawling through it.

Push and Beyar stopped and looked at her doubtfully. "Who was in the lead?" they both said at once.

Grandy laughed. They could have been any two OBees she had seen come into her place in Hardcore almost forty years before. It was a long time since she had thought about Grandy's Place, a long time since she'd first drunk the Sunrise with URdon Wee.

Grandy took Wee's hand and yanked him across Main Floor. Heads turned and eyebrows rose. Occasionally Grandy might pick some incredibly lucky OBee or Catcher as a temporary consort, but it was always more discrete, with Hardcore or the Cage aware of it, if at all, only afterward. Others might be swept away by passion, but Grandy was always in control. For her to storm across Main Floor heading obviously for the Stacks was unprecedented.

As with almost everything else that happened in Hardcore, when fists weren't flying, money was. The shortest odds said Grandy was going to drag URdon Wee up to the top of the Stacks and throw him off. Halfway down the Stacks the attention got to her, and she turned on URdon Wee. "Wipe that silly grin off your face!" she said. Wee wiped it off by bursting out laughing. The odds on the top-of-the-Stacks hypothesis fell drastically.

What was really unprecedented was that Grandy did not turn into the last Uprise but went straight on by it toward the middle wall. Grandy never took a man to her own quarters. If someone struck her fancy, she took a Squeeze like everybody else, so there was no doubt that it was anything but recreational. But by the time she got to the First Door, the entire patronage of Grandy's Place had gone silent in deference to the historic nature of the moment. Even the music stopped, and the couples who perpetually seemed to Dance the Dove on

Main Floor stopped dancing for the first time in anyone's memory.

But at the First Door her fury got the best of her again. She turned on the silent crowd. For an instant she seemed about to condemn them all to a flaming eternity, but the sight of so many heads hanging out of the doors of Squeezes struck her funny and she laughed. Her voice echoed down past the Stacks and out onto Main Floor, as if the place were empty. "If he comes out of here alive," she shouted, "kill him!" The cheers and laughter sounded like an explosion, and it was five minutes before the music could be heard again. By then, Grandy and URdon Wee were nowhere in sight.

Their passage through the manufacturing area was more dignified but not by much. Grandy still dragged him by the hand, and URdon Wee still struggled to keep from laughing. About every fifty feet, Grandy turned and warned him that if he didn't keep a straight face, she was going to go back, but they both knew she was not going to make that walk again for anything. At least twice Wee broke out into open laughter, and almost at the door to her quarters, she turned and kissed him just as she told him to shut him up.

The guards looked at each other with bewildered embarrassment and stood aside. Grandy was obviously not there for business, but it seemed impossible to the OBees that a relative dwarf like URdon Wee could be the object of anybody's pleasure, let alone the finest woman in Hardcore. They looked at URdon Wee as if the whole thing were his way of casting aspersions on their masculinity, and they seemed distinctly inclined to beat some sense into him when Grandy pointed a finger of warning at them. "I don't want to be disturbed," she said.

She looked back at URdon Wee and smiled. "We don't want to be disturbed," she said. The guards nodded and looked fiercely at one another, as if one of them were already plotting to disrupt Grandy's privacy.

URdon Wee could not resist. "Wee don't want to be

disturbed," he said as he went through the forbidden door. The guards prayed silently for the opportunity to kill him.

It was Grandy who was holding back laughter when the door closed behind them. "Wee?" She laughed. "Wee don't want to be disturbed?!" She put her arms around his neck. "You're pretty confident," she said.

Donald Wheeler shrugged. "I've been here before," he said.

"Only in my wildest dreams." She laughed.

"All dreams are one dream," he said. It was the last coherent thing he said for an hour.

Grandy silenced him with a kiss. Her hands moved with a deft precision that left them both naked without moving out of an embrace that seemed more a dance than anything else. When he pressed against her, she felt a warmth she realized she had been looking for all her life. She was no stranger to pleasure, and yet everything URdon Wee did seemed to be done to her for the first time. Each touch seemed to last an eternity, as if it were a fixed instant in time that would never fade. Time seemed to have stopped. Motion became impossible. Each exquisite sensation seemed a discrete instant, perfect and whole in itself.

She felt like an infinite series of holograms set next to one another on an endless plane. Each one focused on a single minute detail. Each whorl in his fingertip seemed the raised and magnified center of one instant. Another instant was in its entirety the flush of sensation that made her thighs too weak to stand anymore. A dozen instants shaped themselves around the bobble and settle of her breasts as she fell back onto the airecline. Others focused on the arch of her lower back and the stretch of her neck, the swell of her abdomen and the tightening of her thighs, the sweat pressed and spread between them. But whatever their focus, each was in itself a complete masterpiece, and any single instant contained more sensation than she had ever felt before in an hour of passion.

But out of the hours of rising and falling pleasure, the

hours of rapture stretched to the breaking point and beyond, the one thing that was overwhelmingly paramount was the feeling of completeness, of absolute oneness with another human being, which she had never felt before and which she had not believed existed. It was that unity, that loss of self into a new entity, which set the tone for her vision when, in the floating rapture of ecstasy spent, in the blissful lull when the selves have not quite pulled back into their separate identities, he placed the vial of crimson haze in her palm.

There was no need to tell her of its dangers. She was not afraid. That she could have felt what she had felt was proof enough for her that her individual self was only an illusion. URdon Wee had awakened her to the infinite nature of the Great Illusion as much as the Sunrise would. She reached up, and her fingers spread across the back of his neck. She pulled his mouth to her and kissed him one last time. Then she lifted the vial to her lips and drank it down.

She nestled in URdon Wee's arms and felt what she had always considered to be reality shift and dissolve. The room, even Donald, became shadows of light, a shifting play of energy in and around itself. When she looked around, she could see through Hardcore; each passage in the growing maze looked like a transparent picture imposed over all the others. She could see the stars shining through the walls and, within the stars, life shining out.

The wholeness she had felt with URdon Wee permeated everything she felt. All time spread before her, past and future, all in the stack of transparent pictures, shadows of the light. Discrete moments flared and went out but remained, nevertheless, another layer in the infinite layering of the World. But it was the unity of all things that struck her most, the inescapable interrelatedness of all events, waking and dreaming, and the unity of the whole into one complex and shifting pattern of the light.

She understood why URdon Wee was always smiling. All things were good; all events contributed to the pattern of *the whole illusion, the illusion of space, the illusion of time, the illusion of death. Connecting all illusions was the benevolent wholeness of things, the essential oneness of the World. Like Wee, she could laugh at what she saw, her own first death, Wee's death, the fact that she would have children but bear none, that she would see them die and be born, that she would take miraculous part in their murders and their resurrections, that they would free the Cage and turn mankind down an irreversible road, that it was all illusion, after all, all a beautiful story that made itself up as it went along and then played itself out.*

CHAPTER
EIGHTEEN

Grandy looked at them proudly. If she did not know they were Beyar, Push and Chancey, she would have believed they were Bruise Hasselpeg; his father, Flush; and Gran. "You've learned a lot in a short time," she said. "URdon Wee will be pleased to hear it."

"*And* see it." It was URdon Wee's voice, but he was nowhere on the platform. It took even Grandy a few seconds to find him in the plants just beyond the rail. He was not even using a holo or a cape to cover himself, and he had probably been in plain view the whole time he was there, if anybody had really looked. Stillness and silence had been enough to make him invisible. Despite all their training at doing the same thing, both the twins and Beyar were astounded.

"How long have *you* been there?" Chancey demanded.

Wee laughed. He was proof that what he had been telling them for months was true: People see what they expect to see, not what's there; reality is an illusion made up of expectation and assumption. "Since before you had a son or a grandson," he said.

He turned to Grandy. "I think they're about ready to travel."

"Travel?" the twins said.

"It's what Skyshockers do," Wee said. They did a lot more. The Skyshockers were the key to Wee's vision of a bloodless Revolution, a Revolution by infiltration rather than confrontation. Bringing it about was a long, slow, almost evolutionary process. It had been going on for a quarter of a century, and it still had almost a decade to run before it could be accomplished without any possibility of failure and with a minimum of bloodshed.

In the short run, the Skyshockers were URdon Wee's intelligence network. They could travel freely anywhere in the League, and they could pass unnoticed anywhere they traveled. Everywhere they went, they gathered information and passed on directions from End of the Sky to the army of conspirators who were at work in every habitat. Guided by Wee's Vision, the Skyshockers carried out the intricate plots that would make the revolution an inevitability.

At any given moment there were at least two performing troupes of Skyshockers in every habitat in the League, although no one knew they were there until they put on their faces and announced a performance. To the inhabitants of the League the Skyshockers were an unpredictable phenomenon whose erratic wanderings sometimes kept them absent for weeks. They would have been astounded to find out that most Skyshockers didn't travel at all but lived permanently in the habitats as Tubers or Corehards or Roundworms, without their neighbors suspecting in the least.

Performing Skyshockers were of all ages, but traveling Skyshockers were mostly younger people serving their apprenticeships in the arts they would need to live a life in disguise. More experienced Skyshockers gradually established several different identities throughout the League, and when directions came from End of the Sky, they took up residence in one of the habitats or commuted regularly between two or three identities in different places.

Some went completely underground and never performed after their initial training period. They lived lives outwardly no different from the people around them. They were Communications Techs in Corporation Headquarters in the Grand Sphere, or finance verification experts in Henson's Tube, or robot mechanics in the Little Wheel; they were vacationing Execs from Earthside visiting the simulated Earth environments of the Big Wheel, or Corehards working on the latest energy satellites off Catchcage. They could be anybody anywhere.

Some, mostly in the Fist, did not even know they were Skyshockers and would not remember who they were until the Revolution had begun. Others knew perfectly well who they were and where the information they gathered was going when they passed it on. The number of Skyshockers in the middle levels of the Fist was growing, and time would move them to even higher positions of power. At the lower levels, especially among the Blues, the number of those who were not Skyshockers but were loyal to the Revolution was already approaching thirty percent. It was part of Wee's Vision that when the inhabitants of the League finally rose against the Corporation, two thirds of the Fist sent against them would be part of the Revolution.

There were even Skyshockers Earthside, working in the Corporation itself. For a decade Skyshockers had been doing the Corporation's most sensitive Research and Development, and during that decade, the Corporation's power had steadily declined. Promising areas of research never seemed to produce, and those that did always took more time than anybody had anticipated, as Skyshockers passed technological breakthroughs on to End of the Sky and told the Corporation the projects needed more work. Their efforts wasted the Corporation's resources while it financed the arming of the League.

Early Skyshockers had infiltrated the Corporation in permanent disguise as Execs who disappeared while on vacation in the League, but once Skyshockers occupied crucial positions in Personnel, they hired other Skyshockers for important positions or changed the records of people they wanted to place in Corporation jobs within the League. In the Corporation's Finance, Security, Communications, Planning, Personnel, and Research divisions, there were already Skyshockers working their way up, working their way in, waiting for the Revolution. Until Wee's followers controlled crucial positions in the Corporation, in the Fist, and in the League, the revolt would not begin. But when it began, there would be no stopping it.

"When?" Beyar said. He was almost drowned out by Push and Chancey wanting to know where and how.

Wee answered them all at the same time. "A troupe comes in tomorrow and goes back to Hardcore with the OBees in two weeks."

"Already?" Grandy said.

Wee shrugged. "They have to go sometime," he said. "They have friends to meet"—He did not wait for the inevitable question and looked at Push and Chancey—"people you must meet now in order to know later."

"Who are they?!" Chancey wanted to know.

"You'll know them when you meet them," Wee said. He looked as if he was trying hard not to laugh.

Grandy knew he was right; there were friends to be met in Hardcore. But there were also enemies. She knew the dangers that lay ahead for them there, and the prospect did not delight her. Wee looked at her and laughed. "It's what we've trained them for," he said.

"They still have things to learn," Grandy said.

Wee nodded. "And where else can they learn them?" It was true. There were some things that only experience could teach and no amount of training could make up for. There were minutes out in the League that would be worth months at the End of the Sky.

It was Beyar who noticed the woman watching them. She stood on a platform a half level up on the far side of a mirror. Her hair was a pale blond, almost gray, but the rainbow from the mirror made it seem all scarlet and indigo. She watched them quietly, intently, as if she had not merely watched them but watched over them for a long time and would watch them a good deal longer.

Push and Chancey followed his eyes. It was hard not to notice her, and yet they had the impression that she could have stood there invisibly for hours if she had wanted to. They looked to Grandy. "Who is that woman?" Chancey said.

Grandy smiled without looking up. "That's my special-sister," she said. "We went to see the End of the Sky together a long, long time ago."

When they looked back, the woman was gone.

CHAPTER
NINETEEN

The wallway went down, and the two young Blues shoved the large OBee into the room. They seemed relieved to be rid of him, and Pock smiled to himself. They were new transfers from Earthside, and they were not used to dealing with prisoners as large as themselves. Much of Earth's population had dwindled in size as the population grew beyond the limits of finite resources, and the poor, who fell most often in their clutches, were mostly scrawny dwarfs gnarled by malnutrition and weakened by disease.

The Blues were used to catching chickens and rabbits. Hool was their first wolf. They had no idea he was, if not a pet wolf, at least a domesticated one. Pock doubted they would have been able to bring him in at all if he didn't want to come.

He was surprised that they had gotten out of Hardcore alive. It would have been considered a great joke within the Fist to take two Fools like that into a place where even veterans traveled in sixes and then send them into Hool's quarters alone to bring him out.

No doubt the other four had waited for them to come flying back out without him before they went in and did the job themselves. None of them knew Hool was one of Pock's

Ears, and he would have liked to have seen the face of the
Bronze in charge of the squad when they came out with their
prisoner.

He hoped their success wouldn't tempt them to try similar arrests on their own. If they did, the knowledge that they
had been unreasonably lucky with Hool would probably be
the last thing they learned. Disappearances of young and
inexperienced Blues in Hardcore came to about two a month,
and he had the distinct feeling that he would not see those
two faces again, unless they remembered the look in Hool's
eyes the next time they went into Hardcore.

It was not an easy look to forget, and the fire of fanaticism that burned in them was something that no longer existed Earthside. There just weren't enough calories to sustain
it outside the Corporation, and within the Corporation it would
have been suspect, even in the Fist. If the two Blues remembered it, they might even live to advance to Bronze someday.

He nodded for them to leave, and they looked as if he
were telling them to leave a wild animal with him. "I'll take
care of the interrogation myself," he said. Hool looked at
them as if he were about to tear their throats out; they saluted
and left. Pock smiled to himself; at least they were developing
a sense of self-preservation.

Even with the wall up again, Hool did not relax. Pock
sat on the airecline. "Six months ago you showed me a holo
of three children," he said. Hool's eyes pierced him. "What
became of them?"

Hool ignored the question. "Found them, have you?" he
said.

Pock ignored Hool. "Children of the Cage . . ." he said,
as if it might jog Hool's memory.

"Children of Wee's Vision," Hool insisted.

"You remember them, then." He doubted that Hool
thought of anything else. "I had reports that two of them died
in the coming of age ritual in the Cage." Hool nodded confirmation. "A boy and a girl. Identical twins," he said. Hool

nodded again. "No bodies were recovered, though..." He left the implication unsaid.

"Suit-split don't leave much." It was not news to Pock: He had cleaned a Bronze off the walls and ceilings the week after he came Up. Some OBee had opened the Bronze's suit with a cutting torch when he had tried to inspect an unpressurized cargo container off Hardcore. He exploded like a balloon full of blood. A week later two Blues had caught the OBee in Catchcage and opened *him* with the same torch. Pock was one of them.

"Convenient," he said. Hool said nothing. "What about the older one? What was his name... Bair?"

"Beyar."

Pock nodded. "Beyar," he said. "What happened to Beyar?"

"Catchround accident."

"You were there?"

Hool nodded. Pock knew better than to ask him if he did it. A holoscan of Hool admitting to the murder of a child would make him a dead man in the Cage and most of Hardcore, no matter how much protection the Fist gave him. He'd never give Pock that much power over him. Still, Pock pressed him for confirmation. "You *saw* it done?" He said it like a trap he was daring Hool to step into.

"He died," Hool said.

"Then how is it I have no report of it!" Pock shouted.

"Nobody noticed."

"Do you think I'm new Up?" he demanded. "A *child* was killed in Catchcage and nobody noticed?"

Hool nodded.

Pock was incredulous. "And they never missed him?" he said. "Never noticed this boy wasn't around anymore?"

"He was sixteen," Hool said, as if it explained everything.

Pock knew what he meant. Children left the Cage at that age to find their fortunes elsewhere in the League. They didn't ask anybody; when they were ready, they just *went*. Nobody kept track of them. But at least *somebody* knew where each of them went, and everybody followed the Exceptional ones. He shook his head at Hool. "This boy was an Exceptional!"

"It *was* done!" Hool said.

"Then where's the body?" Pock shouted.

Hool looked at him as if it were obvious. "Smelter don't leave much."

Pock let his voice drop, as if he was satisfied. "Then they're all dead."

"Dead once," Hool said. "Twice born."

Pock laughed as if it was the most outrageous lie anybody had ever tried to pass off on him. "Are you telling me Wee raised them up? Brought them back to life?"

Hool's eyes blazed with certainty. "The Twiceborn live," he said. "I've seen it."

Hool felt awkward as he passed through the plushness of the lounge toward the middle observation deck of the Torch. Everyone he passed was a Tech. Two stopped to give him directions to the public observation deck a half level down. One little fat Tech with a Control Rod insignia on his worksuit was even about to ask for his authorization to be on the working level before Hool's look and a fear of sudden death turned him back to his business.

It made him angry to feel out of place there, a place he had helped to build. He had been inside the bottom tip of Hardcore before the Torch was ignited; he had laid up the structure for it, had helped put the discharge pins in place. He had been there when there were only a handful of Techs instead of a thousand, and the "flame" was a ribbon of energy scarcely ten feet long instead of ten feet thick. He had a right to be there. Still, he felt like an intruder.

Dreem met him at the door of the Primary Control Deck halfway around the circular corridor that surrounded the observation deck. He found it hard to stay angry when he looked at her. She took his arm and squeezed it. "I'm going to do an Insertion!" she said. Her voice crackled with excitement.

He was glad for her. Only the great and mighty physicists usually put an experiment into the flames. He remembered when it was some expendable OBee who had to get up close to the writhing field of energy and adjust the clamps and standplate so that some concoction the physicists made up would sit in exactly the right temperature at exactly the right angle.

But the flame had been minuscule then, compared to the hundred-yard-long river of energy it had become when Catchcage went operational. Still, it had been big enough to blast an OBee a week when some unanticipated jump in the field let it kink instead of flow. "You be careful," he said. "I've seen men fried from the inside out by that thing." The image of bubbled and blistered flesh, the stench of charred meat, still hung in his mind.

"There's plenty of shielding," she said. "And I'll be wearing an insulation suit." Hool looked dubious. Dreem shook her head in exasperation. "This is the Torch, it's not that jury-rigged sparkler they used to let you OBees play with." She stressed the word to tease him. He knew it made no difference to her or she wouldn't have met the fact of their difference head-on the way she did. "It's completely under control," she said.

It wasn't quite true. The discharge that leapt continually from one discharge pin to the other was relatively stable. No matter how many kidneycars crashed through the Gates empty or overloaded, no matter how much their passage through the magnetic field of the Gates varied, the Great Ball at the bottom of Catchcage took the energy the discharge of their momentum created and sent a steady, even flow up into the Torch.

Some of the flow went up the side conduits to the Smelter, and at the far end of the Torch, the energy that passed through it joined that stream. Energy could be pulled back out of that continual circuit, and the Great Ball held a reserve charge that could be used to modulate the field as well.

But the Techs were not infallible, nor was their machinery. From time to time, especially when something was being inserted deep into the flame itself, discharges occurred that neither the shielding of the insertion vehicles nor the insulation suits could compensate for. There was no way to predict them and no way to stop them. Dreem stroked his cheek. "Don't worry. It's only a Surface Insertion," she said, "hardly a foot deep."

Hool remembered when the whole flame was only a foot wide. It had been more than enough. A Third Level Tech like Dreem should only have been inserting into the Glaze, the haze of energy around the main beam. Only the Chemies and the Physicists were supposed to touch the main field, and most of them did it by guided remote. Except for Wheeler. Even Hool had to give him grudging respect for doing his own "hand work." Nobody in the Cage had done as many Insertions, and nobody worked as close to the energy as routinely as he did. It was probably why his eccentricities hadn't gotten him fired. He'd been working on the Torch from the beginning, and, saint or lunatic, nobody knew more about it than he did. Hool would have been more than happy to see Wheeler "crisped." He didn't like the idea of Dreem taking that risk. "Why isn't URdon the Wee doing it?"

Dreem scowled. "He wouldn't be letting me do it if he didn't think I could," she said. "He had to overrule a lot of people to get me this chance." She seemed more than grateful. Hool's jealousy rose into his eyes. It tinged everything with a green haze.

"Why?" There was a clear implication that he thought Wee's interest was more than professional.

The star over Dreem's eye seemed to flare into nova. "Because I asked him to," she said.

"Why do you want to take his risks for him?" It was

one of those accusations that always started a fight between them.

"Because I want to touch it," she said. "I want to feel what it's like." He should have understood what she felt; he had known the thrill of hazard himself, and in the emptiness between lines of structure he had reached for the infinite enough times himself to know what she wanted. But all he could see was that there was a feeling he could not give her, and URdon the Wee could.

She took his scowl for worry. "He'd know if it wasn't safe." There was a tone of admiration in her voice that made Hool want to kill. He wanted to grab her and tell her just where Wee's holy Vision was going to lead humankind. But he held back, forced himself to be patient. The time would come when he could alter that vision, but he knew he was not at one of those points.

She took his hand. "Just watch me," she said, "and be happy for me."

Hool nodded, and she led him over to the consoles. There were only two other people in the booth, Wee and Grandy. Hool scowled. He wondered whether Grandy was there because of Wee or because of Dreem. They had become close friends since Dreem had started following Wee, and Dreem might have invited her, as well as him, to share her moment of triumph. He tried not to look at Grandy. No matter what he felt for Dreem, there would always be that irresistible longing when he saw Grandy, like the pull of other sequences, other probabilities.

Wee welcomed him and pointed to a chair in front of the console. Grandy sat in the chair on his right. Wee opened the hatch to the Insertion Vehicle, and Dreem gave Hool a final kiss before she dropped through it. She said it was for luck; it felt like it was good-bye. Hool felt a strange dreamlike quality to the moment, and the crimson mist of the Sunrise seemed to be rising around him again. Everything seemed to have an eerie familiarity to it.

Neither Grandy nor Wee seemed to notice it. They were too intent on watching for the Insertion Vehicle to appear in the window on its way to the flame. The window was almost as thick as the glass of the Nearside Window, but they could see perfectly. He looked down the shaft. He could see people on the far side sitting at curved consoles in the two Lower Control Decks.

Each level had its own experiments to conduct, and the Techs were oblivious to anything else. He could see some of the Techs in the decks above and although the top window was just a dark, curving band around the shaft, he knew that the people there were equally preoccupied. Probably the only people watching the sweep of the action around the whole of the flame were standing on the public deck, a half level below.

He had to lean forward to see the discharge pin, fifty yards up the cylinder. Its tip was obscured by the stream of bluish-white energy that ran from it, down the center of the shaft, and to the other discharge pin. The crimson haze made the flame seem purple to him. The round top of the yellow Insertion Vehicle seemed almost orange to him as it emerged just below the window.

Its mechanical arms held a one-foot glass kettle of reddish liquid. As soon as he saw it, Hool knew why Dreem had volunteered. Wee was putting another batch of the Sunrise into the Torch to undergo its mystical change. He felt a cold tingling crawl up the back of his neck; the crimson haze around him seemed to thicken. A vague whispering started in the back of his mind and grew steadily as the bright yellow globe moved slowly out across the emptiness.

Halfway to the flame, the magnetic field that formed a sleeve around the plasma looked like an enclosed glass cylinder. Above and below, all along the hundred-yard column of the flame, different-colored vehicles entered and left it. Every once in a while a bright flash seemed to light up the whole magnetic cylinder like a light bulb as one of vehicles made too much contact with the flame. When Dreem's globe approached

the sleeve, Wee pressed some icons on the control board and a
hole opened in the field just long enough for the vehicle to glide
through it. Even though he knew it was impossible, Hool
heard it close behind her with a hiss.

The globe seemed to approach the flame gingerly, and it
hovered too far away to touch it for a moment. Wee touched
another icon, and the yellow bubble moved closer to the stream
of bluish-white energy. Hool watched the mechanical arms
stretch out, setting the kettle inside the flame. They should
only have unbent a little to insert it a foot, but he watched
with growing uneasiness as they straightened and straightened
until their tips were closer to the center of the flow than the
edge.

The glass kettle was invisible, but he could see the hands
release, and he knew it had been inserted. He waited for the
arms to retract, but they continued to move in the flow, as if
Dreem were bathing her own arms in its unimaginable force.
Only slowly did he realize they were feeling around for
something else. It could only have been another glass kettle
whose transmutation was complete. A double operation like
that was far more dangerous than a simple Insertion, and the
crimson haze seemed to thicken so that he could barely see the
globe.

The arms bent with agonizing slowness as they pulled the
kettle out of the flame. They were almost free of energy when
it happened. There was a bright flash that filled the whole
magnetic cylinder with a fog of white light. A gigantic bang
followed it in Hool's mind. It sounded like the end of the
universe.

He waited for the sleeve to clear. Wee was working
frantically with the controls, and Grandy was halfway up
out of her seat, trying to see out the window. The fog of ions
gradually settled in the sleeve, and vehicles above and below
began entering and leaving it again. Hool searched for
Dreem's bubble.

He found it almost out at the wall of the sleeve, where

the discharge had knocked it. He felt a terrible emptiness. It was the biggest flash he had ever seen in the Torch, and he knew the shielding could not have handled it. Dreem was dead. He was certain of it.

Wee turned the vehicle from the control board and brought it back out through the sleeve. The kettle was slightly askew in its arms, but it was still intact. He guided it slowly toward the window. Hool watched the process without moving. He could not see Dreem in the seat, and he knew what that meant. He felt numb. Even his rage seemed dead for the moment. He watched Wee dock the vehicle, but the whole thing seemed to be happening through a numbing crimson fog that paralyzed him. Wee's voice banged against him twice before he heard it. "Get her out of there!"

Hool looked at him blankly. Wee pointed toward the hatch opening. "Get her out!" Even then Hool did not move. He had seen what a "crisped" body looked like. He did not want to see Dreem like that. He turned away and looked back out the window. The shaft seemed entirely fogged in. Whispers came to him out of it, but he could not hear what they said. When Wee got up out of his seat and started for the hatch, Hool hardly noticed.

He was not sure whether it took them a long or short time to get her body up out of the hatch. All time seemed equally meaningless. He watched Wee lift her up out of the hole like taking a body from a grave and lay her on the floor. She was still wearing the insulation suit, but there were burn marks all over it, and the palms of the hands looked charred. Grandy came up out of the hatch and helped him start to strip the covering off. He wanted to stop her, but the fog held him fast in his chair. It did not even leave him enough will to look away.

Dreem looked as bad as he had imagined. Her face was difficult to recognize. The skin was all bubbled up and blistered, as if it had boiled from the inside out. He thought of how that skin had felt, how smooth and supple. He thought *of how he had watched the flush of her passion spread over that face. The star over her eye was all but gone, melted and cracked like the skin.*

Wee hovered over her. He had brought the kettle up first, and he dipped his finger into it and smeared some of the crimson on her face. Grandy stripped the rest of the insulation suit off her. Her clothes seemed burned onto her skin, and Grandy peeled them away delicately. Hool looked at the body that had given him so much pleasure, that had been so full of life. It was all swollen and blistered.

He wanted to get up and kill Wee when he saw him rubbing the Sunrise over that body, but his inertia held him fast. The whispers held him down; the fog pressed in against him pressing him into the chair. It clogged his mouth when he opened it to curse Wee. Wee's hands moved gently but quickly over every inch of her. Grandy helped roll her over, and Wee spread the crimson liquid over her back, her buttocks, her legs. When he and Grandy turned her back over, the swelling had already gone down, the blisters were gone, and the skin had its original smoothness. Hool blinked his eyes in disbelief. Dreem's face was as lovely as ever. Even the star was where it should have been, as if she had just sprayed it on herself.

He watched as Wee rubbed his fingers across her lips, covering the last parched inch of her. Her breath started again with a sudden sigh. Grandy smiled across her at URdon Wee. Slowly Dreem opened her eyes. Wee's voice greeted her. "Welcome to the World, Dreem Shalleen, who has died the Little Death and the Big. Welcome to the World, Dreem Twiceborn."

Hool felt an overwhelming joy, but it turned to acid in his mouth. Dreem's eyes were full of love and adoration. But they were staring straight into the eyes of URdon Wee.

"Nobody raised them up!" Pock shouted. "They never died!" He tossed three discs on the floor. Three figures blossomed from them. "Or these aren't them."

Hool bent down to see them closely. There were three of them, the right ages, the right sizes. They were dressed as Skyshockers, and everything they did as the holoscan ran was obscured by the disguises. Pock scattered three more holodiscs, and the three figures Hool had left with him stood near the other figures. Pock did not look at them closely. He had watched them for hours before he sent for Hool, but he could not be sure. They *might* be the same children. They were certainly Exceptional.

The version of the news they were performing about a Blue who had leapt or fallen to his death off Fist Headquarters in the Grand Sphere was close to treason, but it was hard to turn away from, and harder still not to laugh at. Whoever they were, they would bear watching. But he wanted to know for sure, and only Hool could be certain.

Hool watched the whole performance before he said anything. Finally he straightened and looked at Pock. "Where?" was all he said.

Pock gave him the answer as if he expected nothing in return. "Hardcore," he said. "Yesterday." Hool nodded. Pock knew there was no use pressing him further. But he pressed him, anyway. Something in him had to know. "And these are your"—his voice said Hool was crazy if he believed such things—"Twiceborn?"

Hool shook his head. "Twice-*dead*," he answered. He was already on his way to Hardcore.

CHAPTER
TWENTY

Push and Chancey waited in the first Squeeze in the Stack for Beyar to get back from "running a crowd." Whenever Skyshockers showed up in a habitat to perform, about half the troupe would scatter throughout the habitat spreading the word that a performance was going to take place. The twins had drawn Main Bay, a large cube made from two docking modules that had been welded together to form a kind of public square back in the days when Grandy was still running Grandy's Place.

Before the Hardcore Massacre, it had housed a large, flat screen on which the LeGrange Corporation News and Entertainment Network had broadcast as much news as it thought was good for the League to hear about. But in the decade since the League's largest uprising the screen had been replaced by a large holoball in which twenty-foot-high figures performed the Corporation's version of reality. The holoball was in the middle of the floor, and OBees walked right through the lower parts of the figures on their way from one part of Hardcore to another. Despite the ball's size, knots of young Corehards lounged around outside it without taking much notice of it.

Traffic in Main Bay was always brisk, and all Push and

Chancey had to do to attract a good-size crowd was a bit of juggling and some minor acrobatics on the girders above the top of the holoball. Push had drawn applause by attaching a piece of Stretch to the girder and dropping down into the middle of the holoscan of Spencer LeGrange explaining the benevolent nature of the Corporation and the enormous benefits the League derived from its association with Earthside.

Every time the figure of Spencer LeGrange opened its hand to gesture, Push would drop down its palm, but whenever the hand started to close, he would jerk on the Stretch and it would pull him suddenly upward, making it look like Old Spence was trying to grab him and failing miserably in the attempt. Using the Skyshocker Soundbox on the girder above, he could drown out the holoscan's real words and replace Old Spence's voice with his own impersonation of it.

Every time he eluded the figure's seeming attempts to grab him, Old Spence's speech would be interrupted with a string of profanity that always trailed back off into what Old Spence was actually saying. Although they may not have fully appreciated the symbolic significance of a Skyshocker continually eluding the Corporation and making it look ridiculous, the OBees found the performance hilarious.

When Push wasn't bobbing up and down out of Spencer LeGrange's grasp, Chancey was providing a satirical translation of Old Spence's speech that left most of the passersby laughing too hard to walk. She ended by doing a few quick handsprings across the main beam and leaving a string of holograms of herself in her wake, each frozen in a different aspect of her flight. When she stopped, all of the three-dimensional figures turned together and directed everyone's attention toward Grandy's, where the real performance would take place.

Things were more difficult for Beyar. He had to work his way through the maze of corridors between Main Bay and the Rim and back again. From Catchcage, Hardcore had always looked like an erratic model of a spiral galaxy seen edge on. The large cube of Main Bay and the cone-shaped ex-mass catcher that had become Grandy's Place formed the center of the thickest point, and the uneven jumble of dormitories and made-over cargo containers above and below them trailed off in thickness in direct proportion to their distance from it. From above it looked more like a spreading stain of metal spilled accidentally in space and left there to congeal.

Even from the side it had no actual levels, because each new square or oblong was grafted onto previous ones at whatever angle suited the welders who connected it. Most of the passageways were formed almost inadvertently by the way the cubicles surrounding it on all four sides were arranged. There were no panoramic vistas or wide highways in Hardcore. Its corridors twisted and turned, rose and dropped without warning. For the most part they were narrow, dim, and congested with angry-looking men and even tougher women. It was said throughout the League that the only way to get from one place to another in Hardcore was to fight your way there.

Push made his way through with music. The holoscan of Nohfro Pock that seemed to run ahead of him continually dodging his blows, and the outraged contingent of the Fist that seemed to chase after him, helped clear the way as well, although more than one OBee refused to get out of the way of even an *image* of the commander of the Fist on general principles. It taxed even Beyar's skill to avoid them while running full tilt through the narrow passageways.

When he did bump into someone, he usually managed to spin off and keep going before they could teach him a lesson in traveling the corridors of Hardcore. However, even the most irate of them would have thought twice before laying a hand on him once they realized what he was. Throughout the League, Skyshockers were considered insane and were treated with either reverence or pity. In truth, most people simply found it easier to excuse Skyshocker behavior as the inescapable eccentricity of those whose journey to the End of the Sky had made them mad than to face the consequences of hampering them.

Almost everywhere it was considered extremely bad luck to harm a Skyshocker, and like most superstitions, it had a solid basis in fact that had been obscured by the passage of time. In the early days of the League there had been those who insisted that the Skyshockers were really the eyes and ears of the Fist, but those who harmed Skyshockers on the basis of those suspicions came to such bloody and brutal ends that such rumors eventually died out along with those who spread them. The "accidents" that befell those who harmed a Skyshocker led to the perfectly logical conclusion that intentionally harming a Skyshocker was suicidally bad luck.

For the most part, however, Skyshockers were liked and welcomed, and what inconveniences they created were tolerated, if not thoroughly enjoyed, throughout the League. Those who were startled or jostled by Beyar's run were generally more interested in where the Skyshockers were going to perform than in getting revenge.

More laughter than curses followed the path of his flight, and it sowed the seeds of a large crowd. Everybody was delighted when a troupe of Skyshockers were passing through. They brought news the way the League liked it, uncensored. If the news was not always true, it was at least always entertaining, and everybody who had nothing that couldn't be avoided headed for Main Floor.

The Skyshockers had two advantages that the LeGrange News and Entertainment Network didn't. The first was that no matter how solid an image a holoscan could throw up, it did not have the same "presence" as a human being. When the Skyshockers told about Spencer LeGrange or anybody else, that person actually appeared, in the flesh, with the help, of course, of the facecase and the Skyshocker gift for mimicry.

The second advantage was truth. Even the parts of their

performance that had nothing to do with events of the day, the "entertainment" portions, were based on the truth of life in the League, although it had to be admitted that as often as not, Skyshockers got to the truth by way of a lie or, as URdon Wee would have it, an illusion.

Still, the LeGrange Network's truth was always further from reality than Skyshocker lies, and although it continued to pass its propaganda off as a literal and objective re-creation of events, few people in the League took what it said at face value. The Skyshockers, on the other hand, never claimed to tell the truth but only to create illusion, which inevitably made their version of events more entertaining.

Beyar got back to Grandy's long before the crowd was fully in place, but already most of the platforms were filling up and the smallest were beginning to overflow onto the ramps. He climbed into the Squeeze along with Push and Chancey and sprawled on the wall-to-wall airecline like a dead man.

The twins were too excited to wait for him to catch his breath. "Did you see the crowd?" Chancey said. "It's bigger than Last Day in the Cage!"

"The Widewall's half full already," Push added, "and the lower shelves on the Inner and Outer walls are packed."

"You should've seen how many followed us over right from Main Bay!" Chancey told him. "And it doesn't even start for another hour!"

"I never knew there were so many people in Hardcore!" Push admitted.

Chancey seemed equally surprised. "Yes, it's not nearly as big as the Cage. You wouldn't think it could hold all of them."

Beyar nodded. "They're packed in pretty tight," he said. The real population of Hardcore was three or four times as large as it seemed at any given moment because most OBees were working somewhere else for weeks at a time. In the Hard Core around Main Bay, old-timers had carved out family spaces almost as large as on Catchcage, but out on the Rim, even those who worked local shifts might share a daily space the size of a Squeeze with two others on a rotating basis.

The dormitories offered even less space per person, and the goal of most young Corehards was to earn their way out of them as soon as possible. Until they could, they spent as much time as possible in Main Bay, or Grandy's, or one of the countless swills out on the Rim where OBees between shifts lost their money and their wits.

Life in Hardcore consisted of frenzied periods of dangerous work laying up structure with long stretches of intense boredom in between. Nothing broke those tensions like a good fight, and nothing broke the monotony like the arrival of a troupe of Skyshockers.

"I hope they like us," Chancey said.

Beyar smiled. "By the time it's our turn, they'll be laughing so hard, they won't be able to stop."

"We're first up," Push said.

"First?!" For all his show of confidence, even Beyar was a little nervous about their first time before a really big audience, and he knew Hardcore audiences were as likely to be hostile as appreciative until their euphorics had a chance to take effect. The troupe usually saved its newest material until after the halfway point, and Beyar had his doubts about how a cold Hardcore audience would take a satire on OBee life like their Hasselpeg family.

Chancey shook her head. "We're doing an impro on the Blue that fell off Fist headquarters."

Beyar shrugged his ignorance, and Push tossed a disc on the airecline. "You better watch this," he said. The figure of I. I. Pontoon, the Network's Eye in the Grand Sphere, stood before him, two feet tall. He was a frail little man with large, protruding eyes that still managed to look beady despite their size. At Pontoon's feet was the badly battered body of a Blue, and behind him loomed the front of the Fist's headquarters within the compound at CORPQ in the Grand Sphere.

The report was a summary of the facts that sounded like it had been written for him by the Corporation News office. The officer had been found on the ground in front of the Fist's headquarters where he had apparently fallen. No explanation was given, and Pontoon spent most of his time on a close-up inspection of the body, accompanied by commentary about the tragedy of the event.

The Blue, R. Cove Hampton, was reported to have served six weeks in Hardcore and two years in Henson's Tube before his recent transfer to the Grand Sphere. Pontoon looked up toward the roof of the building and speculated on Hampton's last moments as he hurtled toward the ground. The report ended with the battered body of the Blue falling almost directly into Pontoon's scanner, and then a multiangled recreation of the impact.

Beyar watched it twice before they started to prepare. They started, as URdon Wee had taught them, by looking at what wasn't there. "They don't say why he was transferred to the Grand Sphere from Henson's Tube." It was an important point. Men were transferred to the quiet of Henson's Tube for only three reasons: as a reward for distinguished combat; as a place to recuperate from wounds received in places like Hardcore and the Sphere; or to await transfer Earthside because they weren't tough enough to make it in the League. "He only lasted six weeks in Hardcore," Chancey offered. Push and Beyar agreed he'd probably been transferred out because he couldn't take it.

"But why two years in the Tube? Why didn't they send him Earthside?" Push had isolated the chief question.

Beyar had an answer. "Family," he said. The twins nodded. Most of the Fist who were not recruited from the League itself came from the hereditary class of professional policemen Earthside. The legalized thuggery of policework had become a family occupation on Earth long before Catchcage was built, and it was common practice to send as many young Blues as possible up to the League for some experience under fire. If the Blue was the latest generation of a police family, he would have been kept in the League to save family pride even if cowardice made it impossible for him to be kept in Hardcore.

"But why transfer him out of the Tube to the Sphere?" Push asked. It was hard to imagine him being afraid in Henson's Tube, the most staid and conservative of all the habitats, and the life of a Blue in the Grand Sphere was not much less dangerous than an assignment in the Cage.

It was Chancey who figured it out. "Blink," she said.

It seemed obvious once she had said it. Blink, or tincture of whitwillow, made perfect sense. A few drops of it in the eyes gave increased alertness and a feeling of invincibility that were usually perceived as extrasensory powers. The Blue had probably begun taking it in Hardcore where every corner posed the danger of an ambush and every contact with the OBees was a confrontation. Whitwillow in a far milder form was readily available in Henson's Tube where even the most reserved drank it daily as tea. It would have been easy to convert Tube Tea into Blink, even for a Fool fresh up from Earthside, and even casual use would lead to addiction in two years.

The side effects of abuse would explain the transfer as well. Too much Blink led to generalized paranoia and blind rages that always ended in violence. The Blink probably made a Hardcore out of Henson's Tube for the young Blue, and repeated violent confrontations with the mild-mannered Tubers would have earned him a transfer to someplace his newly regained aggressiveness could be put to use. A sizable minority of the Fist in both Hardcore and the Sphere were functionally insane from Blink abuse, but it was a useful insanity under the circumstances and one the Fist did not do much to prevent.

"Jumped, then," Push said.

"Probably," Chancey agreed.

"The first time, anyway," Beyar said. The twins stared

at him. He touched the disc, and the last scene of the Eye's report replayed itself. Beyar stopped it as the beaten body hurtled toward the ground. It hung just above them, staring down empty-eyed into their faces.

Beyar looked at them. The twins smiled and nodded. They knew exactly how to play it.

CHAPTER
TWENTY-ONE

G randy's Place was packed. Every platform on the Widewall was so crowded with OBees that they looked like they were going to pull free of the wall and come crashing down. The ramps were equally full, and both the Inner and Outer Walls looked like they were made of people. The Outer Wall was occupied by Hards and Rimrats in from the Rim, and it looked a lot less colorful and a good bit meaner than the Inner Wall.

On all the walls Young Corehards clung to the ladders between shelves, and most of the floor was ringed with them. There didn't seem to be an inch of wall space between the lowest platforms that didn't have some Corehard leaning up against it. Even couples on their way to the Stacks had paused awhile to see the show, and in the Stacks themselves most of the Squeezes were wide-open with layers of young men and women lying on their stomachs and looking down toward Main Floor.

The place was all noise and contrasting music, and the main bank of lights at the top of the arch shone down through a heavy, sweet-smelling mist. Every form of mood enhancer Grandy's Place offered had been sold out, and freedealers who normally did a poor business on Grandy's tiers were overwhelmed with customers. Everyone seemed in a joyful mood, and when the lights blinked off, there was thunderous applause.

When they came back on, the body of a Blue lay on its back in the center of the floor. It wasn't a real body but a humandikin, an almost weightless prop that could give even a faint hologram the bulk and solidity of reality. It lay there alone until the boos and catcalls died down, and then Beyar and Push moved out into the light. Push was dressed as a Blue and walked with the uncertain roll of those recently Up from Earthside. Beyar was a grizzled veteran in a scarlet uniform who had apparently taken twenty years to change the color of the fist in the middle of his forehead from Blue to Red. They approached the body slowly, Beyar shaking his head.

Beyar knelt and examined the corpse's face. He stood up and shook his head. "Damn Blinkers!" he said. There were sporadic cries of indignation from the Blink addicts in the crowd, but they were quickly hushed.

Push leaned down without getting too close to the body, and the crowd laughed. "What's wrong with him?" he said.

Beyar looked away and yawned. "Nothing wrong with him. He's dead." A great cheer went up from the ladders and the floor. Nothing was surer to gain the goodwill of the young Corehards than a scene with a corpse in the uniform of the Fist.

Push moved timidly closer and leaned down toward the body again. "Really dead?"

Beyar went over and gave the face a second, long close-up look. Finally he gave the body a sharp kick that brought waves of laughter and applause. "He's dead." Push turned away. Beyar looked amused. "Never seen a dead man before?"

"Not a Blue."

Beyar gave him a look of long-suffering disdain. "Did you think Blues don't die?"

Push shrugged. "No, but..."

"Did you think they don't Blink?" The Blinkers in the audience cheered. A wave of threats followed immediately, and for a minute the Inner Wall seemed on the verge of civil war. But Push brought their attention back to the body.

"I didn't think they died on the roof of Fist headquarters." There were murmurs of recognition as the audience realized which news event they were watching.

"You oughta wish he didn't," Beyar told him.

"Why?"

"We're not gonna sleep for the next two days."

"You think we'll have nightmares?" Push said. The crowd howled.

"Yeah, we'll have nightmare. Two solid days and nights of making reports and changing them until they come out the way Pock wants them." He turned and gave the body another vicious kick. "Why'd you have to do it up here?!" he shouted at the body. He turned to Push. "Why couldn't he do it on the ground?"

"What's the difference?"

Beyar gave him a look of disgust. "We wouldn't have to carry him down!" he shouted. He gave the body another kick. The audience never tired of seeing it. He went and looked over to the edge of the roof. "And the ground patrol would have to do the reports!" He came back and shouted at the body again. "Why didn't you jump instead?"

Push was incredulous. "You mean he did it on purpose?"

The Red looked at him as if he couldn't imagine such stupidity being concentrated in one person. "Of course, he did it on purpose. He's Hampton; that fifth-generation Fool got Blinked and headhammered those two bankers over in the Tube." He looked at the Blue to see if he got the point. "They took him out of Hardcore because he ran from a Corehard..." A great cheer went up from the Stacks. "They can't leave him in the Tube because he keeps pillaging the Tubers..." There were hoots of disdainful laughter directed at the Tube. "... and they can't send him home alive without embarrassing four generations of the Fist. So what *can* they do with him?" Push shrugged, and Beyar answered the question himself. "Wait awhile until things cool down, and then send him to Hardcore." Another cheer went up from the floor and the Stacks, as if every Corehard was waiting for him to come. "He's dead meat in Hardcore...." Even the OBees cheered. "And everybody's happy."

Push nodded, as if the truth were dawning on him. "So he beat them to it and Blinked himself dead." There was a vague tone of admiration in his voice, as if he admired any Blue who could manage to evade hard duty.

"And left us with a mess to cover up!"

Push looked as if he didn't understand, and Beyar spelled it out for him. "The Fist doesn't commit suicide!" he shouted.

Chancey's voice rang out from the darkness. "Not unless they come to Hardcore!" The entire audience roared.

"He did this on purpose!" Beyar went over to the corpse and kicked it again. The OBees cheered. He turned to Push. "Do you know what this is going to do to your record?"

Push looked nonplussed. "I didn't kill him."

"We *found* him! That's just as bad. No matter how we lie, this thing is going to look like suicide, and Pock won't be able to do a thing about it!" A wave of cheers and laughter washed across the floor. "And he's going to be *mad*, and when he's mad, he's got to bite somebody!"

Push seemed to realize who was going to get bitten. "He's going to blame us because we couldn't cover it up right."

"Worse." Beyar looked like a man facing a death sentence. "If somebody finally does cover it up, we're the only ones who know the truth. They'll send us out to the Rim!" There were hoots from the OBees. The Fist patrolled the Rim as infrequently as possible, and Fist patrols went through the narrow and erratic corridors as if there were a fire burning behind them. It still cost them casualties every time they did it.

"The Rim?" Push said it like a condemned man asking for a recount. "The Rim?" Beyar nodded. Push ran over and kicked the body. "Why didn't you jump?" he shouted. The crowd roared.

He and Beyar looked over the edge of the roof, as if they were contemplating it themselves. Slowly Beyar turned back toward the body with a look on his face that started the Stacks laughing. Push stood at the edge of the roof watching him. Beyar looked back over his shoulder and waved the Blue toward him. There was no need to say anything. They each grabbed a leg and an arm and flung the body up in the air. They vanished while everyone's attention was directed upward.

The body went two thirds of the way up to the arch, and when it reached the apex of its climb, a hologram of Fist Headquarters as high as the arch itself suddenly appeared. The body floated rather than fell back to the ground in front of it. When it hit, there was a crash, like the building had fallen, and the lights snapped off. The applause was deafening, and it went on even after the lights came back on, and what was clearly I. I. Pontoon rushed over to the body.

Chancey's facing was outstanding, and Pontoon himself was impressed as he recorded everything they did for the Fist. The crowd booed the figure of Pontoon soundly while Chancey poked at the body and crawled all over it looking for a better view. Finally she crouched down next to it and let her head hang forward like a vulture. She looked around as if to see that no one was watching, then dipped a finger in the blood and tasted it. There was pandemonium, and it was minutes before the laughter stopped sufficiently for Push and Beyar to come on again, dressed as two Blues from the ground patrol.

Unlike the characters from the roof, the Blues knew immediately what was going on and exactly what it meant for them. Chancey sat scanning the body through a circle made with her finger and thumb; it was something most of them had seen Pontoon do a hundred times, and there were ripples of applause and laughter. When Beyar spoke, Chancey went on lining up views of the deceased, as if she did not hear him.

"It can't be!" Beyar said.

Push stretched his neck to look. "I think it is."

"What kind of a human being would throw a dead body off the roof?"

"Especially after all the trouble it took us to get it up there!"

Beyar scowled at him. "Would you be happier explaining where he got the Blink?"

Push looked offended. He pulled down his lower eyelid and held a dropper above it. There was a wave of applause from the Blinkers on the Inner Wall when he squeezed it. "I offered him a drop. How'd I know he'd do the whole bottle!"

Beyar grabbed the dropper off him and pulled his own eyelid down. The Inner Wall went wild. "The question is, what are we going to do now?"

Push looked over at Chancey, as if noticing her for the first time. "Pontoon's here." His voice was more of a groan.

Beyar looked around, but he was blinking too hard to see. "Where?"

"At the body."

Beyar gave a whimper. "We're going to die out on the Rim." The Outer Wall laughed. He pulled down the lower lid of his other eye and held the dropper over it. The Inner Wall laughed.

Push grabbed the dropper off him. Beyar looked everywhere but at Pontoon.

"What are we going to do about Pontoon?"

Push used the dropper and stood blinking for a minute. When the effects of the Blink hit him, he froze a minute and his face lit up. "We'll kill him!"

"Good idea." Beyar seemed about to do it when a second thought seemed to hit him. "What are we going to do with his body?"

Push shrugged. "Take it up on the roof?"

"And do what? Throw it off?"

Push scowled. "Why do I have to think of everything?"

"Never mind, I know. We'll break him up pretty bad and stuff him under Hampton."

Push looked bewildered. He blinked, and Beyar's reasoning suddenly became clear to him. "Make it look like Hampton fell on him?"

Beyar nodded. They started for Pontoon, but it was already too late. He was looking directly at them through the circle of his finger and thumb, and they knew he was already recording them. Whatever he saw was already as good as in Pock's hands, and even the euphoria of Blink couldn't make it plausible to them that they could kill him now and get away with it. Pontoon offered them an out.

Chancey didn't just sound like I. I. Pontoon, she *was* Pontoon. Pontoon himself was not amused, except when he thought of what Pock's face would be like when he saw the holoscan of the performance. He might even start cracking down on the Skyshockers, and nothing could please I. I. Pontoon more. In the meantime he kept as still as he could and tried to blend in with the crowd on the Widewall. He was halfway up the wall, and if anyone recognized him at the moment, there was a good chance he would go sailing out off the platform toward the floor.

Chancey's voice had the same high-pitched, wheedling tone Pontoon's had. "Gentlemen, we seem to have a problem here."

Push and Beyar looked at each other. "What's that?" they said in unison.

Chancey turned and looked back toward the body through her finger and thumb. "Somebody just threw this body off the roof."

Push and Beyar looked at the body as if they were seeing it for the first time. "He wasn't thrown," Push said. "The Fist doesn't throw its own off roofs."

"The Fist doesn't commit suicide, either," Chancey said. She had captured the whiny arrogance of Pontoon's voice so perfectly that there was subdued applause every time she spoke. "So he couldn't have jumped."

"I think he fell," Beyar said. His tone said Pontoon ought to think so too.

Pontoon shook his head. "No, I saw him come sailing out over the edge, and he did *not* fall." Push and Beyar looked at each other as if they might not even live long enough to go to the Rim. "I just couldn't get in position to record it." He looked at Beyar as if he was perfectly willing to compromise. "I believe we can help one another," he said.

Push shook his head. The Blink was obviously talking. "The Fist doesn't need any help."

Pontoon laughed. It was the kind of laugh that made anyone who heard it embarrassed that a human being could make sounds like that. It provoked loud applause from the Widewall. "Probably not. Except in Hardcore." There was general laughter. "But *you* do. And I have a way out of your dilemma."

Beyar frowned. "What dilemma?"

Pontoon sighed, as if the Blues ought to be smart enough not to make him spell it out. "You just discovered the body of a suicide, or two of your own men murdered him and threw him off the roof. Either way, you're going to be held responsible for not covering it up." Beyar frowned. Pontoon was right, there was no denying it. He waited for Pontoon's offer. "That's *your* problem." He seemed about to wash his hands of the whole affair. "*My* problem is that I didn't get to record that spectacular fall, and the people I'*m* responsible to are going to want to know how I could be this close and miss it."

Beyar looked at Push to see if *he* understood what Pontoon was driving at, but Push looked equally Blinked. Pontoon waited for them to complete the thought for him. When neither did, he went on. "This is where we can help one another." He looked as if he expected one of the Blues to figure it out. When they didn't, he said, "I want you to take the body up to the roof and throw it off again."

Push nodded appreciatively. "That would solve *your* problem."

Pontoon spread his hands, as if the rest was obvious. "I record it coming down and then *I* find the body. That solves *your* problem."

Push and Beyar looked at one another. Beyar said it first. "How are we going to do that?"

Pontoon looked disappointed at their lack of resourcefulness. "You take it in the Uprise, just like you would if you were taking it to the morgue on the top floor. If anybody stops you, you're on your way there. Then you just go one story too high and you're on the roof."

"What if there's somebody on the roof?" Push asked.

Pontoon looked as if it was an obviously foolish question. "Would you stay around on the roof if you just threw a body off?" The answer was obvious, and since they all knew it must have been the roof patrol who did it, they could depend on an uninterrupted hour before the patrol came around again. It was more than enough time.

The two Blues looked at one another for a moment and decided. Without another word they picked up the body and headed for the door of Fist Headquarters. When they went through it, they seemed to disappear, and even those used to Skyshocker stage tricks gave a murmur of appreciation. A few minutes later the body came hurtling down again. This time Chancey stood underneath it, recording its fall as it came. When it landed on top of her, the lights went out and the crowd went wild with laughter.

When the lights came back on again, the crowd would not stop applauding. The thin metal wafers used in the habitats for money came showering down from everywhere. They covered Main Floor like snow, and neither the money nor the applause stopped until Push, Chancey, and Beyar stepped back into the light again. They had already removed part of their facing. It was a mistake.

I. I. Pontoon, the Eye of the Fist in the League, made sure he got a good close-up of each of them for Nohfro Pock.

CHAPTER
TWENTY-TWO

Back in the Squeeze again, Chancey was elated. "They loved us!" she said. It was true, their "Hasselpeg Family" was an instant success and would have made them at least momentary celebrities even if their version of the news hadn't. Half their lines were already part of conversation all over Hardcore, and out on the Rim there wasn't a swill where whoever was buying didn't lift his glass and say, "The Fist doesn't commit suicide," and everybody else didn't respond, "... unless they come to Hardcore."

"It was deafening," Push said. He looked as if the applause were still ringing in his ears.

Beyar was surprised at how much they liked it, but he was even more surprised at how much *he* liked it. He tried to seem unimpressed with their success, but in reality he was as excited as Push and Chancey. He sprayed the resin off his cheeks before he answered. "I wasn't sure they'd like the Hasselpegs," he said.

"People were crying, they were laughing so hard," Push said.

Chancey laughed. "I saw these two Corehards along the wall." She gestured off to her right, as if they were still on

Main Floor. "They were laughing so hard, they couldn't stand up. They kept sliding down the wall."

Beyar dissolved the fiberglass of Bruise Hasselpeg's cheekbones from his face. "We'd be cleaning off blood instead of fiber if they didn't like us," he said.

Push shook his head, as if there was no chance. "OBees like to laugh," he said.

Beyar shrugged. "True. But they don't look far to find an insult." They were both right. For a place where there was so little to laugh about, there was a surprising amount of laughter in Catchcage. But there was even more violence, and it was no exaggeration that one OBee would punch another for letting their shadows cross. They required even less of an excuse for attacking a stranger.

"Those two Corehards were very friendly-looking," Chancey said. She looked at Push. "Do you think we could find them?"

Beyar frowned. They were certainly free to explore Hardcore if they wanted. They couldn't stay in the Squeeze all week, and the troupe usually blended in with the population even when they traveled. Still, something about it made him uneasy. "I don't think we should be too visible," he said.

"We won't go as ourselves," Chancey said. She hadn't even begun to take off her facing, and she still looked like Gran Hasselpeg. The thought of her going like that made even Beyar laugh.

"We'll go as Corehards," Push said. It wouldn't be hard to do. Their capes could be tucked and folded to approximate the right clothes anywhere in the League, and the facing would be no problem. Push and Beyar might have to change themselves a bit, but Chancey had been heavily disguised both times, and it was unlikely she would be recognized. There was no stopping the twins if they wanted to do it, anyway, and Beyar relented. It was foolish to worry, he told himself. They had been trained to handle themselves in the most deadly kinds of situations.

In half an hour they were ready to go. "Do you think they'll still be here?" Chancey said as they left the Stacks.

Beyar shook his head. Once the Skyshockers were gone, Grandy's Place was for people with money to spend, and Corehards were usually less than solvent. "Main Bay," he said. They turned back and went along the Stacks and took the first Uprise to the catwalk above the top row of Squeezes. At the far end of it there was an exit into the upper gallery of Main Bay. Standing on it, the girders Chancey had danced across were above them, but they were still a good way above the floor of Main Bay.

Chancey scanned the knots of Corehards scattered across the floor. The figure of I. I. Pontoon filled the holo, and down near one of his feet she saw what she wanted. She rushed toward the Drop with Push and Beyar right behind her. The ride down was considerably slower than the ride up, and Chancey kept her eye on the base of the holo as they went down. When they got off, she went straight for the group of Corehards gathered around two boys who were apparently brothers.

Beyar frowned. They were obviously First Stock, and First Stock was as close as anyone in their generation could come to being a true OBee. It was more than simply being the offspring of two OBees. When the first waves of Original Builders came up, the suits were less than perfect, and no one knew for sure what the effects of exposure to the solar wind and other radiations would do to the genes of people working Outside so much. The Corporation assured everybody the risks were minimal, but not all the OBees listened. Later it became standard practice, but only a few of the Original Builders stored specimens of their genetic material from which children could later be artificially produced. Children created from it were First Stock. There were not more than a hundred and fifty like them in the whole of Hardcore, and they were the toughest of a tough bunch.

Chancey walked directly up to the fringes of the group

and stopped. The older of the two brothers was giving his opinion of the Skyshockers. He was closer to Beyar's age than hers but not nearly as big. He had square, rugged features and short blond hair. The younger brother was about the same size as Push, and he had quick, bright eyes that zeroed in on her immediately, as if he recognized her. She smiled at him and he smiled back.

The older brother was arguing with another Corehard with a blue arc over one eyebrow. Like most discussions in Hardcore, it was passing rapidly through disagreement toward physical confrontation. There were about nine others in the group with smaller arcs over the opposite eyebrow. It meant they were Rimrats, and a confrontation with one of them was a confrontation with all.

There was continual conflict between Hards from the Rim and those who lived closer to the Core. The older brother didn't seem the least bit intimidated by the fact that he was greatly outnumbered. Reckless courage was required of First Stock, especially in matters of blood and family, class and kind. He pressed the argument, as if he hoped it would come to blows.

The argument was over which of the performances had been second best. All Corehards agreed the high point of the night was the one about the dead Blue, but the Rimrat claimed the one with Spencer LeGrange auctioning off his mother was easily second. The older brother questioned the genetic inheritance of anybody who didn't think the Hasselpegs were the second funniest thing of the night, but the Rimrat said he didn't think it was funny at all. The older brother was incredulous. "You didn't think it was funny, Blue Death?!" He said the name with outright sarcasm. "You didn't think it was funny when the Old Man thought he carried his son home, and the son said he carried his Old Man home, and the Gran said they both crawled home, and they said, 'Who was in the lead?'"

The others in the group laughed at the mere mention of

it, but Blue Death said the whole thing was an insult to the
Rim. The older brother looked around at the other Corehards
and snorted, as if it was not possible to insult the Rim. When
he spoke again, his voice seemed to prod his adversary. "And
you didn't think it was funny when the Old Man said he
didn't do nothin' for a livin' because livin' come natural to
a Hasselpeg, and the old Gran said..."

Chancey finished it for him in Gran Hasselpeg's voice,
but she was careful not to make the impersonation too good.
"It's a good thing, Flush. You'd be dead if you had to *work*
at it." The crowd laughed, and the older brother stopped and
looked directly at her, as if she was interfering in something
very important, but he was willing to make allowances because of her age and beauty.

He didn't say anything else until everybody turned to
look at her, too, and then he turned his attention back to the
Rimrat. "See," he said. His voice was like a shove. "Everybody thinks that's funny, Blue Death. How come you don't?"
He waited for an answer, but as soon as Blue Death was
about to give it, he said, "Maybe you're just too dumb to see
it, halfstock." It implied that half of his genes had been
damaged by radiation.

Blue Death took a step closer to him. Five other Rimrats
closed in behind him. They formed a wall of threat. The older
brother made an elaborate ritual of counting them. "Five more
Rimrats heard from," he said. He looked at them scornfully.
"Five more, Blue Death, and you'll have enough to make
one real Corehard." The five took a second step toward him.
His younger brother reluctantly took his eyes off Chancey
and stepped up beside his brother.

The other Rimrats in the crowd closed ranks and approached from the opposite side. It was the fight every Hardcore night built toward. For every Corehard, life was a dance
of intimidation that eventually led to blows. While they were
still young the blows came from their peers; eventually they

would come from the Corporation, and the odds would be far less even and the outcome far more grim.

OBees accepted life as a test of will and strength and courage; they accepted the lost cause, the lopsided odds, the likelihood of death as opportunities to prove themselves. In Hardcore self-respect had to be earned. Pain was its purchase price, and nothing worth anything ever came free. If the situation had been reversed, Blue Death might have changed his opinion and backed away from the obvious outcome. But the odds were in the Rimrat's favor, and the others were First Stock. They weren't allowed a backward step.

Beyar looked at Push, and Push smiled. He moved quickly through the young Corehards who were backing away from the second line of Rimrats. The crowd drew back until it formed a circle around the brothers and their adversaries. Everything got quiet, and everybody waited for the inevitable. Blue Death took a closing step, but he did not deliver a blow. The brothers obviously had a reputation he was reluctant to face, even with the odds in his favor. He looked like he was debating whether to change his mind or not. He turned his head toward the four behind him, as if he was going to ask their opinion, and then spun around and threw the first punch.

The older brother slapped it aside and came in over it with a right hand that put Blue Death down like Blue Dead. The four Rimrats stepped forward to attack, but only two of them actually moved. Beyar had the middle two by the back of the neck. When they struggled to turn on him, he beat them together a dozen times, as if he were trying to bang the dust out of them, and dropped them in a heap. The older brother had disposed of the other two almost as quickly with a kick and a blow from the back of his hand.

Even though the Rimrats on his side outweighed him by a good fifty pounds each, the younger brother fared even better. Push intercepted two of them. A pair of quick kicks behind the knee left them doubled up on the ground. The younger brother swarmed all over the other two. He was jumping up and down on them when his brother finally pulled him off. He looked at Push and Beyar as if they had spoiled half his fun.

Beyar shrugged. "I liked the Hasselpegs," he said. He put just enough belligerence into his tone to command respect. The older brother glared at him and then broke into a smile. "Wyleeun Wyleeun Gid-e-on George," he said. He nodded toward his brother. "Creetchur."

Beyar nodded to Creetchur. "Beyar," he said. "And Push and Chancey." Creetchur looked at her like his destiny. Chancey only smiled. Men were going to be looking at her like that all the rest of her life. She liked it the way she had liked the applause.

CHAPTER
TWENTY-
THREE

Hool watched the Squeeze from a Squeeze of his own in the top row two stacks down. He had been watching it for five days, and he had seen them come and go dozens of times. He had even seen one or the other of them alone in it, vulnerable to attack. But he had not attacked. One of them was not good enough; it had to be all three. He was patient; if he did not get them in Hardcore, he would get them in Henson's Tube or in the Grand Sphere. But he *would* get them. He could feel *his* moment coming. He could feel the shadow of its approach. When it came, he would move.

In the meantime he followed them everywhere, always at a distance, always out of sight. He had followed them, he had followed the young Corehards they had become friends with, and he knew their routine. He did not know exactly *how* it would unfold, but he knew that the girl would be the key. Her carelessness would deliver them all to him. He had known that much from the moment he had seen her look at the young Corehard.

And he had been right. He even knew when it would

happen. Not an hour before, close enough to hear without being seen, he had heard them make their plans to slip away from the others after the night performance, and although he did not know where they were going, he had a hundred pairs of eyes to watch them with.

For the moment the Squeeze was empty. They were out wandering Hardcore with the brothers, but they would be back soon to begin running up the crowd for the afternoon performance. He had a whole day with nothing to do but wait. His time would come after the evening performance. In the meantime he could relax. He might even sleep. He could use the sleep. For the past three nights he had watched the Squeeze, in case the girl had sneaked out. But she hadn't.

He was about to cloud the front of the Squeeze completely and go to sleep when the woman went by. The sight of her woke him up. At first glance he had almost sworn it was Dreem Shalleen, and he crawled forward and stuck his head out of the Squeeze to get a better look at her. She was five strides down the catwalk and walking away fast. It was not Dreem's walk—it was looser, less athletic, more provocative—but it was a pleasure to watch her walk just the same. He was only vaguely disappointed. It had happened to him before, that feeling that he had seen Dreem again, and he had gotten used to being wrong.

Sometimes it was a woman who didn't look anything like her, but there was still something that reminded him of her—a sidelong glance, the way she held her head, or the swing of her breasts when she turned. In the twenty-five years since Dreem, he'd had his share of recreational moments, but whenever he was with one of those echoes of Dreem, it was always a time to remember. He thought of a Standup on the Great Wideway in the Grand Sphere, and a day in the Subtropical segment of the Big Wheel, an hour in the last recliner on the Catchcage-to-LUNAC shuttle, and a dozen times in the Squeezes right there at Grandy's.

The woman stopped at the Drop at the end of the Stack

and looked back along the catwalk. She saw him watching her and smiled. The smile made him think of Dreem. It was not quite her smile, and it trailed off into a little pout that was definitely not Dreem's, but it was close enough, and he scrambled out of the Squeeze and walked down the catwalk toward her.

He could not say for sure why she looked like Dreem. Her hair was ash blond and much longer than Dreem's had been. But her eyes, at least, were blue, although not the pale blue of Dreem's. Her body was a little fuller than Dreem's, and she might have been five years older, but there was something about the contour of her lips that was wonderfully familiar. Sometimes it was not even that much.

She watched him walk toward her with a kind of hunger. He was used to that. The same menace that made even strangers get out of his way in the corridors of Hardcore was irresistible to some women, especially in Hardcore or the Sphere where women were more direct than in the Tube or the Little Wheel. If she hadn't reminded him of Dreem, he even might have stayed in the Squeeze and waited for her to come to him. But he could tell she was going to be one of the special ones, and they were too infrequent to risk losing.

"You've got a Squeeze," she said, as if all the others were taken.

"Open-ended." He meant that the rental had no time limit. There was a time, back when Hardcore was all there was for recreation, when that would have been the mark of almost unlimited affluence. Most of the others turned over daily if not hourly, and it was still impressive in a minor sort of way.

"A man of means," she said. She had that faintly mocking tone, that Dreem had had when she was teasing him about being an OBee. "Or is it a man of meanness?" She looked at him as if he thought he was a lot tougher than he really was.

It was something a Grander would have said. If she was

from the Grand Sphere, it was certainly from Upside. He had been to the Sphere often enough to talk to a Grander. All it required was never saying anything that could only be taken one way. "A man of feeling," he said. He said it so that it could have meant either a man with feelings or a man who feels.

"Touching," she said. Hool laughed. She was bright in the way Dreem had been bright. He felt a deep emptiness he believed she could fill for a while.

"That's what a Squeeze is for," he said.

She smiled and held up two emerald-green candies. "That's what Rousers are for." Of all the aphrodisiacs sold on the floor of Grandy's, Rousers were the best, and the hardest to come by. He held out his hand and she took it.

In the Squeeze they ate the Rousers. He had intended only to eat half, but he had the whole day before he would need his wits again, and after half of it, she bit her bottom lip and smiled at him almost like Dreem, and he had chewed the other half to turn "almost" into "exactly."

They must have been quality Rousers, the kind that used to flourish in Grandy's Place but hadn't been found there since pleasure moved its capital to the Grand Sphere, because when he embraced her, he slipped entirely into the fantasy that she *was* Dreem. The longing he had learned to live with like the familiar and hardly noticed pain of an old injury began to throb, until somewhere, between the first flood of passion and the last, she *became* Dreem, and the longing was filled.

Hool stood on the first balcony looking down at Grandy. She stood staring out the Nearside Window after the vanished body of URdon Wee. Grief had only made her more vulnerable, and vulnerability had only made her more desirable. Her grief was his joy. Never again would he have to see her adoring URdon Wee, the pathetic clown, the charlatan. Wee, who was nothing compared to him.

That had been the agony of his life; if only Wee had

been a better man, had been some admirable giant he himself could have followed, the rest would have been bearable. But Wee was a joke of a man, a fool, a liar, a weakling. And yet both women had loved him!

That was the unbearable part. Not just that Grandy had worshiped him, but that Dreem Shalleen had loved him as well. All those years Hool had seen that light in Dreem's eyes only when she looked at Donald Wheeler, never for him. No matter how he might raise her passion, no matter how he might figure in her affection, that absolute worship, that complete adoration, was reserved only for URdon Wee.

And when she closed her eyes, when she cried out in rapture, he knew whose face floated in her vision. He knew who came to her in her dreams, and that knowledge had been a torment to him every night for twelve years. And yet he understood it, understood her longing for Wee like his own longing for Grandy; it was not love but the inexorable pull of Wee's vision, the irresistible momentum of moments that were neither Dreem's nor his. And because he understood it, it did not diminish his love for Dreem, and in his secretmost self he knew that her longing for Wee did not diminish her love for him. And yet he hated it and waited for it to be gone, waited for the momentum to shift from Wee's Will to his own.

But even after she had renounced Wee when he married Grandy, even after they had finally left Wee's group, nothing had really changed. He had thought that finally there would be the end of it, that his moment would come: Wee's vision would weaken, and she would see Wee for the pathetic weakling he was, that she would be freed of her delusion that Wee was the mystical figure, that she would finally see Back Toss Hool as he truly was, the best of all men.

But he was wrong. It was not the end. The Light was still there, burning as jealousy every time she saw Grandy, burning as longing every time she thought of URdon Wee. He waited a year for it to be gone, then two, and when she finally married him, he thought, "Finally she's free of it."

And immediately behind it came a second thought, one that should have told him that nothing had changed, "And if she can be free of URdon Wee, why not Grandy?"

But it was not gone even then. Year after Year he waited for it to burn out, waited for the coming of his moment, just as he had waited for it to burn out of Grandy's eyes all the time he had followed URdon Wee, waiting for Dreem to come to her senses. There were so many times he had been certain it had finally gone and he was the only man in her mind, as he was the only man in her bed. But in the odd moment he would see it flare up again, and he would watch her put it out of her mind and watch it creep back in, the unfulfilled destiny, the longing to be to Wee what Grandy was.

And every time he saw that light, every time he saw it flaming in Dreem's eyes or in Grandy's, every time rage choked him until it brought tears to his eyes, he thought of Wee's vision and how he might someday bring it to an end.

But as he stood on the balcony he felt the rage beginning to wane. Wee was dead. Hool's own hand had made certain the kidneycar would split open as soon as it hit the LUNAC Gates. And Wee was gone. Surely his moment was at hand. Soon they would both turn to him as they had always turned to Wee. Soon they would see his strength, his will, his vision, and not Wee's lies and fantasies. With Wee gone he was the only thing they had left, both of them. Finally he would get to consummate his vision. He looked down at Grandy, as if she were already his.

When Dreem Shalleen walked slowly toward her, it made his vision complete. It made him feel avenged to see them staring out into the emptiness URdon Wee had left behind. That emptiness would have to be filled, and he was the only man worthy or capable of filling it. He waited for Dreem to put her arm around Grandy, her jealousy finally gone forever. He waited for them to grieve together before, one by one, they would turn totally to him for solace.

Grandy turned slowly from the window. Dreem was

*almost to her. He waited for them to share the embrace they
would eventually share with him now that they were freed
from the irresistible pull of Wee's Will. He never saw the
electric cane until Dreem raised it, and even then he did not
understand what it was. It was so out of place; some member
of the Fist should have held it, should have shocked two
fighting OBees apart with it, or jolted some out-of-his-head
Catcher into submission. He had never seen one turned to its
full lethal capacity. Almost no one outside of the Fist ever
had.*

*Even when she poked it into Grandy's chest, he had no
idea what it would do, and the white flash as the voltage
arced through Grandy did not make him understand. He
watched stunned as Grandy flew back against the window
and slid down it to the floor. It was incomprehensible that
Wee's greatest treasure could be snatched away from him like
that.*

*Dreem looked down at Grandy, as if she had expected
something to be resolved. When she turned away, he knew
nothing had changed. Wee's Vision was still hurtling forward
under its own momentum; his moment had not come after all.
Neither grief nor rage nor jealousy had made Dreem do what
she did. She had been caught in another irresistible moment in
the sequence of irresistible moments that were part of Wee's
Vision. She turned and looked up at him, as if he alone
would understand. He realized what she intended to do, and
he put his hand out as if he could reach her, stop her. But the
moment was neither hers nor his.*

*Dreem looked at the electric cane one last time. It was
still set for "kill". She turned it in her hand and looked
through the glass window below its tips to make sure it was
fully recharged. Then she looked up at Back Toss Hool one
last time, and he knew that despite everything she had done,
she had truly loved him.*

*She turned the prongs of the cane toward herself and
pressed its points to her chest. There was a second blinding*

flash, and it struck him with full force as only things can strike when it is too late to change them, that for Grandy he had felt the loss of what was Wee's; for Dreem the loss was entirely his own.

She fell dead hardly a body length from Grandy. Hool's agonized "No!" went rocketing out toward her. It seemed to hit the glass and shatter. Only broken pieces of sound came floating back toward him.

He awoke with a start, still reaching out to stop her. The longing for her ached in him. He reached out for the woman, but she was already gone.

CHAPTER

TWENTY-FOUR

They saw a lot of Wyleeun and Creetchur over the next week. Whenever they performed, the brothers were there. So was most of Hardcore. Skyshocker performances changed continually, and although the crowd had its favorites and demanded to see them, at least half of every Skyshocker performance was new. At first they had not mentioned who they were, but even Beyar liked and trusted the brothers, and they were sure Wyleeun and Creetchur were the friends URdon Wee had said they would meet.

Creetchur knew even before they told him. When Chancey said she would see him at the performance, Creetchur winked at her and said he was at least sure *he* would see her. When Chancey was nowhere to be seen in Grandy's the next night, Wyleeun was disappointed. Creetchur only laughed, and when Chancey explained it later, he didn't look a bit surprised. When Chancey asked him how he knew, he said that the first time he had seen Gran Hasselpeg he'd thought of what she had looked like when she was his age, and what he saw in his mind's eye was Chancey.

The brothers took them everywhere in Hardcore, and before the week was up, they knew the place almost as well as the Cage. In deference to their need for secrecy, Wyleeun did all his fighting when they were not around, except for a few very brief encounters over the right of way in the narrower corridors, and Creetchur was too busy thinking up things to amuse Chancey to provoke very many confrontations.

Wyleeun even teased him, as he sealed a cut over Creetchur's right eye, that he was mellowing prematurely. But Creetchur was blissfully happy. Like most Corehards, happiness made him vaguely uncomfortable. He knew it wasn't the natural state of things, and like any force running contrary to nature, it was just saving up momentum to recoil in the opposite direction.

The disaster came after the last performance. Chancey dissolved her facing in less than a minute and bolted from the Squeeze with a hurried good-bye and a promise to meet them in Main Bay. "Don't forget. The shuttle for Henson's Tube goes off in two hours, and the troupe won't wait," Beyar said, but she was gone before he got the warning out. Push was just as anxious to get their last night in Hardcore started, and he waited impatiently for Beyar to get finished. Beyar was much faster at it than he had once been, but dissolving his facing was still a painstaking ritual, and he finally told Push to go on without him and that he would catch up shortly.

Push was halfway gone before Beyar called him back. "Chancey left her facecase," he said. It was something no Skyshocker went anywhere without. Beyar tossed it to him with a frown. Push laughed and mumbled something about the carelessness of women in love as he left. Push was probably right, but Beyar could not escape a sense of foreboding about it. It followed him all the way to Main Bay, and when he started across the floor, it made him turn back and look up to the gallery. What he saw there chilled his heart. Against the railing, looking directly at him, was Back Toss Hool.

Beyar hurried across the floor to the far side of the holo. He looked back through it to keep sight of Hool coming down the Drop, but Hool was not there. It worried him more than pursuit. He was still looking back when he slammed into someone coming the other way. In Hardcore a collision meant a brief scuffle and a long apology at best, and he did not have the time for Hardcore fun. He prepared to dispose of whoever it was in the quickest possible fashion, and it was all he could do to stop the blow before it hit Wyleeun.

The Corehard laughed. "You're becoming an OBee," he said. He seemed pleased about it, as if he thought it might somehow keep them there longer. It was not something one man said to another in Hardcore, but he had come to feel like Beyar and Push were almost as much his brother as Creetchur, and he was going to miss them.

Beyar looked frantically for Push and Chancey. "Where are the twins?"

Wyleeun frowned. "Push's over there. We're going out to the Rim. Creetchur and Chancey left already. We're going to meet them there."

"How long ago?" There was a hint of panic in Beyar's voice that did not go unnoticed.

"A little while before Push got here." He shrugged. "Fifteen minutes maybe." Beyar brushed past him toward Push. Wyleeun turned to follow. "Whose way are you in?" The corridors of Hardcore were often too small for more than one person to pass, and the right-of-way belonged to the stronger. If Beyar was concerned, somebody big and mean must be coming through, and even the bravest OBees sometimes decided to rest in an alcove rather than insist on the right-of-way when a man who commanded respect came through.

Beyar's answer was directed more at Push. "Back Toss Hool," he said.

"That old ghost?" Wyleeun said. A ghost was anybody who didn't have the weight to force his way through a crowded corridor. "We'll stuff him in an alcove." It was what any OBee would do to someone who didn't clear the passageway when they should have. But it did not sound like Wyleeun really thought they could do it. First Stock was one thing, but Hool was one of the Original Builders, and even the oldest and hardest of the OBees took an alcove when Back Toss Hool wanted to pass.

"Did he see you?" Push asked. Beyar nodded, and Push looked around apprehensively.

Beyar turned to Wyleeun again. "What's the quickest way to the Rim?"

There were no direct routes in Hardcore, but there were at least twenty ways to the Rim that were more direct than others. Wyleeun pointed to a medium-size doorway directly across from them, but he grabbed Beyar's arm when Beyar started for it. "He wouldn't go that way." He pointed to a narrow opening closer to the Uprise. "Not enough alcoves," he explained.

Beyar knew what he meant. The narrower passageways would give Creetchur more opportunity to get close to Chancey when they had to give way to some OBee, and more chances to assert himself when they ran into Corehards. With a little luck he might even run into a small pack of Rimrats. Beyar hoped they wouldn't run into Back Toss Hool. He followed Wyleeun to the opening and looked down the tall narrow passageway. It was a tight squeeze for a Corehard, and any full-grown OBee would have to go sideways. "Are they all like this?"

Wyleeun shook his head. "If he goes the way I think he'll go, some are Tights," he said. "Some are Realtights." It was the difference between a passageway a grown OBee could fit through sideways and one an adult wouldn't even attempt. They had been through both before, and to a Catcher the widest of them were claustrophobic, but Beyar looked forward to the narrowest because he could be sure Back Toss Hool would not be hiding in one of the alcoves.

Push asked the crucial question. "Is he after us or Chancey?"

Beyar tried to think like Hool. An OBee would have come right down the Drop to the floor of Main Bay after

them and then pursued them through the passageways until
he caught them. But Hool was as much a Catcher as an OBee,
and his attack would be more subtle, more strategic. Beyar
had felt Hool's presence long before he saw him; it meant
that he had been watching them for a while. Probably he
knew about Creetchur and Wyleeun as well and had been
waiting to catch them alone and pick them off one at a time.

"Both," he said. He was sure Hool had not accidentally
seen him from the gallery. The question was why Hool had
let him know he was there. The answer came with the question. Hool had probably seen her leave with Creetchur; he
wanted them to know he was after Chancey so they would
have to split up to find her before he did. That way he could
wait for them in the Tights and pick them off one at a time.
He could take the opener to the Squeeze off one of their
bodies and wait for Chancey inside it when she came back
to get her things for the shuttle.

"How can he be following both of us at the same time?"
Push said.

Wyleeun had an answer even Beyar hadn't thought of.
"Hool's from the Rim," he said. Push looked puzzled. "All
Rimrats are the same pack," Wyleeun said. He didn't need
to say that while Hool was following the three of them,
Rimrats were probably following Creetchur and Chancey.
There were enough of them to cover most of the routes to
the Rim, once they knew Creetchur's general direction, at
least, and they would know where to corner him. Two of
them could probably close off a Realtight where maneuvering
was difficult and Creetchur would be at a disadvantage. At
least they could do it long enough for a Squeal to bring in
reinforcements.

Beyar was impressed; it was a much sharper insight than
he had expected from a Corehard. He turned to Wyleeun; it
would be an insult to warn him directly that Hool would kill
him if necessary. "It's Hool's passage," he said. What he was
really saying was that even First Stock weren't expected to

commit suicide, and Wyleeun could walk away without losing anything in Beyar's eyes.

Wyleeun shook his head. "Not until he earns it," he said.

Beyar nodded down the passageway. "We'll need the alcoves to get a new face," he said. Wyleeun nodded and went down the corridor with Push close behind him and Beyar walking backward to protect them from behind. The passageway was short, but light from the far end did not come far enough down it to make it more than dim, and the green, luminescent frames of two alcoves on the right-hand side stood out sharply. Beyar took the first and Push the second. They hung their capes across the opening, took out their facecases, and went to work.

Wyleeun went back to the entrance and leaned up against one wall of the passageway. He folded his arms across his chest and waited for someone to try to pass. He looked as if he hoped it would not be Back Toss Hool. Beyar was finished almost as fast as Push, and when he was done, he went down the passageway to get Wyleeun. The young Corehard started at his approach and took a step to knock him down. It was a perfectly reasonable thing to do to a Rimrat.

Beyar backed off a step and smiled. "I'll take the door," he said. "Second alcove." Even hearing his voice, Wyleeun had to look at him twice to be sure he wasn't one of the Rimrats he had had the argument with when he'd first met Beyar. "It's *me*," Beyar said finally. Wyleeun gave a short laugh and shook his head in wonder as he slipped past Beyar and down the passageway.

In a few minutes two more Rimrats left the second alcove and joined the first at the opening of the passageway. Then the three of them disappeared into the narrow darkness.

CHAPTER
TWENTY-FIVE

Chancey followed Creetchur through the second straight Tight. They could walk normally but not abreast. It was a long one and very dim. Creetchur paused before every alcove and held up his hand for Chancey to wait. When he was sure it was empty, he moved quickly past it and watched while she came in front of the opening.

The alcoves were rarely more than two feet deep, but they ran the height of the corridor. Two people could stand comfortably in them, three if there was a necessity, and there were usually clusters of them. They were usually offset, so that if there was one on the right wall, there was another on the left but either farther down or farther up the corridor.

Chancey had gotten used to traveling them, and it no longer seemed like the walls were moving together when she was in the middle of one. At first she had wondered how anybody could stand living that way, but she had grown fond of the adventure they always presented. She liked the way the corridors rose and dropped and twisted, and turned suddenly without reason.

She liked the fact that no part of Hardcore seemed on a level with any other part, and the sheer absence of specific design delighted and fascinated her. Catchcage was open and green and beautiful, but the hand of a single planner was obvious everywhere from the way the buildings were designed as three-leafed clovers to the way the clovers were arranged on the tiers. But Hardcore seemed to have been grown rather than built, and she loved its variety.

Traveling with Creetchur gave her ample opportunity to get the feel of Hardcore's dark twists and turnings. Going with Wyleeun meant brisk walking down as many wide corridors as possible, with only brief shortcuts through a Tight or a Realtight. Travel with Creetchur meant more climbing and crawling than it did walking, and he was always finding obscure side trips even his brother didn't know about. She doubted that there was a square inch of the Mazes Creetchur hadn't been over, and every time he took her somewhere, they got there almost twice as fast as Beyar, Push, and Wyleeun.

"Where are we now?" she asked.

Creetchur looked up and around, as if every place had a signpost. "Ten North, Eight East on Level D."

"About halfway to the Rim," she said. Creetchur had been pleased when she'd picked up his way of measuring things so quickly. North and South ran through the long axis of Grandy's Place. East and West ran through the axis of the Widewall. The bulk of Hardcore lay east of Grandy's, with the biggest part of that to the northeast. Each unit was one fifth the length of Grandy's, and the levels represented one cargo container above or below a line drawn through the center of Grandy's.

"Right," he said, "*if* we were going to the North Rim, but where we're meeting Wyleeun is closer to east than north."

She was used to Creetchur's roundabout, but quicker, journeys. At the end of the Tight they stepped into a Wide, a long corridor about half the length of Grandy's that ran straight down between two stacks of houseblocks three made-over cargo containers high. Eight people could walk comfortably side by side down its entire length before they would

have to choose among a dozen different-size openings heading
off in different directions. Half the population of Hardcore
seemed to be trying to make headway along it.

But they only went a little way down it before Creetchur
took her hand and led her in to a wide alcove. In the corner
of it he knelt and slid aside a square screen set in the floor.
He climbed down the ladder, and Chancey followed him
without protest. One of the things she liked about Creetchur
was that you never knew what was going to happen next with
him. The new passageway was low enough to touch the
ceiling on, but it was wide enough for them to walk side by
side.

The only light was the luminous paint that covered it.
The top and bottom were yellow, and the sides were dark
blue. They seemed to diminish in the distance until they came
to a point. Creetchur pointed to it proudly. "The Gideon
Gideon Gid-e-on George Undershaft," he said. "Longest line
of sight in Hardcore."

Chancey smiled. It would have been an air duct in most
habitats, and even in the Cage it would not have been a great
vista, but she appreciated it like a native of Hardcore. "It's
beautiful," she said, and it was, in its way. The longest,
straightest place in Hardcore and not a soul on it.

"We named it for our Old Man," he said. It was what
every Corehard called their father. "He built it," Creetchur
said proudly. "It used to be used as a transportation track
between loading docks before the other habitats were built.
People built up all around it and forgot it was here. Wyleeun
and I are the only people that know about it." He was sharing
a very private part of his life with her, and Chancey knew
it.

She looked down the dwindling focus of the corridor.
"It doesn't *feel* like it's even in Hardcore at all." She was
afraid she'd insulted him as soon as she said it.

But she needn't have worried. Creetchur seemed enormously pleased that she could feel the difference. "I knew

you'd be able to feel it," he said. "Wyleeun thinks you have to be First Stock to feel it, but I knew you were special."

He took her hand and led her down the tapering corridor. It widened as they went, but always the end of it seemed narrowed to a point. When they got to the middle, Creetchur stopped. He pointed back where they came from. It, too, was just a point where yellow and blue planes converged.

"The Old man brought us here to learn to feel the Spin," he said. The whole irregular mass of Hardcore turned on the axis of Main Bay and Grandy's Place, but it turned erratically—not enough so that the gravity varied by more than a percentage point of Earthside-plus, but enough to feel the difference when the momentum of its turning torqued the cells.

Creetchur sat down and patted the floor beside him for Chancey to sit. "The Old Man says the Spin is a physical expression of the Cosmic Momentum."

"Like the Ring in the Grand Sphere," she said.

Creetchur seemed a little insulted by the comparison. "*That* measures Luck," he said. "*This* measures life."

"The momentum of events," she said. He was surprised that she understood, and relieved. "Hard times make the pressure of the Spin go up; good times make the pressure of the Spin go down."

Creetchur smiled. "You sure you're not First Stock?"

"I *am* First Stock," she said. "Just not from Hardcore."

He held her hand, and they sat side by side in silence for a long time. The Spin slowed way down. She leaned over and kissed him, and the wobble of Hardcore seemed perfectly balanced for the first time in its history. They seemed for a while to be floating free, perfectly in balance with the Spin.

And then there was a lurch, as if Hardcore had shifted gears, and the Spin grew until they felt it would crush them. Creetchur had never felt it so keenly or so strongly. It was like the weight of all the hard luck, hard times, and death that had been suffered since Hardcore began was concentrated and focused just on them. Even after they pulled themselves free of it, the impression lingered, a kind of dread, a deep and irrefutable feeling that something was terribly wrong. They stood. "I think we should go," Creetchur said.

Chancey nodded. "And find the others."

In the silence footsteps moved toward them from the far end of the corridor, heavy solid footsteps, like evil walking in a human shape. They looked at one another and began to run. Behind them the footsteps began to run as well.

CHAPTER
TWENTY-SIX

Back Toss Hool watched Beyar cross over into Main Bay from the Stacks, as he had watched Chancey and then Push come the same way. He could feel *his* moment building; very soon he would be able to short-circuit URdon Wee's vision for good. The world seemed full of ironies to him, but he did not have URdon Wee's cosmic humor to put them into perspective. Very soon he would kill three children in order to save the world, and if he was remembered for it at all, it would only be as a murderer, and the worst kind of murderer at that. The best he could hope for was to be remembered as a madman or to be unremembered at all.

It did not worry him that he had killed one of them already and it had accomplished nothing. He had been wrong; it had not been *his* moment, and Wee had been able to reverse it. He even understood the why of it. Every moment sits in an infinite stack, touching on all sides, moments of equal probability. All things that can happen, *do*. Happen and continue to happen, perfect globes without beginning or end, each one discrete and complete in itself. He had seen them in his vision, had seen the writhing beam of light that connected them into one awareness, one sequence that became one reality.

But, in truth, only the awareness moved, only the Light, illuminating the holograms of possibility into the solid forms of reality; giving Essence, Existence. His vision was one path of the Light. Wee's vision was another path. Both were true, both real, both destined to form a sequence of events all participants would think the single and only reality. But *he* knew it was not so.

He knew that the Light could be deflected from its path to form another reality, that it was not bound by limited laws formed by limited awareness. When the Light entered an event, within the bubble of that occurrence its path could be changed, not in *every* event, not even in most, but in some. In events of special significance the angle of déflection could be changed, and the Light would emerge, not into the twisting chain it had started to form but into another chain, another universe, another sequential reality.

That was what gave him both the hope and the courage to do what he had to do. If there was an event the Light could not emerge from, it could not enter all the events connected with that event. It must come out some other way, form other connections, actualize different possibilities.

Far down the snake of Light was the absolute dead end of man's annihilation. Unless he turned that path aside somewhere in the range of events his own Light connected into a reality, mankind would end. Everything that had been suffered would be for nothing; everything that had been achieved would be lost.

So his destiny was clear to him: He must deflect the Light from the series of events in which the children grew to adulthood and carried out their destinies, to free the League and start mankind down the chain of possibilities through which it would come to its ultimate end. He must deflect the Light from those events, keep it from making those potentials into actualities. He must stop that chain; extinguish the Light from all possible events in which those children existed.

For the good of all other children yet to be born, he had to destroy three. It was a terrible thing to do, and yet he knew he must do it. As surely as he knew he must close off the Light from all events in which he himself existed as well. When what he had to do was done, to prevent the Light from changing its trajectory, from doubling back through him to regain the trajectory he had altered, he would have to reject the Light from himself. He, too, would have to die.

Because he had lived in Hardcore so long, and because he had come from Hardcore's equivalent on Earth, he did not admit even to himself what he secretly hoped: that he would transcend his death, that he would emerge from it in a new sequence, a sequence in which he would be reunited with Dreem Shalleen to fulfill all that had been denied them in the unfolding of Wee's Vision. But whether he emerged in a new universe or not, he expected to die in his present one. It was a price he was willing to pay to stop Wee's Vision.

He tapped the electric cane impatiently on the railing as he watched Beyar cross the floor of Main Bay. A modified version of the canes that were once the sole property of the Fist were becoming commonplace throughout the League. A touch from the twin points at their tip could produce pain, temporary paralysis, or unconsciousness, depending on the voltage setting, but only the Fist had ones that could kill. For anyone else the penalty for having an electric cane with lethal force was immediate execution. Hool didn't care. It was the weapon Dreem had used, and that made it the perfect weapon for his revenge.

He waited until Beyar looked up. Then he tapped his temple with the end of the cane in mock salute and started along the gallery toward the Drop that would take him to the first of the corridors leading toward the Rim. His plan was Hardcoresimple. Find the girl, kill her; wait for them to come looking for her, kill them. There was no need for subtlety. It was *his* moment. He could not miss. He could feel it even in the Spin. Wherever he went, they would come to him, or he would come to them, but their meeting and its outcome were inevitable.

The first Rimrat met him at the bottom of the Drop. He looked at Hool with a mixture of awe and terror. Hool waited for him to talk, but he seemed unable to speak. "Which way?" Hool said finally. The Rimrat pointed straight outward, parallel with Grandy's. "How far?"

The Rimrat finally found his voice. "A Wide, three Tights, and two Realtights."

It was nearly useless information. Depending on where the Realtights were, it could mean twice as long a trip for Hool. Tights were no problem; they would clear the moment he stepped into one. But there was no way to get through the Realtights. "How long for *me* to get there?"

The Rimrat seemed bewildered. He looked at Hool as if trying to figure out which of the passageways he could fit through. It was too complex a problem for him, and finally he just shrugged. Hool contemplated strangling him. "Where were they seen last, then?"

The Rimrat looked relieved to finally have something he could answer. "Crossing Three Door Wide into the Realtight at the Near end." Hool knew where it was. The Near end was the one closest to the Rim; the Far end was always the one closest to Grandy's. The Realtight connected with a second Wide just beyond a string of cargo containers that had been made over into houseblocks.

He wedged himself sideways into the first Tight across from the Drop. It was a short one, and it was empty when he went in. Halfway through it somebody started to come in at the far end, but one look at the bulk blocking it and the OBee stepped back out and went to try his luck farther down.

Hool came out of it in to Makeaday Wide. It was only a three-person Wide and it did not run very far, but a Narrow at the Far end took him to another Wide running at a right

angle, and two more Narrows finally put him onto Three
Door Wide. He looked around for the Rimrat that should have
been waiting for him. There was no one there. He walked
almost to the Near end before he found him. The Rimrat was
leaning up against a wall, watching an alcove across the street.
He stood up straight when he saw Hool. He looked as if he
wished there were some sort of salute he could give. "They're
in that alcove over there," he said.

Hool looked at the alcove with a frown. It looked empty
to him. "How long?" he said.

"Fifteen minutes," he said. "Maybe twenty."

"You look away ever?"

The Rimrat shook his head vigorously. "Not for a second," he said. "Two went in, none came out."

"Did you check to see if they're still in it?"

The Rimrat looked confused. "Watch. Don't touch," he
said. They were Hool's orders. There were big penalties for
failing to follow Hool's orders, and few rewards for personal
initiative. Simple obedience was all most Rimrats could handle. Hool let it pass.

Sometimes he wondered why he was not afforded better
materials in his efforts to stop the end of humanity. The
Rimrats made him wonder if the salvation of humankind was
such a noble goal, after all. It didn't matter; even if the race
deserved to die, he would still prevent it just to spite URdon
Wee.

Hool walked directly to the alcove and stuck his head
in. He knew what he would find. There was a recess on the
left side that went behind the wall, but there was nobody in
it. He looked up. Three feet above his head there was a duct
opening. He dug his elbows and knees into the wall and lifted
himself up. The duct ran parallel with the Wide for a few
feet, then turned right. Hool tried to remember what the next
space over was. Unless the duct branched again, it should
have been Ten Body Narrow. He would have to go all the

way back down Makeaday Wide and take a Narrow across to it.

The walk took him longer than he expected. Some OBee with too much swill in him wouldn't yield the passage and had to be stuffed into an alcove. He was very awkward, and Hool had to break some things to fit him in. It was a nuisance, and he stepped into Ten Body Narrow in a bad mood. There were about twenty people in the Narrow, but one by one they got a good look at him and ducked into alcoves. He made good time down the Narrow.

The Rimrat at the far end was a little brighter than the last. He had seen them cross the Narrow into a Realtight, and he knew the series of Tights and Realtights that ran in that direction. He even knew where they would come out, Long Walk Wide. The news was good and bad. There were a number of Rimrats on Long Walk Wide, but it was going to be a roundabout to get there. Even with the alcoves filling in front of him like a precision drill, it would take him fifteen minutes to get there, and even then he was going to have to take a Tight.

He didn't like Tights; he had to go through them sideways, and it put one string of alcoves always behind him, making him inspect them over his shoulder as he passed. He was likely to go right past anybody less than shoulder-high. He doubted that the girl and the younger OBee even knew he was following them, but if they did, they'd be hard to find crouching in a Tight.

The others were too far behind him to try to ambush him, but a Tight would be the perfect place for it if they did. Moving sideways made him vulnerable. He would only be able to move forward or back, and without room to maneuver the electric cane would be useful in only one direction. Even changing it from one hand to the other would have to be done by lifting his arms over his head, making him open to attack, especially from the alcoves behind his back.

They might not succeed, but they were perfectly capable

of trying it, if they caught up with him. Wyleeun was First Stock, and Push and Beyar were very well trained. On the way to *his* moment even *he* might have vulnerabilities.

When he got to Long Walk Wide, there were two Rimrats waiting for him. They fell all over each other trying to report to him. What they said, as far as he could make out, was that the girl and the young OBee had gone into an extrawide alcove at the Far end of the Wide. When they didn't come out after fifteen minutes, the Rimrats went looking for them but they were gone, and the Rimrats were sure they didn't slip out of it unnoticed.

They showed Hool to the alcove. It took him only a few seconds to find the screen they had overlooked. He slid it back and looked down into the shaft. It was going to be a tight fit, and he would have to drop right down it instead of using the ladder. It didn't look more than ten feet deep, and he could use the rungs of the ladder to slow his fall at least partway down. He pointed to the shaft. "Get the rest," he told the Rimrat. "Nobody in, nobody out."

The Rimrat nodded and started his Squeal. Its ultrasonic beam went out to every Rimrat in the vicinity. Hool handed him the electric cane and lowered himself into the shaft. There was not even enough room to look down, and he had to let himself drop with his arms straight up over his head. It made him land flat-footed, and the landing jarred his neck and made his teeth hurt.

He waited impatiently for the Rimrat to drop the electric cane down to him. He had to back out into the passageway and lean in to catch it. When he turned and looked down the dwindling blue-and-yellow distance, he smiled. It was the passageway of his vision, and he knew that if they were still in it, he had them. He had to crouch to move down it, but even if they ran, it was a long way to the other exit and there were no alcoves in between. He was sure to catch them. It would probably be years before anybody found the bodies.

CHAPTER
TWENTY-
SEVEN

Hool had a good head start on them, but Wyleeun was confident that they could overtake him. He was not so confident about what they could do about it when they did. They passed quickly down the corridors. In the Narrows there was little need to check the alcoves; they were sure Hool would not recognize them in the crowd even if he were lying in ambush.

The Tights were even safer; Hool could not fit into most of the alcoves in them, and even if he could, the most he might hope to get in such a narrow space was one out of three of them. They looked so similar that in the dim light it would have been foolish for Hool to risk an attack and end up getting the wrong one. But the Realtights were safest of all because Hool could not enter them, and they were vulnerable only when coming out, and even then there was little risk because they came out one at a time, and Hool could never be sure which one was Wyleeun.

The Realtights were the quickest route, anyway. Where Hool had to travel the length of a Wide to find a crossing

Narrow and then probably come partway back, they simply cut across the shortest distance. Wyleeun's path was longer than Creetchur's, and there was none of the duct travel Creetchur used, but by traveling up or down the Verticals where there wasn't a Realtight, they went almost as fast as Creetchur had traveled.

Every time they crossed a Wide on their way to another Realtight, they saw Rimrats. They seemed to be everywhere, and it was obvious that they were watching for Creetchur and Chancey. It was Hool's only advantage: he at least knew if he was on the right track. They had to guess.

They got all the way to Three Door Wide before they ran into trouble. They came up out of a Vertical into an alcove on the Near side of the Wide, and they stepped out of it right into a pack of Rimrats. It would have been no great problem if the Rimrats hadn't been the ones they had had the fight with the first day they came. And even then they might have passed undetected, if they had re-faced themselves as generic Rimrats. But Push had chosen a specific face, and both he and Wyleeun looked exactly like Blue Death. It was Blue Death they came face-to-face with when they stepped out of the alcove.

Nothing moved for a full half minute. Blue Death stared at Push. He stared at Wyleeun. His own face stared back at him. He turned and looked at the two Rimrats nearest him and cocked his head, as if to ask them if he was seeing right, but he could tell by the look of utter bewilderment on their faces that they saw it too.

He looked back at Push and Wyleeun as if he expected something to have changed, and then he looked at Beyar as if he were afraid he was going to see his own face looking back at him again. Beyar looked exactly like the Rimrat who stood behind him.

Blue Death looked from face to face again, and suddenly it fell into place. He almost got the word *Skyshockers* out of his mouth before Wyleeun's fist hit him in it. The blow made him look even more puzzled for a second, but the second one cleared his mind of all questions and left him lying facedown in the Wide. Even without the element of surprise the odds would have been in their favor. There were scarcely a dozen Rimrats, and although they were tough, they were no match for Wyleeun, let alone Beyar and Push. Wyleeun was an explosion of kicks and punches. Push was equally dynamic. Only Beyar worked methodically through his allotted foursome.

There were only two left standing when one of the original victims managed to overcome his pain enough to start his Squeal. Its sound was well beyond human hearing, but it rang in the earplug of every Rimrat within two hundred yards. Push dropped the last two and turned to Wyleeun for directions. He was surprised to see Wyleeun dash back into the alcove. He looked at Beyar for an explanation, but Beyar only shrugged until he looked down the Wide. Rimrats were coming out of Tights and Narrows all up and down Three Door Wide. They bolted back into the alcove and down the ladder after Wyleeun.

At the bottom of the ladder Wyleeun took a Realtight that led back under Three Door Wide. It was all quick turns and sudden dashes until he stepped into a narrow alcove and began pulling himself up the inside wall. Push and Beyar watched him disappear into an opening before they realized what he was doing. As soon as his feet disappeared, Push was up after him and Beyar immediately after that. They crawled a long way before they tumbled out into a small room. Wyleeun held up a finger for silence and climbed back up to listen at the crawl shaft.

Beyar looked around the room. It was a Pack, a blind cube with only the one exit, formed inadvertently when four houseblocks were welded into place at a different times. It was an easy place to defend but a bad place to be stuck in. Wyleeun finally stepped down from the opening of the shaft. Push and Beyar looked to him for an explanation.

His voice was quiet but not quite a whisper. "One of those halfstocks started his Squeal," he said. He looked at Push to see if he followed and then added, "Ultrasonic alarm brings Rimrats running from everywhere." He looked around the room as if he expected them to start dropping out of the ceiling at any minute. "Can't hear it without one of these." He pointed to the tiny plug in his ear. "Good thing to have if you go to the Rim much." He didn't say where he'd gotten it, but Beyar assumed somewhere there was a Rimrat without one.

Beyar took out his facecase. "Time to be someone else," he said. Push took his out as well.

Wyleeun shook his head at Push. "I thought you looked familiar," he said. He laughed. "I wish Creetchur could have seen the look on Blue Death's face." Beyar looked at Push and they both held up their mirrors in front of Wyleeun. His mouth dropped open. "I don't believe it!" he said. "I look just like him. No wonder he looked brain-fried." He looked at himself more closely and shook his head, then he put a finger to his ear and stopped as if listening. He frowned. "I thought they'd turned it off," he said.

Beyar was already at work on his own face, and Push began removing the fiber and resin from Wyleeun. In a few minutes he started to reapply it. "Make me somebody I don't know," Wyleeun said. "It's bad enough having to look like a Rimrat without having to look like Blue Death." Push smiled and went on with his work. Beyar finished his own face and took over working on Wyleeun while Push remade his own face.

In the end they still looked like Rimrats but none they could expect to run into. Push started to put away his facecase, but Wyleeun put a hand on his wrist and turned the mirror toward himself. He took a long look and pointed to the blue arc over his left eye. "Put two little white stars here," he said. "That'll make us look like we're from Mid-Rim." The section of the Rim directly out from Main Bay was far enough away for them to be strangers but near enough for them to be passing through on their way to Grandy's.

Wyleeun stepped up and listened at the shaft again. He listened to the plug in his ear and then nodded for them to follow him. At the end of the Realtight they went down two more Verticals and then rose through another Vertical all the way up onto the Far end of Ten Body Narrow. Wyleeun poked his head up out of the top and looked around, but he was already standing in the Narrow before he saw a good reason for staying where he was. Not twenty yards away, Back Toss Hool stood talking to a Rimrat.

Wyleeun motioned Push to go back down the Vertical. He stepped into an alcove as Hool turned and started down the Narrow. When he was past, Wyleeun stepped out and watched him go, and when he turned right onto Crosswalk Narrow, Wyleeun knew exactly where Creetchur and Chancey must be.

He climbed back down the Vertical. Push and Beyar were waiting for him at the bottom. "I know where they are," he said. "The Undershaft. It's a long, low Narrow that nobody else knows about. Runs under Long Walk Wide, and then some. It's a special place we used to go all the time when we were little. Creetchur probably took Chancey there."

"How do you know?" Push asked.

Wyleeun smiled. "Because that's where Back Toss Hool is headed. I saw him turn onto Crosswalk Narrow."

"Can we get there before him?" Beyar weighed the alternatives.

"Easy."

Beyar looked at Push; they were thinking the same thing. "Does he have to go through any Tights?"

Wyleeun traced all the possible routes in his mind. "He doesn't *have* to. But he looked like he was moving pretty fast, so he'll probably risk one."

"Which one?"

Wyleeun frowned. "There's three at least, but the most

likely one is the one that connects Long Near Narrow and Long Walk Wide."

"Can we get in it before he does?"

Wyleeun looked as if he knew what Beyar was thinking but wasn't sure he agreed with the risk. "We can beat him to Creetchur easier," he said. "And if we miss him in the Tight, we might not."

"A Tight's the only place we have a real shot at him," Beyar said. He looked at Push. "We have to get that cane away from him."

Push nodded. "We'll take him. Let Wyleeun go on ahead to the Undershaft and warn Creetchur and Chancey."

Wyleeun shook his head. "You can't take him by yourselves," he said. "We'll be lucky if all three of us can do it."

He was right and Beyar knew it. "Are there alcoves for all of us next to each other?"

"Two on one side, one right across, halfway down the Tight." It was one of the few places in Hardcore where the alcoves were opposite one another. "Hool's right-handed," he said. "He'll go through facing the single alcove. We hit him front and back; the hand with the cane in it should be right in front of the second alcove." He looked at Push. "Just grab it as it falls," he said.

He expected Push to argue for a place in one of the attacking alcoves, the way Creetchur would have, but he didn't. It was the most reasonable setup. Wyleeun and Beyar were the biggest and strongest, and Hool was a very big man. Push's quickness would be largely nullified by the cramped quarters, but it made him the ideal one to grab the cane as it passed. There were no easy stations. There was plenty or risk to go around. Push nodded his agreement, and they set off through a series of Verticals and Realtights that brought them up on Long Walk Wide.

They came through the Tight from the far side, facing the way Hool would come through. They were hardly in place when a body filled the doorway at the Long Near Narrow end. The man came into the passageway sideways, facing the left wall. He held an electric cane out in front in his right hand. He moved quickly, the way an OBee would in a tight space. Wyleeun would be facing him, Beyar at his back. They had the sequence of their attack timed perfectly.

When the man passed between Beyar and Wyleeun, they struck. The alcoves were not deep, and there was little room to cock an arm or leg for a blow. Beyar had to turn sideways at the last instant to strike. The side of his foot smacked down into the man's leg directly behind his knee, caving it in. He hit the other knee immediately after it. The man fell to his knees, his hand dropped toward the floor, but Push was waiting. As the cane arced past his alcove he snatched it out of the man's hand.

Wyleeun and Beyar's timing was equally good. As the man dropped to his knees his head came into range for Wyleeun, who jammed the heel of his palm into the man's face just above his nose at the same time Beyar drove his fist into the back of the man's neck. The man was very big with a thick OBee neck, but the two blows hitting him from opposite directions snapped it back. He collapsed forward toward Wyleeun's alcove, and Wyleeun shoved his head to the side. The body followed it and fell heavily on the arm from which Push had snatched the cane.

Wyleeun was out of his alcove in an instant, clambering up over the man's body; he grabbed its hair and pulled the head up. He looked at Push. "Flash him," he shouted. It never occurred to him for a minute not to kill Hool. When Hool regained consciousness, he would certainly make a career of trying to kill them. If *they* didn't succeed, *he* certainly would. "Right between the eyes," he said. He lifted the man's face and twisted it toward Push.

Push raised the cane to poke its prongs into Hool's face, but he did not complete the motion. "What are you waiting for?" Wyleeun shouted.

Push let his hand drop. "It's not him," he said.

Beyar scrambled up beside Wyleeun. Wyleeun twisted the head around as far as he could. It was not Hool. He and Beyar looked at one another. It meant Hool had taken another Tight. He was ahead of them once again.

Wyleeun let the man's head drop and climbed across him. Beyar and Push were right behind. They came back out onto Long Walk Wide at a dead run. Wyleeun let out a groan. There were already half a dozen Rimrats blocking the alcove where the Vertical into the Undershaft was, and more were coming down the Wide every second.

CHAPTER
TWENTY-EIGHT

Grandy and URdon Wee watched Hool disappear into the alcove from the top of a storageblock near the end of Long Walk Wide. Grandy looked at him. "He'll catch her if you don't do something."

Wee only smiled. "Not one of *my* moments," he said. Grandy knew the explanation. Every moment was a bubble of probability; every individual was a beam of light the thickness of their Will. The light pouring into a moment determined its actuality. In some moments the force of URdon Wee's light, URdon Wee's Will, determined what became "real"; in others it was the combination of light from other entities—Beyar, Push, Chancey; even someone just passing by might shift the moment one way or another. Some moments were even determined by Back Toss Hool. What gave URdon Wee his edge was that he alone knew which moments were which.

Grandy looked worried. "Is it one of Hool's?" she said.

URdon Wee seemed on the brink of chuckling. "Not necessarily," he said.

"Good," Grandy said, "then it must be mine."

Wee shook his head. "No," he said, "it's Dreem Shalleen's."

Under Long Walk Wide, Chancey's specialsister made her way through a crawlspace. A short Vertical and a very long Realtight put her on a ladder at the far end of the Undershaft. She dropped down it almost without touching the rungs. At the bottom she took out her facecase.

She could see them coming into sight down the passageway. It rattled with the sound of cries and footsteps, small footfalls almost on top of one another, others almost on top of them, and others still, echoing from behind almost out of sight. She felt the bubble of the moment around her, illuminated by *her* will only. Soon the light of others would flow into it; how and where that light would flow out was indeterminable. She spread her cape to give substance to the illusion of the end wall in front of it and waited for the instant when the momentum of the event could be changed.

Chancey felt as if she had been running for hours; there had been a burning in her throat almost since they started, but it had solidified into a lump that blocked her breathing. Her chest hurt and her legs felt weak, as if her knees were going to cave in with every step. Her feet were almost too heavy to lift, and they had gotten heavier every time she looked back.

At first there had been only sound, the shuffling beat of footsteps coming from back down the passageway out of sight. But gradually a figure had emerged, gaining on them, out of the horizon where all the planes formed a single point. No matter how fast they ran, it gained on them. Soon it seemed to fill the entire passageway. She recognized it immediately as Back Toss Hool.

If he had been able to run fully upright, he would have caught them easily. She kept looking for an alcove as they ran, hoping there might be a way up. There was no breath left over for Creetchur to tell her there was none, but she knew by the way he ran, pulling her by the hand, looking only straight ahead, that the only other exit would be at the far end of the passageway.

It was equally clear to her that they were not going to make it. Even when she saw the end wall of the passage with the ladder just short of it, she knew Hool was going to overtake them. They were still a long way from it when Creetchur yanked her past him and turned.

What he intended was obvious. He was First Stock after all. He had planned from the beginning to go down fighting while she escaped. She wanted to stop, but she knew Creetchur's only chance was for her to keep running so that Hool would be more interested in getting past him than killing him. She ran, looking back over her shoulder every few steps.

Creetchur threw himself in front of Hool knee-high. His head and shoulder hit bone, and the impact burst in his head. But it upended Hool, and his momentum drove him flying over Creetchur. He hit on his face and slid down the passage. Creetchur shook off his dizziness and scrambled after him.

Hool was on his knees, fumbling to get the electric cane free of its bindings. Creetchur sprang on his back, wrapping an arm around his throat and pounding him in the face with short, curved blows. His knee kept banging Hool's arm, knocking it away from the handle, but Hool kept reaching back for it.

Finally he had hold of it, but as he pulled it free Creetchur's knee hit him behind the elbow and the tips of the cane struck the side wall. There was a white flash and the cane recoiled, leaving a scar of burn down the wall. Creetchur jammed his knee into the back of Hool's elbow again, and the cane clattered away toward the end wall.

Chancey saw it, stopped, and started back. Hool forced himself up off one knee and threw himself backward on top of Creetchur. It knocked the wind out of Creetchur, and he fell off onto the floor. He wanted to roll away and get back up, but he couldn't breathe. He kept making little involuntary noises every time he tried to inhale, but no air came in, and his chest would not fill. He wished Wyleeun was there to push down on his diaphragm and get him breathing again; he tried to do it himself, but it was too late.

Hool was almost at the cane. Chancey was still ten yards away from it. There was nothing for her to do but stop herself and turn. Her momentum carried her skidding toward her death, but she finally slowed, stopped, turned, and ran. Hool looked back toward Creetchur, struggling to get to his feet. There was no time to kill him if he still wanted to get Chancey. He sprang after her.

She sprinted toward the ladder; it was close but still too far away. Her hair flew out behind her as she ran. Hool pounded after her. His feet seemed to be landing in her footsteps, and the sounds of her running was muffled under his. Every step he took landed farther up her shadow. She could hear the pounding of his breath. The ladder was just ahead when he leaned forward, reached, reached, and finally grabbed her by the hair. Her head jerked backward, and she broke her stride. Hool yanked her to a stop. He pulled her head back and raised his cane.

She heard Beyar's voice, but he was much too far away to do anything. Hool hesitated, listening to the footsteps too far away to stop him, close enough to be next. In a moment he would have them all. He could feel *his* moment shimmer around him. The end wall seemed to dissolve in front of him; in its place stood Dreem Shalleen.

CHAPTER
TWENTY-NINE

Wyleeun followed them back into the Tight. Long Walk Wide was crawling with Rimrats. "Is there another way in?" Beyar said.

Wyleeun shook his head. "Too far. It's a good hundred yards beyond the end of Long Walk Wide. He can't stand all the way up in the Undershaft. If we're going to catch up to him, it's through there." He pointed to the alcove across the Wide.

Push was already changing his face. Wyleeun looked at him. "We'll need a Squeal," he said. Beyar stepped past him to the doorway of the tight. He stepped outside and waved the first Rimrat by to follow him. Then he darted back in before any questions could be asked. The Rimrat hesitated, then trotted across the Wide and into the Tight.

One step inside and he tried to step back out, but Beyar had him by the throat. Wyleeun was supposed to stun him with the electric cane, but he was still trying to figure out which way to turn the voltage ring when Beyar ran out of patience and put the Rimrat to sleep himself. It was messier and it wasn't as quick, but it *was* effective.

Wyleeun took the Rimrat's Squeal. "There's a Realtight

about twenty yards down," he said. "In the second alcove on the right there's a Vertical. Wait for us at the bottom."

Push nodded as he took off the last bit of fiber. He rearranged his cape to look more like a Corehard's clothes than a Rimrat's. "You ready?" Wyleeun asked. Push nodded.

They started shouting, and Push burst out of the Tight and ran down Long Walk Wide. Beyar and Push were right behind him. The crowd across the street was moving to cut him off when Push darted into the Realtight. Beyar and Wyleeun were right on his heels. They were lucky; the Tight was empty. Wyleeun was faster, and Beyar was two steps behind him going into the Realtight.

About half the Rimrats from near the alcove were five steps behind Beyar. He stepped into the first alcove and twisted the voltage collar toward "stun." Then he stepped back out and poked the first Rimrat in the chest with it. He went down as if he'd been clubbed, and the two behind him went tumbling over him. A half dozen others piled up on top of them. Beyar was long gone before they untangled themselves and dragged the unconscious Rimrat out of the way.

By then Beyar had caught up with Wyleeun at the bottom of the Vertical, and the three of them were on their way through a Realtight under Long Walk Wide. Halfway down it, Wyleeun took a short detour down another Realtight and stuffed the Squeal up in a crawl shaft before he turned it on. The Rimrats coming down the Vertical followed it and milled around the Realtight looking for it.

Wyleeun and Beyar came back up onto Long Walk Wide out of an alcove almost directly across from the Realtight. They had Push by the arms, and Beyar was doing a good job of seeming to kick him. They shoved him through the crowd of Rimrats into the alcove. Beyar slid the screen back out of the way before one of the Rimrats grabbed his arm. "*No*body in," he said.

Beyar gave him a murderous look. "Hool *wants* him," he said.

It was too confusing to the Rimrat. He repeated his orders. "Nobody in, nobody out!"

"Hool *said* to bring this one to him right away," Wyleeun said. He shoved Push to Beyar, who began to put him down the ladder. The Rimrat made a grab for Push. "Nobody in, no—" Wyleeun stuck him under the chin with the cane before he could finish. He jerked back into the wall of the alcove, as if he'd been punched, and fell flopping at the bottom of the wall.

Wyleeun gave Beyar a look that said Rimrats never learn. He turned the cane toward the other Rimrats. They took it for a sign of authority and stepped back. Beyar followed Push down the ladder. Wyleeun dropped the cane down to Beyar and turned to the Rimrats. "*Now*, nobody in, nobody out," he said. The Rimrats nodded, and Wyleeun dropped down the ladder.

Push stepped out of the alcove at the bottom of the ladder. He could hear running footsteps echoing back from far down the passageway. More than one person was running, and he knew Hool must have caught sight of Creetchur and Chancey. He could see Hool's back almost at the point where the walls converged. Push began to run before Beyar got out of the alcove.

The others followed him. Hool had a good head start, but they did not have to run crouched over as he did, and after fifty yards they could see him plainly. After a hundred they could see flashes of Creetchur and Chancey dashing just beyond him, but they were still far behind them when Creetchur turned and toppled him.

The fight gave them a chance to close some of the distance, but they were still nowhere near enough to help before Hool was up and running again. Wyleeun stopped to help Creetchur as they passed; Push and Beyar kept running. But it did them no good: when Hool caught Chancey, they were still too far away to do anything about it but shout helplessly for Hool to stop. The flash of the cane was like the end of the world.

CHAPTER
THIRTY

Back Toss Hool stared at the figure of Dreem Shalleen. She looked exactly as she had when he had first seen her more than twenty-five years before. Even his memory had not adequately preserved how beautiful she was. The crimson star that covered her eye, the scarlet and indigo of her hair, the pale blue of her eyes—all seemed so much more vivid than even the best of his bleached and faded memories. It made him ache to see her again.

But it did not entirely surprise him, except in the way OBees were always surprised when the best that they had hoped for actually happened. He had know that *his* moment was special, that it controlled the normal flows of space and time. In *his* moment not only the reality of the future but also the rules of reality would change. Things that were to be would not be, things that had happened would unhappen, everything would be changed, nothing would continue as it had been.

Beyond *his* moment, all events derived from *his* moment. What had gone on before it was irrelevant; all new events could contradict all old events, outcomes could occur without antecedents, effects without causes. Strange and disordered sequences that functioned according to their own inertia, regardless of the momentum of other events, would occur and become the paths of new realities.

That had been his great hope: to reach the one moment where all things could be changed and to leap not only beyond his life, but to another life, one in which there was and would always be a Dreem Shalleen. More than his desire to save humanity, more even than his hatred for URdon Wee, his desire for Dreem Shalleen had moved him down the long years of failure and frustration, of empty longing and aching loneliness. And now that the moment was before him, he felt vindicated and complete.

Dreem held out her hand to him, and he could see in her eyes what was and was *not* necessary. There were understandings within *his* moment that had been impossible outside of it. That he change the moment was more important than *how* he changed it. It was only necessary that the flow of things be changed, that the sequence be significantly altered. He let go of the child's hair.

He marveled that it had escaped him all along that he had been going about it the wrong way. He did not have control over the participants of Wee's vision; he could never change the way *their* momentum flowed. He could only change *his* momentum. It was why *his* vision had been a mystery to URdon Wee, because it was *his,* just as the moment was *his.* He had, and had always had, one power and one power only, the power to change *his* direction, to end *his* participation in the chain of events that led to mankind's ultimate destruction.

It was not necessary to block the progress of the light by ending the chain of possibilities that flowed through the children of Wee's Vision; he could divert it simply by ending the possibilities that flowed from *him.* He knew enough of Wee's vision to know that he persisted in it, that Back Toss Hool was a part of it all the way to the revolution and beyond. *That* was all he had to change. It would not even matter if the children of Wee's Vision grew up and toppled the Corporation; it would not matter if they freed the League; it would not even matter if they turned mankind's path outward to the stars and beyond, *as long as he was not part of it*.

Once he had eliminated his effect on that chain of events, it would alter everything. He would have altered one of the lines of force that led to that fatal intersection; it did not matter whether he altered it by an hour or a minute, a mile or a parsec; the event would not occur. The chance encounter with the alien life form that would destroy mankind would not occur.

He twirled the cane toward himself with a laugh and touched its tips to his forehead. There was a blinding flash of light, and Back Toss Hool was gone.

The light broke up into a dazzling shower of lights. Each one shone for a single, but complete, instant, connected by a chain of light to other events stretching toward infinity. In every one he looked at, he saw himself and Dreem Shalleen. Behind him, dwindling into the darkness, were other chains of instants, terrible moments leading only to destruction. It did not matter. Back Toss Hool never looked back.

CHAPTER

THIRTY-ONE

Grandy came down the ladder first. The flat, sharp smell of something burned hung in the air like streamers trailing down from the thin haze trapped just below the ceiling of the passageway. Dreem Shalleen knelt on the floor, holding Back Toss Hool's head in her lap. Chancey stood with her head against Creetchur's chest, sobbing softly. Beyar and Wyleeun and Push stood catching their breath just beyond Hool's feet. All faces turned toward URdon Wee as he came down the ladder. He was the only one smiling.

Chancey looked at Hool's body. Her voice was filled with bewilderment. "Why did he *do* that?"

"Love," Grandy said.

"And duty," URdon Wee added.

"Duty?" Creetchur shouted. "Love?" He looked at Wyleeun as if he thought URdon Wee and Grandy were both crazy. "He tried to kill Chancey!" he said.

Wee smiled. "There are no villains, only unrecognized heroes."

Beyar tried to explain it to him. "He wanted to stop URdon Wee's Vision from coming true," he told Creetchur. Creetchur frowned. Beyar tried to make it plainer. "He wanted to change the future. If Push and Chancey and I don't live to fight in the revolution, everything will change and the League will never be free."

"The League will never be free, anyway," Wyleeun scoffed.

Wee laughed. "It will *now,* thanks to Back Toss Hool, and you and your brother will stand with Push and Chancey in front of the big holo in Fist Headquarters and tell Spencer LeGrange to his face that the League is free and there's nothing he can do about it."

Creetchur looked as if he liked that version of the future, but he felt obligated to back up his brother. "Nobody knows the future," he said.

"URdon Wee does," Push said.

Creetchur started to argue, but Chancey had the answer for him. "It's like reading the Spin," she said, "to know where the flow of things is going. But URdon Wee can just read it further ahead than we can."

Creetchur looked willing to accept the possibility, but Wyleeun was still unconvinced. "Then why did he kill himself?"

Wee smiled, as if the reason was obvious. "He found a better way to change my vision," he said.

Beyar was incredulous. "Then your Vision *won't* come true?"

Wee laughed. "Not the way Hool was afraid it would," he said. "He changed *that* possibility. But it *will* come true. And it will come true *because* of Back Toss Hool, not in spite of him."

"But you said he was trying to *stop* it," Wyleeun said.

"He was."

Wyleeun looked as if he was sure Wee had lost the argument. "Then how could he be a hero?"

Wee shrugged. "Sometimes unrecognized heroes don't even recognize themselves." Wyleeun shook his head, and Wee tried again. "If we stretch a tether between us," he said, "and we have to keep it centered over a point for a certain period of time, can I do it pulling by myself?"

Wyleeun saw the analogy. "I'd have to pull against you," he said.

"And if only *I* knew that everybody's life depended on it being centered?"

"You could tell me," Wyleeun said.

Wee smiled. "And if I told you, but you were convinced that everybody's life depended on your pulling the whole tether over to your side?"

"You'd have to pull just as hard as I did."

Wee nodded. "Why?"

Wyleeun looked as if he understood. "Once the pulling started, if either of us stopped pulling, everybody would lose."

"And if you pulled with all your strength for as long as you could and the tether stayed centered, would you be any less of a hero because your reason for pulling was wrong, even though your intention was good?"

Wyleeun conceded the argument. "Hool thought everybody's life depended on having things his way?"

Wee nodded. "He believed that if there was a Revolution and the League finally freed itself, mankind would start to explore the stars and eventually run into an alien race that would annihilate it."

Wyleeun saw the reasoning. "And if he killed off important people in the Revolution, while they were still young, there wouldn't be one in . . ." He looked at Wee for the date.

Wee smiled. "Less than a decade," he said.

"And we'll be there?" Creetchur said.

Wee smiled. "At the very moment the League declares its freedom."

Wyleeun shook his head. "But why did Hool kill himself?"

Beyar had the answer. "He must have been there too!"

Wee nodded. "And at a dozen potential turning points along the way."

Push saw it too. "And if he wasn't there, it would be the same as if we weren't there. Everything would be different."

"And if you change one part of the future, you change it all," Chancey said.

"All you can really change is the present," Wee said. "But a different present means a different future."

Chancey shook her head. "Then Hool really *was* an unrecognized hero."

"Even when he was trying to kill us," Push added.

Wee shrugged. "What else can you call someone who gives their life trying to save everyone else?"

They looked down at Hool's body. Beyar shook his head. "I never thought I'd be sorry he died," he said. The others nodded their agreement.

URdon Wee threw back his head and laughed. "Nothing stays lost," he said.

CHAPTER
THIRTY-TWO

URdon Wee took the vial of Sunrise and knelt beside Back Toss Hool. The boys helped turn him over, and Wee rubbed the Sunrise on Hool's wound. Dreem held his head in her lap, waiting for his eyes to open. When they did, she was the only thing he saw.

He smiled and closed them again, as if he were afraid she would disappear. Dreem leaned forward and kissed his forehead and said, "Welcome to the World, Back Toss Hool, Who-Has-Died-the-Little-Death-and-the-Big. Welcome to the World, Back Toss Twiceborn."

He opened his eyes again; there was a tear in the corner of one. "It really *is* you," he said. "I was afraid..." He let it go, something out of a past he did not want to remember. He shook his head in amazement. "Then death really is just a dream."

"Life's the dream," URdon Wee said. "Death's a waking. Nothing's what it seems."

Hool turned his head. When he saw Wee, his face dropped. "All for nothing," he said with a groan. He thought of their quarter-century of opposition. Twenty-five years of wasted effort. There was no rage left in him, only sadness, weariness, and defeat.

Wee laughed. "All to get *here*," he corrected.

Hool shook his head sadly. "Is that what it was for? To come back in *your* Vision."

"Why *my* vision?"

"There's no URdon Wee in *my* vision," he said.

"True," Wee said, "And no self-sacrificing Back Toss Hool in mine."

Hool frowned. "What, then?"

Wee shrugged as if Hool should already have known. "Every event is a composite of wills. Vectors of opposing forces." He pointed to Hool's shadow as he had so many years before. "In your vision the League is never free." He pointed to his own. "In mine, mankind eventually meets its annihilation." He stepped forward until his shadow fell across Hool's creating a darker third shadow where they overlapped. "The beat phenomenon," he said, "a vision made of the interaction of your Vision and mine, your will and mine. In *our* vision the League becomes free, mankind goes out into space, but it doesn't show up for its rendezvous with its death."

"Then everything that happened..." He said it as if he were afraid to hope.

"...was the path to getting *here*," Wee said. "All of it was necessary to reach this joining point, where a new future could be made. Without all that preceded it we would never have been *here*."

Hool could see that it was true. He had never thought of a combined vision, offering the best of both, and yet so much was different from his own vision and so different from what he knew of Wee's vision that he knew it must be true.

He was not sure whether he was still in the same chain of events he had burned himself out of toward the vision of Dreem Shalleen, or if it was an alternative world, and he did not care. Dreem Shalleen was in it. He was finally URdon Wee's equal. Even Grandy was alive and well. He was surprised that he thought of her only as a long-lost friend. And when he looked at Dreem, he could see that what he had thought he had seen in her eyes when she looked at URdon Wee was not there and never really had been.

He looked at the children smiling down at him. He was relieved that he was not a murderer, after all. If it was a new universe, he did not really care; mankind faced no eventual annihilation in it, he was sure of that. If it was an illusion, it was no more so than the universe he had left, and this one was much happier. He decided to stay in it.

Wee offered Hool his hand. Hool took it, and Wee helped pull him to his feet. He looked around at the children, half afraid to face them because of what might have been, but he could see that they understood it all as well as he did. He smiled at URdon Wee. "Why are we standing around?" he said. "We have a Revolution to prepare."

Wee smiled. "And you three have a shuttle to catch," he said, looking at Beyar, Push, and Chancey. "There's still a lot of work for you to do as Skyshockers."

Creetchur frowned. Chancey stroked his cheek. "I'll be back," she said. Creetchur did not look satisfied. "We have a future together," she said. Creetchur smiled. The Vision was his vision as well now. Even Wyleeun seemed to accept the truth of it.

Hool put his arm around Dreem Shalleen. "I've missed you for a long, long time," he said.

Dreem raised an eyebrow of indignation. "You call this afternoon a long time ago?"

Hool was astonished. "That was *really* you?"

Dreem nodded, as if he should have known. Hool looked at her cautiously. "Have you ever been in a stand-up on the Wideway in the Grand Sphere?"

Dreem smiled. "Or in the last recliner on the shuttle between Catchcage and LUNAC?"

They both began to laugh.

URdon Wee and Grandy went up the ladder last. Grandy stopped with one foot on the first rung. She turned and looked at URdon Wee. "You know," she said, "I haven't seen Grandy's Place in a long time. After the shuttle goes," she said, "maybe we should take a Squeeze."

URdon Wee smiled. "I knew you would say that," he said.

Grandy laughed. "Of course, you did," she said. "After all, it's still *your* illusion." But the way she laughed made him wonder if, in reality, it wasn't really *hers*.

At the same moment that Beyar, Push, and Chancey boarded the shuttle for Henson's Tube, Spencer LeGrange opened a board meeting at Corporation Headquarters Earthside. He was completely unaware that his days were numbered.